# THE FAKING GAME

## PORTIA MACINTOSH

B

First published in Great Britain in 2023 by Boldwood Books Ltd.

Cover Design by Alexandra Allden

Cover Illustration: Shutterstock

Every effort has been made to obtain the necessary permissions with reference to copyright material, both illustrative and quoted. We apologise for any omissions in this respect and will be pleased to make the appropriate acknowledgements in any future edition.

A CIP catalogue record for this book is available from the British Library.

Paperback ISBN 978-1-80426-679-3

Large Print ISBN 978-1-80426-680-9

Hardback ISBN 978-1-80426-681-6

Ebook ISBN 978-1-80426-678-6

Kindle ISBN 978-1-80426-677-9

Audio CD ISBN 978-1-80426-686-1

MP3 CD ISBN 978-1-80426-685-4

Digital audio download ISBN 978-1-80426-683-0

Boldwood Books Ltd
23 Bowerdean Street
London SW6 3TN
www.boldwoodbooks.com

*For my Joe*

# 1

'How lucky am I? Having all these grandkids when some poor people don't have any.'

My eyes roll so far into the back of my head they actually end up back where they started, before anyone else has a chance to notice. My Auntie Mary says this all the time and, if you don't overthink it, it sounds like a lovely remark on how she has two grandsons and another on the way. But this is my Auntie Mary, a relative so villainous there's no money Disney wouldn't pay for the rights to her, and when she says these words she fires them like bullets, her gun usually aimed squarely at my mum.

'I know, aren't you lucky,' my mum replies genuinely.

My gaze darts around the village hall until I finally focus on my younger brother, Oliver, only to find him staring right back at me, his eyes wide with horror. We've always had that knack siblings often have for being able to have entire conversations, in split seconds, with nothing but a look.

Oliver is twenty-six and in the middle of a PhD, so I don't think anyone expects him to be starting a family just yet. But then there's me, a thirty-two-year-old – a whopping one year older than my cousin, Flora, who is expecting her third child – who is so very clearly the real target in Auntie Mary's crosshair when she starts banging on like this, but if my mum isn't going to rise to it then neither am I. I sip my drink and look around the room, admiring all the blue balloons, imagining tying a bunch of them to my body, like I'm the house from *Up*, so I can rise above all this shit. I hear South America is lovely this time of year.

'Three boys,' my mum says with a smile and a joyful sigh. 'Flora is going to have her hands full.'

'It's doable, if you coordinate it right,' I joke, mostly for my brother's amusement.

My mum just about stifles a grin but Auntie Mary tuts. They're so different, not like sisters at all, to the point where I wonder if they might not even be related. Mary is a year or so older than Annie, my mum. When I'm trying to work out why my mum turned out warm, friendly and loving like my grandparents, I mentally float the idea that perhaps Gran and Grandad – I don't know – thought they couldn't have kids, so they adopted my auntie, but then fell pregnant with my mum soon after. To be honest, I think I just like the idea that I'm not genetically tied to her in any way, and know that none of that is true.

Auntie Mary, with her knack for injecting unnecessary discomfort into conversations, is a real joy at parties.

'Flora is a fantastic mum,' Mary insists – not that anyone implied she wasn't.

Right on cue, Flora hurries over with her youngest, baby Sal, held high above her enormous bump, and her other little boy, Vince, toddling along with her, holding her hand. Sal is about to turn one, Vince is two, and for some reason she's going for some kind of New York Italian mafia boss theme when it comes to naming them. I wouldn't be surprised if her newest recruit was a Carlo or a Fredo or a Don Vito Corleone himself.

I know, I know, it seems like I'm making fun of them, but trust me, it's the only way to get through family events like this. Just smile, make your silly little jokes in your head, and remind yourself that if friends are the family you choose, then family are the friends you don't choose, and there's not much you can do about that.

'Mum, can you take Sal, I need to take Vince to the toilet,' Flora says.

'Of course,' Mary replies. 'Come here, my little soldier. Where is Tommy?'

'He's playing pool, in the next room,' Flora tells her.

Ahh, Tommy. Good old Tommy, Flora's husband, a man who very much believes in gender norms where men are men and women are women. The men drink and play sports, the women look after the kids. He's very much the same, whenever we go to their house, sitting in his chair, reminding himself that he's the man of the house, while 'her indoors' cooks and cleans and raises his kids. Honestly, if I had to live with a man like that, I would be in prison by now.

'Are you guys having a nice time?' Flora pauses to ask us.

'Yes, lovely,' my mum replies. 'You've done such a good job with the decorations.'

We're in the village hall, which Flora and Tommy have hired out for the occasion. The hall has been transformed with decorations in celebration of Flora's baby boy – who I think is due in a couple of months, so February or March. From the moment you step inside, a wave of blue hues washes over you. Cobalt streamers cascade down from the ceiling, crisscrossing the room, forming a captivating canopy that lowers the height of the room significantly. Balloons in various shades, from baby-blue to navy, occupy every other available space.

'You've got the entertainment sorted, right, Cara?' Flora

checks – asking me in a way that suggests there is a strong chance I may have let her down.

'Of course I have,' I reply. 'Oliver and I sorted it together. Millsy is picking it up on his way here.'

'Joe isn't here yet?' she replies, her eyes widening. 'I told you, no one was to be late today.'

'Well, he is coming here from LA,' Mum politely reminds her. 'He's coming back a day early, just for this.'

And don't I know it, because we had to eat the cost of his non-refundable, non-amendable ticket, so that he could be here.

'Joe won't forget, will he?' Mary chimes in, also sounding like she strongly suspects he will.

Joe Mills, my boyfriend, has always gone by the name Millsy. You know what lads are like, they get a nickname when they're younger – either a twist on their surname or something completely random – and it stays with them forever. Of course, in his professional life, he's Joe, but to me, to his family, to his friends, he is Millsy. Not to Mary and Flora, though, who insist on calling him by his 'Christian name'. Mary even trialled calling him Joseph, to make things extra formal, until I repeatedly pointed out that the name on his birth certificate is in fact 'Joe' and not 'Joseph'.

'He won't forget,' I say simply.

Flora practically drags Vince to the loos while Mary makes her excuses and wanders off with baby Sal. Now it's just me, Mum and Oliver.

'Where is Dad hiding?' Oliver asks.

'If it weren't December, I would say outside,' Mum replies. 'He'll be hiding in a corner or watching the boys play pool. Go see if he needs rescuing.'

Oliver nods and heads off to find him.

Mum wraps an arm around me and gives me a squeeze.

'I'm proud of you,' she tells me. 'You're getting very good at ignoring all the silly remarks.'

'Ahh, well, I learned from the best,' I reply. 'I don't know how you put up with them. I can't imagine Oliver being like this, but I'm not sure I would put up with him if he were.'

Mum just shrugs.

'I'll always keep the peace, for your gran's sake, and I know you would do the same with Oliver – not that I can imagine it either. You're both so mature.'

'Ah, mature, but not popping out babies on the regular,' I joke.

'Well, I can't imagine it's easy, when your boyfriend has been in LA for six weeks,' she replies. 'Is he on his way?'

'Yeah, I had a message from him, he said he needed a shower before he came, but he's bringing the game with him.'

'That's good,' she replies.

I don't know how I wound up being responsible for the entertainment today. I suppose it's because, in spite of everything, I do still try with them, even if they don't make it easy. Look at when Flora got married back in 2020, and she wound up with no one to put her party favours together the day before *the* big day, it was me who stepped forward to do them, even though Flora had invited my ex-boyfriend to her wedding and sat him at my table.

Flora asked if we would take care of the entertainment for today, so I came up with an idea, Oliver found a place that could make it, and Millsy is going to be bringing it. I glance at my watch. I thought he would've been here by now.

'I suppose we should mingle,' Mum says. 'Come on, let's grab a blue cupcake.'

'Or a blue egg mayo sandwich,' I say with a laugh.

Yes, even a large chunk of the buffet is blue. I imagine if anyone arrived in so much as a pink outfit they would be told to leave, or asked to change. I'm lucky I'm allowed in, given that my long blonde locks have a very subtle rose gold toner through them, but I would never be let off the hook for attending so easily, otherwise I would've come dressed as Barbie, if it saw me turned away at the door.

Over at the buffet table we happen upon Uncle Paddy – Mary's husband – and Emma, one of Flora's friends.

Uncle Paddy is a small, round man with a commanding physical presence that matches his in-your-face personality. His bald head gleams under the hall lights, giving him a polished, almost comical appearance, and he wears the kind of glasses that make him look like he needs his hard drive checked – not that he could begin to know how to work anything with a hard drive in it.

'...and back then I was a young lad with a brilliant mind, hidden away in the corners of a rough neighbourhood. I was a mathematical prodigy, solving complex equations left and right, but keeping it all a secret,' he explains.

'Wow, really?' Emma replies, her eyes wide. 'I had no idea you were so smart.'

'One day, fate brought me face to face with a renowned professor,' Paddy continues. 'He discovered my exceptional talent and wanted to help me unlock my full potential. We embarked on a journey of intellectual exploration and self-discovery and...'

Paddy's voice trails off as he notices us watching.

'Oh, Annie, Cara, hello,' he says.

'Hi,' I reply.

The thing you need to know about Paddy is that he has never had an original idea or experience in his entire life – unless you count the idea he has where he tells people entirely fabricated anecdotes about himself that he has lifted entirely from movies and books. Honestly, he isn't even subtle with it. Take today's tall tale, which is so blatantly the plot of *Good Will Hunting*. Although I suppose it's more subtle than the time he tried to tell Millsy he was once part of a team trying to catch a great white shark off the coast of New England.

'Is it time for the entertainment?' Paddy asks.

It looks to me like the entertainment is already well underway.

'Millsy is on his way with it,' I reply.

'I don't know, that no-good boyfriend of yours,' Paddy jokes.

'Millsy is great, isn't he?' Emma chimes in.

I don't know Emma all that well, only through Flora, but I do know that Millsy is never short of female attention, which is *just great* for me.

'He is,' I reply with a smile.

'Honestly, you two are just, like, the perfect couple,' Emma says with a sigh. 'Everyone thinks so. You're so lucky.'

I smile again, softer this time.

'Oh, it makes us all sick,' Paddy continues – still hopefully joking. 'I bet you've been going mad, with him being in LA so much, when you're usually joined at the hip.'

'Well, we're adults, we're dealing with it,' I point out.

I'm relieved when I notice my phone making noises. I take it from my bag to see what it is.

'Oh, that's him now,' I say. 'Right, I'd better go set the entertainment up.'

'Don't keep us waiting,' Paddy sings. 'We're all excited to see what you've come up with.'

And don't I know it! Although it doesn't feel like people are excited to see what I've come up with, it seems like they're excited to see if I fail. Well, I'm not going to give them the opportunity. I've gone all out for this one. I looked into games for baby showers and it seemed like one thing a lot of people played was a take on 'pin the tail on the donkey' but with a baby, and baby-type items like dummies and rattles and stuff. Oliver agreed to help too, so he found us a company that made custom games, and I found someone who made high-quality AI images, who used photos of both Sal and Vince as babies, and made us a sort of projection of what the new baby could look like, which we then sent to the custom game people. Honestly, it's going to be amazing, so unique, so special – I don't know how anyone is going to find fault with this, although lord knows they'll try.

I make my way towards the door, to see if I can catch Millsy before he joins the party – well, I haven't seen him for six weeks – but then I spot him.

The doors swing open and he strolls through in what seems like movie-style slow motion. Time seems to slow down, and if this were a movie, a collective sigh would escape the lips of anyone lucky enough to witness his grand entrance.

Tall, dark, and devastatingly handsome, Millsy has always commanded attention, and in a seemingly effortless manner, which just makes it all the more attractive. His well-groomed, tousled brown hair falls perfectly into place, and blows lightly in the wind, which is probably something to do with the breeze coming in from the chilly December weather outside, but from here it looks like there's a Hollywood-grade wind machine pointing at him.

When I first met him, I always thought he reminded me of Jason Momoa but, these days, over three years later, he's maturing into a cross between Jason and a sort of Matthew McConaughey type, but peak Matthew McConaughey, from his dreamy romcom era, before the infamous 'McConaissance' of the 2010s. With his impossibly dark brown eyes and his deliciously deep dimples, Millsy is somehow only getting more attractive as the days go by. Seeing him, in the flesh, after six weeks apart feels like someone simultaneously slapping me across the face, punching me in the chest, and kicking me between the legs.

He spots me and waves with his free hand. His other, thankfully, is holding a large cardboard envelope. Oh, thank goodness, he's brought the game.

As he walks over to me, I feel my tongue swelling in my mouth. I don't know what to say, I feel like an awkward teenager again. But then Oliver spots him too and hurries over.

'Millsy, you got the game,' Oliver says, as the two of them arrive in front of me at the same time. 'Phew. I think Auntie Mary and Flora were gunning for Cara over it.'

'It's right here, mate,' Millsy reassures him. 'Although I haven't checked it, if you want to do the honours.'

Millsy hands the envelope to Oliver and then turns to me.

'Hi,' he says simply, flashing me that trademark grin of his.

'Hi,' I reply, smiling back, my cheeks warming for the occasion.

'I—'

'Have you—'

'Erm, guys,' Oliver interrupts us talking over one another. 'Is this what you were after?'

Oliver is holding the large board to his chest. As we both go to look at it, he holds it away from his body just enough for us to see it.

'Fuck!' I blurt. 'Fuck, fuck, fuck.'

'Wow,' Millsy adds. 'That's... yeah, wow. That's not what you asked for?'

'No, unbelievably, that's not what I asked for,' I reply. 'Oh my God, Mary is going to kill me. She's going to actually murder me, right here, in front of everyone, just weeks before Christmas.'

'I thought it sounded odd,' Oliver says cautiously.

'What do you mean?' I reply. 'What did you ask for?'

'Exactly what you told me,' he insists. 'You said you were sending a photo and you wanted a pin-the-tail-on-the-donkey type thing.'

'Yes, *type thing*,' I reply. 'Is that all you said? You didn't say you wanted a baby version.'

'Of course I said I wanted a baby version,' Oliver replies. 'And... I guess that's what you've got?'

It never ceases to amaze me that, for someone doing a PhD, and being the smartest man I know, Oliver can be quite stupid sometimes. Although I suppose it's not all on him, perhaps the person who made this... this monstrosity took the request a little too literally.

As requested, there is a large board with the AI baby on there, and it really does look like a cross between baby Sal and Vince when he was that age. But this adorable, crawling baby has had some adjustments. It has large donkey ears, big goofy donkey teeth, and a removable donkey tail for partygoers to take turns at trying to pin in the right place – as though there's a right place for a tail on a baby.

'No one can see this,' Millsy says, taking it from Oliver, placing it back inside the envelope.

'Shit,' I say under my breath. 'What are we going to do?'

'Joe,' Auntie Mary says brightly. 'And here you are, better late than never, is that the entertainment? Can I see?'

'No,' I insist quickly, reaching out to grab the envelope, holding it to my body, partially so Mary can't see it, but also as some kind of shield for myself.

'That's just instructions, for the games,' Millsy says. 'The rules and what have you. Cara has commissioned a series of party games, designed specifically for a baby shower.'

Auntie Mary raises an eyebrow at me.

'I see,' she says. 'Well, how thoughtful.'

She says this begrudgingly, almost suspiciously, but I suppose we are acting rather odd. Oliver is low-key breaking a sweat.

'Shall we get set up then?' she suggests. 'Now you're here.'

'Sure thing,' he replies. 'Just let me hug my girlfriend hello, hmm? It's been six weeks since I saw her last.'

I allow my protective cardboard barrier to fall to the side as Millsy approaches me. He wraps an arm around me, placing it on the small of my back as he pulls me close. With his free hand, he rests it lightly on my face, as though he's pulling me in for a kiss, but then he whispers into my ear.

'Go hide that in the car, I've got an idea.'

I allow myself a premature sigh of relief. If there's one thing I can always count on Millsy for – and he can always count on me for – it's our ability to get one another out of scrapes. We have, of course, usually caused said scrapes, but it's the way we've always had each other's backs that got us together in the first place.

When he releases me, he holds my hand for a moment, giving it a squeeze, but as I feel the plastic press against my skin, I realise it's the car keys he's giving me, so I can hide this hideous donkey monster baby designed to look like a member of Flora's family in the car, before later taking it home to burn so that no one can ever see it. My God, imagine if Flora did see it, or Auntie Mary, bloody hell, she would hit the ceiling, and the only thing stopping her murdering me when she came back down would be how tangled up in all the sparkly blue decorative shit she would be. I just know that they would all think I had done this on purpose, to ruin the shower – as though that is a thing that real humans do in real life. I remember when I dyed my hair a deep, dark shade of red and they said I was doing it to ruin Flora's wedding. Unhinged.

Venturing out without my coat, I feel the chill of the December air. Something about the cold weather makes me feel a little panicky. Our winters, while not that bad compared to other countries, somehow feel unescapable. The dark nights set in so quickly, the first daylight of the day feels as if it's never going to arrive, and the weather is far from a picture-perfect snow scene from a postcard.

With the donkey baby safely locked away in Millsy's boot, I return to the party, just in time to see him placing an arm full of toilet rolls down on the floor at Flora's feet.

Oh, God.

'Toilet roll?' Flora blurts at him in disbelief.

'Yep,' Millsy says with a confident smile. 'We have a series of fun games all planned out. I'll be the games master, so everyone else can have fun. So, everyone needs to get into two teams, and then for the first game you'll need to break off into pairs inside your team.'

Everyone does as they are told. Millsy has a natural ability to put everyone at instant ease with his disarming smile that reaches his dreamy eyes, drawing people in like moths to a flame.

He hands me a few loo rolls.

'What are you doing?' I ask him quietly, for some reason smiling, because it's been a while since we did this.

'Making it up as I go along,' he whispers back. 'Hand out these toilet rolls.'

Our hands linger over a loo roll. So romantic. But then I do as I'm told, handing out the toilet rolls – which I'm guessing we're going to need to replace from a store cupboard somewhere – making sure each couple has one.

My mum smiles at me as I hand one to her.

'Oliver told me what happened,' she says with a sympathetic

smile. Then she nods towards Millsy. 'You've got yourself a good one there.'

I look over at him as he starts the game. He really is something.

'Okay, so the aim of the first round is for one person to use the toilet roll to make a nappy for their partner,' he explains. 'You only have so much time and the three teams who have made the best effort will get points. Is everyone ready?'

I glance around the room, wondering if this might be considered too 'low brow' for Auntie Mary, but everyone seems to be into it.

Cheers echo around the hall, confirming that everyone who is playing is ready.

'Go!' Millsy commands as he starts a timer on his phone.

I wander over to him, to talk to him while everyone is distracted. Now that the crisis has been averted, it's back to reality.

'You promised you wouldn't be late,' I utter, my teeth clenched together to try to contain the annoyed feeling that is growing inside me.

'Well, when you're taking an exhausting eleven-hour flight, and then travelling from London to Leeds in the middle of the day, there are lots of things that can delay you,' he points out, also quietly, but through a smile. His voice is tinged with a touch of amusement. He isn't going to let his audience see his face slip.

'But you must've arrived home hours ago,' I point out.

I know that I should let it go, at least until later, but I just can't seem to. My words are dripping with a mix of disappointment and accusation.

'I had some work to do, and I needed a shower,' he says, although it sounds like he's making excuses.

'Okay, but I thought the whole point of you coming back was for time off work,' I continue.

For a fleeting moment, Millsy's smile wavers, his defences go down, exposing a glimpse of weariness, strain and frustration. But then, almost instantly, his smile returns, and his protective shield goes back up.

'Cara, do we really have to do this here? Now? We haven't seen each other for six weeks, we're at a party...'

The weight of his unfinished sentence clouds the air between us.

I chew my thumbnail as I think about what to say. He's right, we can't do this here. Probably best I go get a drink, calm down, and leave him to run the game in peace.

When Millsy left for LA six weeks ago, we knew how long it was going to be before we saw one another again, but this past week in particular I've been worrying, wondering what it would be like. I've been excited too, though, to see the man I love, and seeing him walk through that door I fancied him just as much as I ever have – if not more.

Everyone thinks we're the perfect couple, and we probably were, once upon a time, but not any more. We have a secret, one that we've been keeping from everyone who knows us, and it's a secret that we're going to have to keep for a while longer. I don't know how we're going to come clean, or when exactly, but everyone is going to find out sooner or later that Millsy and I broke up, six weeks ago, and that we're only pretending we're still together for the sake of those around us.

But no one is going to find out today, though, or for the rest of this year if everything goes to plan, so I guess we'll cross that bridge when we come to it.

## 2

I wake up the same way I do every day. I stretch, rub my eyes, and then glance at the empty space next to me in bed. I run my hand over the sheets, feeling the emptiness of the space Millsy used to occupy. Even here, in my childhood bedroom at my parents' house, I still feel it. Well, when you're in a relationship for three years, you get used to sharing a bed with someone, and while occasional nights away for work don't disturb you at all (sometimes you even relish the idea of having all that space to stretch out for a night or two), there is something about knowing just how permanent that empty space is that hits you like a tonne of bricks, every morning, and it makes for one shitty start to the day.

Millsy needed to be back in Leeds for some work thing early today, so it made sense for him to go back to Leeds last night, whereas I had already floated the idea of us staying at my parents' house – almost as a reflex, because that's exactly what we would usually do – so I decided to still do it any way. To be honest, I'm kind of relieved. I hadn't expected it to be so awkward, so quickly, when I saw Millsy again after all these weeks of not really talking (well, other than swapping a few messages, to figure out how we make sure Christmas wasn't ruined for both our families), so starving off that inevitable uncomfortable first conversation where we sit down and make a full (and final) plan for the holidays is fine by me. I know I'll have to face it later today but, for now at least, I'm happy to maintain a blissful ignorance.

Something about waking up in my childhood bedroom makes this all feel real, as though I'm slipping back to basics, regressing to my sad single girl form. Well, I say 'sad single' because that is the way you're meant to feel, right? But in reality, I have nothing but happy memories triggered by this room.

My bedroom is a quirky blend of the confusing mix of geeky and girly interests I had as a teenager. Every inch of the space reflects my personality. Soft pink-painted walls serve as the backdrop, but then they are layered with posters and stickers of retro video games and pictures of planets and stars.

A large old wooden desk dominates one wall, its surface still cluttered with an assortment of puzzles, brain teasers, and board games. Rubik's Cubes, jigsaws, dumb little things from Christmas crackers, my old electronic Lights Out game (that I'm delighted to say still works) – anything I could problem-solve, anything I could get myself lost in. I've always needed answers to questions and solutions to problems – and when I don't get them, I grow frustrated and get low-key obsessed. I've managed to turn it into a career, designing escape rooms, so I suppose it's only fitting that I'm turning my own break-up into some kind of problem-solving game – or one hell of an extreme escape room.

A large pinboard still hangs proudly above the desk with a collage of faded disposable camera photographs still up there, hanging on by some seriously ancient BluTack. I can see my childhood friends smiling over at me from the photos, so I smile back, even though we're not really friends any more. I never saw it becoming an issue, when they all chose to throw their efforts into getting married and starting families, whereas I was more motivated by the idea of starting my career and seeing where I could get with that first. I don't know why they decided that the route I was taking was leading me too far away from them to still be friends, but they made the invisible walls of their 'Mummy Club' impenetrable if you were missing that one vital part of the dress code, that one must-have accessory: a baby. Still, I'm sure they're all happy now, and I am – well, I was until my break-up, at least, but work is going well, so focusing on my career was definitely a good call for me.

I pull myself out of bed and walk across the purple carpet over to the window where I glance out over my parents' perfectly picturesque views. My mum and dad's large detached house is nestled amidst the rolling green hills of Haworth – the Worth Valley steam train line actually passes the bottom of the back garden, which made growing up feel a little bit like I was starring in my own modern-day take on *The Railway Children*. It's so beautiful here, like living in a postcard, one 'wishing you were here' in rural paradise. It's funny how growing up somewhere so seemingly remote made me crave the idea of the hustle and bustle of the big city, which is why I couldn't wait to escape to Leeds in my twenties.

It's funnier still that now, with my impending break-up with Millsy, I'm going to have to give up living in the flat we share (but he owns) in the city and potentially move back here while I find somewhere new. I suppose I could live anywhere I wanted, I'm just not sure where that is any more. What I have – or had, anyway – was what I wanted, I really don't want to give it all up.

I slip on my trusty dressing gown – the one with the decade-old Dream Matte Mousse foundation stains from when I used to absolutely cake myself in it as a teenager – and make my way downstairs, the delicious smell of my mum's cooking growing stronger with every step that I take.

I know that, were I to tell my mum about my break-up, she would be an absolute dream, a whirlwind of support. I don't think there is anything she wouldn't do to make me feel better, and I just know that my break-up would have one hell of a menu, but that's almost the reason I'm not telling her, why we're not telling anyone. The problem is that Millsy and I had no idea we were going to break up, until we did – but obviously no one goes into relationships thinking about when it will end.

So, naturally, when talk of Christmas came up, and someone suggested we all have our first big family Christmas together – my family and Millsy's family – at Millsy's grandma's big, beautiful house on the side of a loch in Scotland, everyone was so excited for it. Plans were made, food was ordered way in advance and, to be honest, even when Millsy and I did break up, it felt like there was an element of bluff calling, of the stress from both our jobs putting strain on our relationship, I don't think either of us thought this break-up would actually take... and now here we are, just a few weeks before Christmas, with nothing to do but go with it – well, not unless we're willing to ruin Christmas for everyone by either having to cancel it, or making everyone feel really uncomfortable with our break-up hanging over the day like an unwanted, uninvited guest. The only real option is to fake it. It's not easy, though, living a lie, and I've been doing it alone so far which, to be honest, is probably easier, because I only need to get my story straight with myself. It's probably hardest in situations like I'm about to walk into now, when it's just my parents and Oliver, the people who know me best, who are the ones who can usually read me like a book.

I feel the warmth the second I arrive in the kitchen, not just from all the cooking, or the heating that my mum likes to keep on at full whack, but from my happy family who are all tucking into one hell of a breakfast spread.

'Here she is,' Mum says with a smile. 'I kept plenty of food back for you, in case you fancied a lie-in, but you've timed it perfectly. Come on, sit down, grab a plate.'

I don't need telling twice.

Annie Brooks, my mum, is like a human ray of sunshine. She is a petite lady, just about making it over the five-foot mark if she stands on her tiptoes, proving that sometimes great things really do come in small packages. She has sleek chestnut-brown hair, a warm smile and twinkling eyes, giving her this magical ability to make everyone feel instantly at ease.

Everyone but my Auntie Mary, of course, who seems to take all my mum's wonderful qualities as somehow personally offensive to her. I often wonder if perhaps, given that it was always just her and my mum growing up, Mary viewed my mum as this annoying benchmark, someone she felt like she needed to live up to, but who she couldn't be bothered to try to compete with.

Oliver and I are similar, in that it's just the two of us, but we've never felt like we needed to compete with one another. I don't resent how smart he is, I just make sure I'm always on his team when we do quizzes. But with Auntie Mary, everything my mum does offends her – even silly things, like Mum dying her grey away, whereas Auntie Mary has a full head of grey curls, so she constantly berates my mum for her 'vanity'. Mary could dye her hair, but she doesn't want to, but you better believe she's going to be inexplicably mad at everyone who does.

I sit down next to Oliver, reminding myself how lucky I am to have a sibling I have such a good relationship with.

'Good morning, Dr Brooks,' I playfully tease him.

'Erm, I'm not quite a doctor, not yet,' he reminds me. 'I could still mess it up.'

'You're not going to mess it up,' my dad insists, unwilling to even joke about such a thing.

Oliver raises his eyebrows and shovels a large piece of pancake into his mouth, lest he say another word. I genuinely believe he hasn't actually ruled out bumbling the PhD he's been working on for years, but there's no way he isn't going to smash it.

Oliver, who stands tall at around 6'1, cuts a striking yet unassuming figure. His general vibe combines intellectual wit with understated confidence, but he's definitely one to use his words wisely, and even he knows a debate with Auntie Mary will never be worth his breath, especially when she's being 'that way out' – a phrase my mum and gran have always used to describe her fun little moods.

He wears his chestnut hair neatly blown back which, coupled with his round-rimmed glasses, somehow gives away the fact that he is an academic. He's growing a bit of a beard – or trying to, at least, he'll be the first one to tell you he can't seem to get beyond the stubble stage. It suits him, though, adding a touch of maturity and sophistication to his otherwise youthful appearance. The interesting thing about Oliver is that he somehow boasts confidence while lacking self-confidence – meaning he can talk to a room full of people, just not about himself.

'How's your business thing going?' my dad asks me from over his newspaper.

Ted Brooks personifies the quintessential Yorkshire dad, as if he stepped right out of an episode of *Emmerdale* (or what someone like me, who hasn't ever watched an episode of *Emmerdale*, would imagine, at least). With his unwavering strength and stoic silence, he's your classic Yorkshireman, only breaking said silence to deliver straight-talking statements that cut through any pretence or seriously dad-y one-liners. He's a master of frugality, meticulously watching every penny (for himself and those around him), unless it involves splurging on prime cuts of meat or speciality pints of beer.

Unsurprisingly, Oliver gets his height from our dad, who is way over six foot, but he's a friendly giant, a teddy bear disguised as a mountain, and a joy to be around. The only thing he loves more than his family is cracking terrible jokes, and while I may not have inherited his height (at 5'7, I stand somewhere in the middle, between my tiny mum and my towering dad), he has most definitely passed his wit and sarcasm on to me.

However, being a sixty-something Yorkshireman means that he doesn't always find 'modern' versions of things all that easy to understand, like tech, or women, and so my 'business thing' as he calls it is really something he struggles with.

My job, for the best part of my twenties, has been designing escape rooms for a popular company in Leeds. I would come up with the concepts for the rooms, the blueprints for them, and then the puzzles that would be inside them. However, about a year ago I had this big idea, a way to take escape rooms outside, and so I decided to quit my job and go it alone. I found someone to work with on the techy side of things and, finally, I think we're getting somewhere. I'm meeting Charlie, my tech guy, in Leeds later today to hopefully iron out the last of the kinks. I'm nervously excited to try the final version.

'Don't call it a "business thing",' Mum ticks my dad off. 'It's an... AI? Erm...'

'AR,' I correct her with a smile. 'It's an augmented reality escape room, that you can play in the city centre with nothing but your phone. Think of it like a treasure hunt, with clues, that takes you around the city's landmarks.'

'So, what, you're going to leave stuff lying around in the city?' Dad replies.

'No, it's all in an app,' I explain. 'So you'll follow a clue, to where you think the right place is, then when you get there you'll point your phone at it, and while you're looking at it through your phone, you'll see things on your screen, that look like they're right there in front of you.'

Dad looks none the wiser.

'It uses GPS,' Oliver joins in. 'Like your satnav. So when you arrive at the right location, your phone will show you things in the right place, and if you're right, you'll get the next clue.'

'Oh, right, okay,' Dad says. He thinks for a moment. 'Why?'

I snort, causing the sip of tea I just took to almost shoot out of my nose.

'For fun, Dad,' I say simply. 'All of this is for fun.'

'Your dad thinks barbequing meat is the height of fun,' Mum teases.

'You've never complained about my sausage before,' he replies to her, deadpan.

Oliver and I laugh. I can never quite tell if they're always intentional jokes, or if Dad just often says the wrong thing, but that just makes it all the funnier.

'Anyway, it's a shame Millsy couldn't join us for breakfast,' Mum says, changing the subject. 'We've missed him. When do you think we'll see you both next? We need to make the most of him, before he jets back off to shoot his movie.'

My heart jumps into my mouth. I don't know how to answer that. If nothing were wrong then we would probably be here tonight, for dinner, because Millsy is as obsessed with my mum's cooking as I am, but the thought of having to fake it any more than is absolutely necessary terrifies me. It's going to be exhausting doing the minimum.

'Well, I've got work today,' I say. 'And we're going to a wedding the day after...'

'Don't forget, we're planning family Christmas on the 6th,' Mum reminds me.

I pull a face.

'I know, I know, but I find it all easier when you're here,' she says.

'Then I'll be here,' I reply. 'What could be better than sitting down with Mary and Flora to try to come up with a plan everyone is happy with?'

'You could repeat Mary's words back to her and she wouldn't be happy with them,' Dad jokes.

'You could have some fun with that,' Oliver chimes in with a cheeky smile. 'Any time you don't like her ideas just agree with them and watch her change her mind.'

I laugh, but that might actually work.

'Well, I'd better get a move on,' I say as I load my plate up with round two. 'After this, of course. But I need to try to catch Millsy before I head out to work. But I can let you know when we can make it over.'

'Do,' Mum replies. 'Otherwise it's going to be family Christmas – oh, actually, we've got Sal's first birthday before that.'

'Yay, a one-year-old's birthday party,' I say sarcastically. 'Can't wait.'

It's strange but, when I was with Millsy, I never used to dread dumb family events. Well, when you have an ally, someone by your side to have a laugh with, there is no wedding, birthday or gender reveal party you can't endure. Everything was always so much fun with Millsy, and you could guarantee we would get into scrapes, like donkey-baby-gate last night, but we would always have a laugh as we teamed together to put things right.

With one last season of events to attend together, I can't help but think about future events – about future life, really, and what it's going to look like without him, and it really, really doesn't look great.

## 3

I step out of Leeds station, my senses immediately overwhelmed as I try to merge with the bustling crowd of shoppers and busy workers hurrying about during their lunch break.

Leeds is always busy. It's a beautiful, vibrant city that seems to grow and grow by the day. I used to live in the City Heights building, before Millsy and I became flatmates, which sits right between Northern Ballet and Leeds Playhouse, with views stretching right across the city centre. There are plenty of iconic places to spot in the Leeds skyline. Both the Victoria Gate and Trinity shopping centres have such striking architecture, the Town Hall and the Civic Hall both have ornate towers that reach for the sky, and then there are the super-tall buildings like Bridgewater Place (also known as The Dalek because, well, it looks just like one) which towers over the city at over 350 foot. I visited a friend in the City Heights building recently and couldn't believe it when I saw how much the skyline had changed in just three years, with skyscrapers pinging up everywhere, making the original landmarks that little bit harder to pick out.

I love Leeds. It's a city that never seems to slow down, that is bursting with an infectious energy. I mean, go to any gig, and feel yourself getting enveloped in the hug of a 'Yorkshire, Yorkshire, Yorkshire' chant. The streets are alive with a diverse mix of people, everyone immersed in their own world, hurrying along with intense purpose or not a care in the world. It's especially busy today, given that we're in the first week of December, and the Christmas shopping rush has begun. Despite the chaos that comes with it, I can't wait to do my own Christmas shopping here, and to visit the legendary German Christmas market when it makes its return this year, because it is such a vital part of the Leeds Christmas experience, to ride the carousel with a hotdog in one hand and chocolate-covered marshmallow in the other. I can't get excited about Christmas yet, though, not until I've sorted a few things out.

Millsy owns a penthouse apartment, on the top floor of a small building just across the river from Leeds Dock. It's a great spot, quieter than being in the dock itself, just outside the chaos of the shops and the bars, with stunning views of the river and canal, and the Royal Armouries museum. Our balcony is directly across from the museum's pièce de résistance, the Hall of Steel, a glass tower full of weapons that looks so beautiful when it's lit up on a night-time.

I walk along the side of the River Aire, which snakes through the heart of Leeds, until I reach my destination: home. Well, home for now, at least.

I turn the key in the lock before stepping into our apartment, which once felt like a sanctuary from the rest of the world. This place has been my home for three years, and Millsy isn't a monster, so he suggested I keep living here until at least the new year. I can't imagine living anywhere else now.

For the first time in weeks, the familiar scent of Millsy's aftershave greets me as I walk through the door. God, I've missed that smell. It lingered for a while after he left, like his ghost, until it gradually faded away like some kind of weird grieving process – one that I'm going to have to start all over again.

As I close the door behind me, the usual air of peace and quiet settles around me, but only for a second, because I can hear something. It's a faint murmur, barely audible amidst the silence. I squint, as though that's going to improve my hearing, but as I make my way further down the hallway, it gets clearer. Voices, coming from the spare bedroom – the room that used to be my room, and the room that Millsy has agreed to sleep in for the time being.

I take off my shoes and tiptoe towards the bedroom door.

'I just... I don't know what to do,' I overhear Millsy say. 'It's not easy, when you want someone, so, so bad, but you can't have them.'

My heart thumps hard against the wall of my chest. Is that really how he feels?

'But you can have me,' a female voice replies, winding me, knocking me sick. 'I'm all yours. You've had me before and you can have me again. So, come on, take it.'

My jaw drops. There's a woman in there with him. In our apartment, not twenty-four hours since he landed back in the UK.

'Oh, I'm going to take it,' he replies. 'I'm going to take all of it.'

For someone so horrified by what she can hear going on, on the other side of the closed bedroom door, I surprise even myself when I barge into the room, practically tearing the door from its hinges, opening my mouth to say God knows what, but I'm no sooner through the door when I'm stopped in my tracks.

'Cara,' Millsy blurts, standing up from where he was sitting on the bed.

A petite, unrealistically attractive brunette woman in her

early thirties sits opposite him, a pile of papers between them. What the hell?

'I didn't think you would be home so soon,' he continues. 'We were just, er, we were working.'

Millsy looks like a rabbit caught in the headlights.

'Hi,' the woman says to me. 'I'm Tally.'

The first thing that strikes me – well, after the fact that she looks like she could be one of the Kardashian-Jenners – is her LA accent. He's brought her home with him.

'Hello,' I say, my manners like a reflex.

'I'll be back in a minute,' Millsy tells her. 'I'll just fill Cara in.'

'Sure,' Tally replies, wincing playfully for effect.

I walk out of the spare room, across the living room and into my bedroom. Millsy is only a few steps behind me.

'What the hell is going on?' I ask him. 'Who is that?'

'That's Tally,' he replies.

'I know it's fucking Tally,' I snap before pausing for a moment, telling myself to calm down. 'Who is Tally?'

Millsy exhales deeply, running a hand through his hair as he sits down on the bed. On our bed. Well, his bed. Oh, boy.

'It's the movie,' he tells me. 'Things are not going well.'

When I met Millsy, he very much kept his work life to himself, to the point where I was suspicious about how he made his money, until one day I learned the truth: Millsy was a body double in movies. So if they needed a perfectly toned arse for a shot in an action movie, or an up-close torso for a romance scene in one of those sexually charged Netflix mum-porn series, Millsy was the guy they went to. Of course, he wanted to be a 'real' actor, and not long after we got together, he finally landed his big break, playing a villain in a superhero movie. Of course, the whole thing was mocap, so you couldn't actually tell it was Millsy in the movie, which is the reason why he and his agent think his big movie career never took off, even though the movie itself was a hit.

Things were quiet for a while, and we were happy, life was simple again. But then his agent put him forward for a role, playing the lead in *Chaos of Desire*, a biopic about the late, great country music star Billy Gill. I'm no country music fan but even I know Billy Gill, the one who had an affair with his musical rival's wife for years, before falling victim to various addictions and tragically taking his own life. And while there were a whole host of Hollywood A-listers vying for the role, the people managing Billy's estate decided that they wanted Millsy, because he looks exactly like a young Billy Gill, to the point where it's kind of creepy. It's hard to believe things aren't going well, when he's not only a great actor, but a twin of the character he is playing.

'What do you mean?' I ask.

'You know we're supposed to start shooting, in the new year,' he replies and I nod. 'Well, for some reason, try as I might...'

Millsy pauses for a second. He looks almost embarrassed.

'I just can't do the accent,' he blurts. 'The Southern drawl. I can't do it.'

'You weren't even doing an accent,' I point out.

'Tally said I should familiarise myself with the lines in my own accent first,' he says. 'Yes, I am *that* bad.'

'How bad can you be?' I reply. 'Even I can do it.'

I blurt out a few random lines I've heard Elvis say, unsure if that's even the correct accent, but I vaguely hit the right notes.

'Oh, I'm going to take it,' he says, delivering the line I heard him practising through the bedroom door. 'I'm going to take all of it.'

I can't hide my cringe and Millsy pulls a face back at me, as if to say he told me so.

'It's not that bad,' I lie, because it is bad, it's really bad – he sounds fresh out of an episode of *Fargo*.

'Well, it needs to be perfect,' he says, agreeing to disagree. 'This biopic is supposed to be a poignant, unforgettable watch – a celebration of music, resilience, and the enduring impact of a true legend. It's not going to be that if I sound like an Irish cowboy with a cold.'

I can't help but laugh at his choice of words.

'I know, I know, but it's not funny,' he insists. 'If I can't get it right, they're going to replace me. So I've got the holidays, to master the accent, and that's where Tally comes in. They've assigned her to me – she's a voice and dialect coach – to shadow me, to help me learn the accent, and to keep using it.'

'In the bedroom,' I can't help but point out, although I do my best not to sound jealous.

'That was just to keep out of your way,' he says. 'I don't want you feeling like you can't spend time in the living space.'

'Feel free to use the living room,' I reply. 'I'm hardly in these days.'

An absolute lie.

'Okay, thanks,' he says.

'God, you're not going to be method acting, are you?' I reply. 'Give me a heads up if you're going to start shagging other people's wives and slapping me when you've had too much to drink.'

I'm sort of joking but, if he is method acting, it's worth noting that fame turned Billy Gill into an arsehole.

'Not method acting, as such,' he quickly insists. 'I won't be staying in character. Just staying in vocal character, I suppose.'

'So you're going to be talking like *that* all Christmas?' I reply in disbelief.

My God, perhaps I'm lucky we're separated, imagine him

talking like that in the bedroom. Well, he's talking like that in the bedroom now, in a literal sense, but you know what I mean.

'With Tally shadowing me around, teaching me, keeping me in check, it should get better,' he says.

'So, what, is she here for like a week?' I ask. 'Because you know we've got so many plans, and you did promise me you wouldn't be working, and—'

'Cara,' Millsy cuts me off. 'She's here for Christmas, until I go back to LA, to help me get this right. There are millions of dollars riding on this project, if I don't do as they say, they'll replace me. I can't say no.'

A perplexed expression takes hold of my face, a mixture of irritation and bewilderment contorting my muscles, working them like a puppet on a string.

'Sorry, are you telling me she's spending Christmas Day with us?' I reply. 'This random woman I just found in your bedroom?'

'This random woman is Tally, a highly skilled voice and dialect coach, and she's worked with A-listers – I'm lucky to have her,' he insists. 'But, yes, she's spending Christmas Day with us. She's spending every day with us. I have to get this right, Cara. I'm not wasting this opportunity.'

'What, so she's coming to the wedding?' I reply. 'To the birthday parties and work dos, and to stay at your gran's house?'

'I don't have a choice,' he insists kind of weakly.

I suppose he doesn't.

'Bloody hell, Millsy, people are going to think we're some kind of throuple,' I blurt.

'Well, if the idea is to pretend we're still together, that might help,' he half-jokes. 'Look, I'm stressed with work, you're stressed with work, it will be a good distraction for everyone around us. And if I'm busy with Tally then that means you can get on with your life, talk to new people, not have to sit with me everywhere we go.'

I don't let it show but that one hurt. I wanted to sit with him everywhere we went. What is he doing, trying to encourage me to get on with my life? Should I be getting on with my life? I was going to wait at least until our break-up was official. Oh my God, has he moved on already?

'We can still do what we planned, though,' he continues. 'We can keep our separation a secret, until after Christmas, because you're right, there's no sense in ruining it for everyone else, and making things awkward over Christmas dinner. That's still what you want, right?'

I sigh.

'Everyone is going to be gutted. I think my family loves you just as much as they do me,' I tell him. 'But... Right, yeah, okay. She's not staying here, though, is she?'

I can't help but sound suspicious.

The news of this random woman infiltrating our holidays has caught me off guard. I had secretly hoped that perhaps Millsy and I could find a way to mend our relationship in the run-up to Christmas, that our break-up wouldn't ever need to be official, but now this. Is it some sort of sign, from the universe, that things are really over? Millsy is certainly making it sound that way. And, am I mad, or did I sense some kind of tension between Millsy and Tally, which only makes the situation even messier? I can't believe she's going to be hanging around us, that we're not going to get much time alone, time to realise how good we are together, because we were so, so good together.

'No, she's staying in one of the hotels, just down the river,' he replies. 'But, Cara, I'm going to have to spend a lot of time with her. I need to get this right. But you're still busy with work, aren't you?'

'I am,' I reply. 'Speaking of which, I'd better get a move on, get changed, and head there now.'

'Right, well, I'll let you get on,' he says.

Sitting here in our old bedroom together, the place where we used to hang out in bed, watch Netflix, eat pizza, roll around together until the sun came up – I can't help but feel a strange mix of nostalgia and sadness. Every corner of the room holds memories and, my God, if these walls could talk they would probably be enrolled in some kind of therapy. It's funny how this just doesn't feel like our room any more, already, we'll never share the bed we're both sitting on together again. What a bittersweet reminder of what we had and what we've lost.

Millsy pulls himself to his feet and heads for the door, stopping as he reaches it, his gaze falling to the floor, the unmistakable sight of a man's T-shirt (one that he instantly knows isn't his) catching his eye. It's a sports top, in bright colours, one of those muscle-hugging, masculine-fit tops. Millsy's brow furrows inquisitively, and he turns to face me, curiosity etched on his face.

'Whose is that?' he asks, gesturing towards the discarded top with a quizzical expression.

I feel a slight pang of nervousness – I don't know why – but I quickly compose myself and try to sound casual with my response.

'What's that? Oh, it's Charlie's T-shirt, Charlie from work. I borrowed it after getting caught in the rain one day, and I haven't had a chance to return it yet.'

Millsy's eyes narrow ever so slightly, his thoughts concealed. I wish I could read his mind right now, does he believe me, is he bothered? I sense a flicker of curiosity mixed with something else. Perhaps a tinge of doubt or suspicion is lingering in the air.

Millsy nods, not saying a word, before heading back to the spare room where Tally is waiting for him.

I stare at Charlie's top. This is what happened, we were out in the city, mapping out an area of the game, and the heavens opened, soaking us both. I was wearing a white T-shirt which went completely see-through, and Charlie had a spare, clean gym top in his bag, so he gave me it to wear.

My first reaction was worry, not wanting Millsy to think I've had another guy in here, but after seeing that look on his face, I don't know, maybe I want him to be bothered.

I can't think about this now, I really do need to get to work. I'll go out, leaving Millsy and Tally alone in the bedroom, and get on with my work, without worrying or giving them a second thought.

Of course I will.

# 4

Heading back out into Leeds city centre, I find myself striding purposefully through the busy streets, and the only thing racing faster than my thoughts is my heartbeat – although that could have something to do with the fact that it is pretty much all uphill.

I'm running late – I'm always running late – so I cut through Trinity as I often do, not really considering the fact that a shopping centre in December couldn't ever possibly be considered a shortcut. Still, it's nice to admire the Christmas decorations and the twinkling lights on the stunning glass atrium roof above. But it no sooner swallows me up than it spits me out on Albion Street, right in front of Starbucks, so I grab a couple of coffees.

I'm meeting Charlie, the genius I have been working with on my augmented reality escape room, to doublecheck a clue placement outside the Town Hall, and it's a chilly day so I know he'll appreciate a warm drink.

Coffees in hand, I continue my uphill journey – it's quite poetic, really, because everything feels like an uphill journey at the moment. I can't get Millsy out of my mind. Thinking about him, our break-up, the fact I've left him alone in our flat with Tally. Honestly, it's only really occurring to me now that I've seen him in the flesh, but I've been subtly but confidently deluding myself that by the time he got back we would probably just pick up where we left off and be fine again. It's been running in the background, like an app you forget to close, one that is slowly draining your battery. And now here I am. And it really does feel scarily real.

I try to feed off the energy that the city pulses around me, to get my head in the game, to do whatever I need to, to find a way through these next few weeks and whatever they may bring with them. Despite the crowds and the chaos, I keep my head high as I walk confidently, my eyes fixed firmly ahead – not just to the Town Hall, but to the future. With each step I take, I remind myself of the strength and resilience that lies within me, reassuring myself that I am capable of overcoming whatever obstacles may come my way and that anything is possible if I want it enough, and I am ready to face whatever the world has in store, and... and I just tripped over seemingly nothing, almost landing face down on the floor in a pool of my own latte. Thankfully I find balance again, in all ways possible. I just need to take things a day at a time, see how it goes, and not worry too much about the future just yet.

After weaving through a maze of bodies, I finally emerge from the chaos of the shops, popping out right in front of my destination: Leeds Town Hall. The grand Victorian building stands tall and majestic, its stone façade decorated with intricate carvings and imposing columns. And then there are the lion sculptures, which stand proud out front, almost as though they're guarding the place.

As I near the bottom of the stairs, I notice a crowd of tourists gathered in front, laughing and posing for selfies. And then, amid everything, I spot Charlie, his familiar face like a beacon of warmth and friendliness – just what I need right now.

Charlie, dressed in a warm winter coat and a woolly hat, clutches an iPad in his gloved hands. When he spots me among the crowd, his eyes light up. He waves me over with a sheepish grin, eager to get away from the selfie-taking tourists and crack on with the task at hand. It might be my concept, but it is Charlie who has brought the game to life, and he's just as passionate about it as I am. I suppose, in a way, he's the game's daddy. There's no way I could have made it alone.

'Hello, Cara! Fancy bumping into you here,' Charlie exclaims, his voice playfully sarcastic. 'And you brought friends.'

Charlie nods towards the two coffees in my hand. I can't help but chuckle.

'Well, my friends almost didn't make it here,' I say. 'Neither did I. It's wild back there.'

With his wavy chestnut hair, playfully tousled and falling wherever it wants, Charlie possesses a boyish charm that seems to have been pulled straight out of an indie movie about an awkward but handsome nerd. His eyes, a gorgeous shade of hazel, try but fail to hide a mischievous sparkle, always making it seem like he has something up his sleeve – and sometimes he literally does, with his passion for magic tricks. He's definitely a nerd after my own heart and a real asset in an escape room. It's no surprise we hit it off right away.

One of the things I like the most about Charlie is that he's a cool nerd, like me – or like I like to think I am, at least. His coat is stylish, and hangs effortlessly from his lean frame in that cool way some people just can't fake. But this isn't a geek chic persona, he is truly a big old nerd, and big old nerds are my favourite kind of people.

'Well, here's your coffee,' I say, handing it over.

'And here's where we're at with the app,' he replies, turning the iPad for me to see.

'Wow, I can never get over how amazing it looks,' I blurt. 'I'm almost sad we made it, because we know all the answers, it means we can't really play it. Imagine it, though, solving riddles and puzzles while interacting with the real world, it's like being inside a movie.'

The idea is that the app will guide players through historic landmarks, quirky hidden spots, and charming nooks of Leeds. We've packed it with surprises, challenges, and even a few cheeky Easter eggs for those keen-eyed explorers. But, like I said, we both know all the answers like the back of our hand.

'Perhaps, when we're less busy, we can come up with a version for each other,' he suggests. 'That way we can at least get a taste of what it's like.'

'I'd love that,' I say with a smile.

I would definitely say our professional relationship has blossomed into a friendship, but how could it not, when we have so much in common and spend so much time together?

'And the good news is that I think I've sorted the problem we were having,' he continues. 'See.'

Charlie holds the iPad up in front of us, pointing it at one of the lion sculptures. Looking at it through the screen, the lion disappears, being replaced by a statue of a man on a horse. It's all to do with the next clue but locals will instantly recognise the statue as The Black Prince from City Square. Then, when players get there, the next clue will appear where the statue, which is over a hundred years old, is pointing. It's all coming together so well.

'You've smashed it,' I say proudly. 'My God, did you ever think it would work?'

'Of course,' he replies. 'Didn't you?'

'I mean, I hoped it would,' I reply. 'But I never think things will work out.'

'That's the spirit,' he cheers, once again breaking out that trademark playful sarcasm. 'Shall we give it a play-through, just in case?'

'Why not?' I reply.

Charlie stops in his tracks, as though something has just occurred to him.

'Sorry, no, your boyfriend gets back today, doesn't he?'

'Yesterday,' I reply.

'Then forget this, go, spend time with him,' Charlie insists.

No, I haven't told Charlie, I really haven't told a soul.

'It's okay, he's working,' I insist casually. 'I'm just getting in the way.'

'Okay, cool,' Charlie says, never one to pry.

As we make our way along the Headrow, to the starting point, we chat as we weave through the crowds.

'Look at them all,' Charlie says with faux disgust. 'So organised.'

'Is a few weeks before Christmas organised?' I reply. 'Because I am in no way ready for it and it's starting to worry me.'

'Oh, you won't believe how much shopping I still have to do, Cara,' he confesses. 'And my list seems to grow longer every day. I swear, I'll be running around like a headless chicken until Christmas Eve!'

'I always think I am the queen of procrastination – until I chat to you,' I reply with a smile, raising my voice as we stroll past a particularly noisy bar. It's never too early to start drinking around the holidays, is it?

'You're the queen, I'm the king,' he replies. 'It's a miracle we got this app done, when you think about it.'

'True,' I reply. 'And I suppose we could always do our shopping online. Click, click, click, click – boom.'

'What? No way,' he scoffs with a smile. 'I know, we're living in a digital world, and I'm a digital boy, but you can't do your Christmas shopping online.'

'Why not?' I enquire in disbelief.

'Bah, humbug! That's why,' he insists. 'There's something festive about the chaos of the high street, something that truly captures the spirit of Christmas like nothing else can. It's not Christmas unless you're physically wrestling the last roll of wrapping paper from someone in the wasteland of the festive aisle. Plus, I enjoy the challenge of finding the perfect gift amidst the madness.'

'Okay, well, if you're going to make it sound like an escape room, then of course it's going to sound appealing,' I concede. 'But, seeing as though I'm spending Christmas in Scotland, I can't quite leave it until Christmas Eve.'

'In that case, if you need a shopping buddy, just shout,' he replies. 'It will force me to do mine earlier too.'

'Thanks, I might just do that,' I reply. 'And I can still find a way to get us into a physical fight, if it's not quite the same without it.'

'Aw, thanks,' he jokes. 'Right, we're here.'

'Okay, fire her up,' I say excitedly. 'Let's take it from the top.'

'Let's go,' he replies. 'And there's a perfectly placed Starbucks between two clues, so the next ones are on me.'

'God, I love this game,' I say through a laugh. 'Let's do it.'

Charlie hits the start button and we begin our adventure. I know, we already know all the answers, so it's not exactly a challenge, and all the bugs should have been caught by now, but it's just fun spending time with Charlie, and a nice distraction from what's going on at home.

Ergh, I wonder what *is* going on at home.

## 5

As I step into the warmth of our penthouse apartment, a chill runs through me, almost as though my body is trying to shake off the cold at the door. My hands are frozen, my feet aching from the long walk, and I can't think of anything better than thawing myself out fully in a nice, warm bath – hopefully it will melt the stress of the day away too. But as I make my way towards my room, something catches my eye and stops me in my tracks.

There, on the sofa at the other side of the large open-plan living space, sit Millsy and Tally. I do a double-take when I notice Tally with a towel wrapped around her head. What on earth has she been doing? Why has she washed here when she has a perfectly fine hotel room just down the river from here? My mind races with possibilities, and suspicion clouds my thoughts. What have they been up to while I was out working with Charlie?

As I listen to their conversation, the two of them unaware I'm standing behind them, I notice they're talking about work at least.

'Y'all reckon I got it this time, Tally?' Millsy says.

I swear, I see Tally flinch.

'Remember to soften those consonants and elongate the vowels,' she replies. 'Give it another go.'

Millsy sighs, frustrated.

'Howdy, y'all, I'm Billy Gill,' Millsy says, his attempts falling flat and sounding more like a caricature than an authentic accent.

'It takes time, Joey,' she insists, patting his leg with her hand. 'Don't worry, we'll get there together.'

Joey! She calls him Joey? The fact that she doesn't call him Millsy, like everyone else, or Joe, his actual name, freaks me out a little. She already has her own nickname for him.

'It's like my tongue refuses to cooperate,' Millsy replies.

'Come on now, we both know you've got a fine working tongue in that mouth,' she says, in a flawless accent, but it's the words she says that leave me gobsmacked. I drop my keys on the hardwood floor.

They turn their heads simultaneously, their eyes widening as they realise I'm standing there. Millsy looks worried, as though he might be wondering just how long I've been spectating.

'Cara, hi,' he blurts.

'Oh, hello,' Tally adds, switching effortlessly back to her own accent.

'Hi, yeah, sorry to interrupt,' I reply, although I can't take my eyes off the towel on Tally's head, my imagination running wild. She must realise I'm staring.

'I hope you don't mind, Cara,' she starts. 'Joey mentioned I could use your bath since my hotel room doesn't have one, and the cold weather has been quite a challenge for me. It's a real drag, I don't know how you live here all year round.'

'I didn't think you would be back from work so soon,' Millsy says.

I can see that in his eyes.

'We're just finishing up here,' he adds.

'No worries, take your time,' I insist.

I notice the top part of a cupcake on the island – sort of the top centimetre or two of cake with the icing still neatly piled on top. I grab it and take a bite.

'Oh, that's Joey's,' Tally ever so helpfully points out.

'Oh, no, it's fine,' Millsy tells her. 'I don't eat the icing when I'm cutting, old habits die hard, so I leave it for Cara.'

'You eat his icing?' she asks me, like it's gross and gluttonous.

'I do,' I say proudly. 'And now I'm going to have a bath. Bye.'

'You might want to wait,' Millsy replies, stopping me almost immediately, so I snap around to look at him.

'What?' I ask.

'Joey, it really is best if you try to keep the accent,' Tally tells him gently. 'It's only going to make it harder for you, if you have to keep switching back and forth between the two.'

'Right, okay,' he replies in his own accent. Then he turns to me and forces himself into character. 'Y'all might want to wait a bit for that bath. Seems to me like the hot water might be all out.'

Awful, terrible, cringe of an attempt at the accent, but the fact that he's saying that to me, and in that stupid voice, makes my blood boil.

'Then I guess I'll have a cup of tea,' I reply. 'Leave you two to work on... that.'

'I know it's totally weird,' Tally says, obviously picking up on the tension. 'It's so important, though. Joey needs to practise his accent, and we're working hard on it.'

'Practising... in our living room... with a towel on your head,' I mutter quietly, so that only I can hear, as I head for the kitchen.

As I fill the kettle, I wonder to myself how many times you would need to boil it to get a warm bath from a tank of nothing but cold water. Probably too many times to make it worth it.

I've no sooner clicked it on when Millsy appears next to me.

'Well, hey there, miss,' he says, in his terrible accent, with a playful smile.

'Can you knock that off, please,' I insist.

'Sorry about the hot water,' he says, assuming that's why I'm annoyed. 'I had a shower earlier. I meant to hit the boost button before you came home but I didn't think you would be back so soon.'

'Yeah, you said,' I reply. 'It's fine.'

'Were you planning on going out tonight?' he asks.

'Going out? Where would I be going?' I reply, almost suspiciously. Does he want me to go out, to get me out of the way?

'Oh, I don't know. I just thought maybe you had plans,' he replies. 'That you might be having a bath to get ready to go out.'

'No,' I reply, a little too quickly perhaps.

I watch as Millsy seems to attempt to analyse me with his eyes. It's as though he can tell something is up, but can't quite put his finger on what perhaps.

'Are you seeing someone?' he asks, but then he quickly backtracks. 'Look, Cara, if you're seeing someone, that's okay. You don't have to hide it from me. We're not together any more and I'm a big boy.'

I pause for a second. I just, wow, I don't know. He sounds so... okay with it all. I wasn't expecting that. It's almost as though he wants me to move on. Wait, does he want me to move on? Is this his way of encouraging me, or letting me know that he has moved on? I glance back across the open-plan room to where Tally is sitting, her comments about Millsy's tongue echoing in my brain. Is something going on between them?

'So you've taken me having a bath and turned it into that I'm seeing someone?' I reply, scrunching my face at my own confusing choice of words. I'm not even sure that makes sense, but he knows what I mean. 'It doesn't sound like you care much.'

'I'm just saying, it's a while since we split, if that's what you're doing, I'm not going to say anything,' he insists, trying to calm things down.

My God, why does it seem so much like he wants me to move on?

'Millsy, if you want me to move on so badly then fine, I'll do it,' I reply. 'I hope it makes you happy, now go back to your lesson, before your teacher tells you off for slipping back into Sean Bean.'

Sean Bean isn't even from the same part of Yorkshire as us, but my point is made.

'Cara, I didn't mean...'

'Honestly, just go back to your lesson,' I insist. 'I think it's time I moved on too.'

Millsy sighs and heads back to Tally.

I mean, I don't really think it's time I moved on, but perhaps Millsy needs to see me moving on and realise what he's missing – or, I suppose, if we aren't going to get back together, then the sooner I get back on the horse the better, because if I remember right you have to kiss a lot of frogs (or pretend you can't because you have a cold sore coming, you can just feel it) before you meet a prince.

So moving on, or going through the motions of moving on, is what I'll do.

Sadly, I only know one way to do it...

## 6

One of my all-time strengths has to be that, even when I'm not running late, I'm constantly thinking of ways to ensure I'll be running late later. Absolutely fantastic trait to have, I must be a dream to know.

It's the day of our friends' wedding – Peri and Connor, one of the couples from our boardgame group – and even though I knew I should be getting ready, I just couldn't stomach listening to Millsy and Tally over the breakfast table. Look, I can't say for sure that they're flirting, and they are working on his accent, but they're clearly having so much fun with it, and given that I'm not a part of it, and don't know what half of what they're saying means, it feels like their own little secret club that I'm not a part of. Prolongation and diphthongisation? What? It reminds me of when my brother and I used to speak in Pig Latin so that our parents didn't know what we were saying. I feel like I'm getting a taste of what that must have been like for Mum and Dad and, I have to say, *it'syay eallyray issingpay emay offyay.*

So, with some Christmas presents that I ordered online to collect from town (I know, I know, bah, humbug!), I made my excuses. Even the thought of sharing a taxi with them made me throw up in my mouth a little, so I told them I would have to meet them there. I just can't believe that all of a sudden we have to cart this random woman around with us – and I really, really can't believe Peri and Connor were happy to add her to the guestlist last minute.

This wedding has been a pain in my arse since day one. Peri and Connor are our friends, and I love them, but what is it about weddings that makes people take the piss? It's hard enough when people set dress codes – and even restrictive colour schemes – and then expect you to go out and buy all new specific stuff just for one day, but Peri and Connor have taken things a step too far.

Like us, the happy couple loves puzzles and games and, as such, decided that it should play a big part of their wedding day, so after the ceremony (which is for close family only) we're all heading to the reception at some old English country house, for a murder mystery-themed party. Each to their own, and I always do my best to accommodate any wedding outfit requirements (apart from that time Auntie Mary suggested I lose weight so that I could fit into a bridesmaid dress), but we were all given really specific characters to dress up as.

While we were assured not to worry, we wouldn't have to source our own outfits, we should simply send our measure-ments to the wedding coordinator who would make outfits for us, we did still have to pay for them ourselves. So Millsy was cast as a gangster, with his outfit being some kind of 1920s mob boss suit, and his outfit turned up just fine. I, on the other hand, was cast as a French maid, and my dress turned up with a hole in it. It's okay, though, because I sent it back, and Peri said it was being couriered here this morning, and that she would have an outfit for Tally to wear too. She said it was a case of the more the merrier, as far as bringing Tally along goes, but you've got to wonder how many people RSVP'd yes to this.

With my hair and make-up good to go, I head into the living room to find my dress but there's no sign of it. I assumed Millsy would have signed for the delivery for me while I was out, because it should definitely be here by now.

I hurry into the bedroom and grab my phone from its charger. I find the wedding coordinator's number and hover my finger over it. I was told to call her, if there were any problems, but only if it was absolutely necessary. To me, no outfit is absolutely a necessary reason to call, otherwise the biggest mystery at the wedding is going to be the disappearance of my dress, and why I turned up in my normal clothes.

'This better be good,' the coordinator answers eventually.

And hello to you too.

'Hi,' I say, not as able to cut to the chase as easily as she is. 'It's Cara Brooks, my outfit for Peri and Connor's wedding was supposed to be delivered this morning, it doesn't seem to have turned up.'

'Wait,' she says – is she talking to me?

I give her a few seconds and I'm about to open my mouth when...

'It says delivered and signed for,' she replies. 'It might have gone to the wrong address. Have you checked with your neighbours?'

'Not yet,' I say. 'What if they don't have it?'

She sighs.

'I could—'

'Do you know Dresstination on Headingley?' she interrupts.

'I do,' I reply.

Anyone who has ever done an Otley Run pub crawl knows the fancy-dress shop in Headingley.

'Right, I'm going to call ahead, and have them put you one aside, they'll let you change there,' she says. 'Luckily a French maid is one of the easiest outfits to find – you're not unique at all.'

I frown to myself.

'Right, okay, thanks,' I reply. 'I'll get going.'

The wedding coordinator hangs up without saying goodbye. Then again, she is probably busy.

I throw on a tracksuit and book myself a taxi. So now I need to go to Headingley first, which is on the other side of Leeds to where I am supposed to be going, but I don't have much choice, do I?

I hurry down to the taxi and give him my instructions. The driver laughs when I say that I'm going to a wedding via a fancy-dress store – until she realises I'm not joking, and then she laughs even harder.

Why do I have a bad feeling about this?

# 7

As I step out of the taxi, the majestic English country mansion comes into view, its grandeur only accentuated by its wintry surroundings. It's a beacon of warmth and light on an otherwise dark and gloomy day.

The air is crisp but the weather is otherwise okay – no snow to trap me here, or ice for me to stack it on as I walk towards the door, so that's good.

I am no sooner greeted at the door when I am invited to check my coat. I really, really don't want to surrender my coat, but what choice do I have? As I remove it and hand it over, I notice the hostess's eyes widen, only for a split second before she snaps back into professional mode, but I definitely spotted it. It's not like I can blame her, though, I would probably react in a similar way, if I saw someone in an outfit like this standing in front of me at a wedding. I suppose I should be thankful, that the wedding coordinator was able to arrange an outfit for me at the last minute, but that is the problem with it. It's not just that it's very cheap, low-quality material – but know that it is – it's more the fact that this particular French maid's outfit is more like the kind you would find in an adult store – short, tight, and low-cut. It's very risqué, to put it politely, and something that might be more appropriate for a more intimate setting, but it feels completely wrong (in so, so many ways) for a wedding.

'The bar is through there,' she instructs me. 'Drinks are being served while we wait for the bride and groom to arrive.'

'Fab,' I say, trying to muster up a smile.

As I head for the bar, I catch my reflection in a large gold-framed mirror. God, it's worse than I remember it looking when I tried it on. The black dress clings to my body, mapping out my figure in detail, and the hemline is a touch too short for comfort. I tug at the fabric, a last-ditch attempt to try to make it cover more skin, but it doesn't work.

I hover at the door. Okay, so I look like a stripper, but I'm probably overthinking it. Everyone here is in costume, everyone probably feels a bit daft. I'm not really going to stand out, am I?

Here goes. It's showtime.

As I enter the room, it's as if a spotlight is shining on me, my outfit seemingly drawing everyone's attention. It's one of those cliché record scratch moments, where conversations pause and music stops playing but I could be imagining that last part.

I mentally beg the earth to crack open and swallow me whole, but nothing happens. The room quickly returns to its lively chatter – probably when they realise I'm not actually a stripper, so nothing to see here, and so I make my way over to Millsy and Tally. The first thing I notice is that Tally is dressed as a French maid – one that covers all her bits and pieces, so she's got me beat there.

Millsy raises an eyebrow, clearly taken aback by my attire.

'Cara, what... what are you wearing?' he asks, baffled but mildly amused.

'Oh, this old thing?' I joke. 'This is the emergency French

maid's outfit I had to pick up from a fancy-dress shop, because mine was supposedly delivered and signed for this morning, but I couldn't find any sign of it at home.'

'No, well, only one outfit arrived, so we assumed it was the last-minute outfit for Tally, and that maybe you had gone to collect yours, and... oh.'

I feel my cheeks flush with a mixture of embarrassment and a little bit of anger.

Tally chuckles, her eyes twinkling mischievously as we all come to the same realisation.

'Oh, hon, I think there may have been a mix-up. I'm guessing this outfit was meant for you and mine never showed up. I thought it felt a bit roomy on me.'

I bite my tongue.

'You've always been great at turning heads,' Millsy offers up with a smile.

'And you've never been good at staying in vocal character,' Tally ticks him off. 'Come on, now. If you want to go down an octave it's going to take work.'

'I didn't realise it was going to hurt my oesophagus so much,' he replies – then he realises he's still speaking in his own accent, so he tries again. 'I didn't realise it was going to haaaa—'

Stunning.

'Millsy, can I have a word with you?' I ask. 'In private.'

'Sure thing,' he says, sounding like Borat for absolutely no logical reason. It's almost as though his vocal cords are panicking.

My annoyance rises to the surface as I enter the next room with Millsy. This is supposed to be our friends' wedding, a special occasion for us all to celebrate, and here I am, feeling like a bystander in my own life. And to make matters worse, Tally is here, dressed in my outfit, and standing by Millsy's side as if she belongs there.

I realise we're in the wedding reception room so I don't venture much further inside than just through the doorway. Millsy grabs a couple of welcome drinks from a server to bring with him. He hands me one before removing the glacé cherry garnish from my glass and dropping it in his, because he knows I don't like them.

For a moment I just stare at him, hoping he'll take the lead, that he'll say something that makes me feel better about all of this.

'What's wrong?' he eventually says, as though he has no idea what on earth I could possibly be wanting to talk to him about. He's using his own voice, at least.

'What's wrong?' I repeat back to him. 'What's wrong is that I can't believe Tally is here, wearing my outfit, acting like she owns the place – or like she owns you, at least. This is our friends' wedding, their big day, we're not on the set of a movie.'

'Cara, come on,' he replies, frustrated. 'You know we have to get the accent right, you know the situation. It's not like we planned for all of this to happen this way.'

The fact that he's even pointing that out makes me suspicious.

'But over Christmas?' I reply. 'When we've got so many plans, so much going on, so much we need to talk about...'

'I know it's not ideal, but my entire career is riding on this, you understand that, right?' he says. 'This is all I've got going for me, I need to put all my eggs in this basket – where else am I going to put them?'

I want to say I will happily take his eggs, and give him mine, but that doesn't make a tonne of sense, and I can't exactly ask him to bail on his career for me. I haven't been doing that for him. I went to LA with him, for his first movie, but then when it was back to reality I got back on with work, began working on the app, and when that started taking up a lot of my time, that's when we realised we were going to have to try the long-distance thing for a while. I didn't entertain abandoning my career to go with him, and he didn't ask me to. There's nothing I can say.

'I know that,' I reply. 'But, come on, she's using my bath, she's wearing my clothes, she's your bonus plus one to the wedding. It's weird.'

'The Cara Brooks I know doesn't worry when another girl uses her bath,' he points out. 'Come on. And she's not wearing your actual clothes. You hate that outfit.'

'I hate this one more,' I say, frantically gesturing up and down my body with my hands, as though that somehow helps me prove my point.

Millsy goes to run a hand through his hair, like he always does when he's stressed, but stops himself when he remembers that he's got it slicked back for the wedding. He's always had long-ish hair but he's growing it longer to play Billy Gill, so he's having to keep the length twisted up in a low bun. It's grown quite a lot, since I saw him last. He looks so different.

Ruby, a friend of Millsy's from before I met him, always tells me about how he used to wear a topknot, back when they were trendy. She tells me they were serial daters, only out to have a good time, in what they call their 'young and stupid' phase, but then Ruby got married and Millsy wasn't far behind her, wanting to settle down. I know it sounds silly but something about his hair longer again, seeing this ghost of Millsy past, I don't like it. I don't like what it signifies.

'I know I sound like a kid but... it's Christmas,' I protest.

'You're right,' he replies. 'You do sound like a kid.'

Ouch. I can't do this right now, so I try to leave, pushing past him.

'Cara, wait,' he insists, obviously feeling bad, reaching out to take my arm but I shake him off.

We collide with some kind of easel with a thick framed photo standing on it, or it was until we knocked it off.

Millsy is down like a shot, picking up the frame as I return the easel to its standing position.

'Don't worry, it's not broken,' he reassures me as he picks it up.

'It sounds broken,' I reply.

We both peer inside, behind the perfectly intact glass, to see where the noise is coming from.

'Oh, God,' I blurt as my eyes finally figure out what they're looking at.

It's a jigsaw puzzle – well, it used to be. Although I suppose it is still a jigsaw puzzle, it's just no longer a completed one. Some chunks have held together but others haven't. I've no idea how many pieces I am looking at.

'Shit, it looks like the seating plan,' Millsy says.

'Shit,' I echo back at him. 'We're going to be in so much trouble. When Peri and Connor find out they're never going to speak to us again.'

'*If* they find out,' he replies.

'Well, they're definitely going to notice,' I point out.

'Unless you put it back together,' he adds. 'Come on, you're a puzzle master. I've seen you make short work of any jigsaw put in front of you.'

'Yeah, for fun, with a picture for reference, without the worry that the happy couple is going to walk through the door any second...'

Right on cue, we hear cheers from the next room. Peri and Connor must have arrived.

'Come on, if anyone can do this, it's you,' he says encouragingly. 'I'll man the door, make sure no one comes in.'

'So as always, we're relying on your mid-level charm and my top-tier intellect to get us out of scrapes,' I reply, daring to joke just a little.

'Hey, if it ain't broke... then we'll probably break it on the most important day of your life,' he replies through a smile. 'You've got this.'

I nod to myself, psyching myself up.

Okay, okay. Some chunks are still intact, and the backboard is still sticky, so it shouldn't be a problem putting it back together, it just needs doing. Obviously it's a seating plan and not a beautiful puzzle so it's not easy to separate it by colour.

Millsy stations himself by the door, arming his charm and wit, ready to take out anyone attempting to enter. It feels like old times, the two of us causing havoc, frantically trying to make things right again. I don't just miss it, I miss him.

The clock is ticking. I know I have to work quickly to piece together the seating plan before the newlyweds make their grand entrance. God, I know they love puzzles, but even I think this is a bit much. I just need to try to relax, to get into my rhythm.

I scan the array of fragments, searching for the edges and corners to form a foundation. I stick the matching pieces onto the backing board as I find them and thankfully they hold. The puzzle gradually takes shape, revealing the intricate seating arrangements and table numbers.

Piece by piece, I connect the sections, my fingers like lightning as they find and place each piece. The room next door hums with excitement and anticipation as the distant sounds of laughter and music drift in, reminding me of the celebration unfolding just beyond the door, and that the guests will surely be pouring in any moment. The volume increases for a second, as Millsy opens the door to peep through.

'Peri and Connor are getting closer,' he says. 'How's it going?'

I press the last piece into place before cautiously lifting it up, scared it might all come unstuck, but it holds.

'Done,' I tell him.

Millsy hurries over and helps me put the frame back on the easel. I swear, it isn't more than thirty seconds before Peri and Connor walk through the door.

'Well, well, what do we have here?' Peri says, her voice laced with amusement. 'Have we caught you in the act?'

She winks, clearly teasing us.

'You joke but you know what these two are like for sneaking off for a shag,' Connor adds. 'You can't keep them off each other.'

Millsy and I exchange a glance. He looks amused, whereas I feel the tinges of embarrassment creeping in.

I chuckle, trying to disguise my nerves.

'Oh, you know us, Peri. Always up to something,' I joke. 'Actually, we were just checking the seating plan, making sure there's enough room for Tally.'

'Is that what they're calling it these days? Checking the seating plan?' Connor jokes.

'We can't thank you enough for fitting Tally in,' Millsy adds. 'This is all... a lot. I shouldn't even be speaking to you in my real voice right now.'

'Well, we had to do some manoeuvring, but the wedding coordinator sorted it,' Peri replies. 'Oh, speaking of, Cara, she told me about the situation with your outfit. I'm so sorry but, hey, at least you look great in it.'

I am so relieved that my out-of-place outfit isn't ruining her big day. Now we just need to make sure the seating plan holds.

I glance at it, to make sure it's still hanging in there, and it is but something on it catches my eye.

'Oh,' I blurt. 'Millsy and Tally are sitting on a different table to me?'

'Yes, well, we needed to make some last-minute changes to fit Tally in, and we know Millsy needs to work closely with her on his accent. So, I thought it would actually be a good idea for them to sit together. A little practise session on their fellow tablemates.'

'Oh, okay,' I reply. 'So, where am I sitting?'

'Seeing as though you're around this big lump all the time, and he'll probably be working, we thought you might relish the chance to meet some new people, so we sat you at the singles table,' Peri says. 'Hey, you get to pretend you're single again, won't that be fun?'

No. Not at all. Not even a little bit. The bloody singles table!

'Yes,' I say, trying to laugh it off.

Unbeknownst to Peri, her well-intentioned gesture has only made me feel worse. Tally is sitting in my seat, with my man, in my outfit, at my friends' wedding. And I'm on the singles table.

'You never know, you might meet someone,' Millsy jokes.

I muster up a laugh. Was that a joke for our friends or yet another reminder from him that I should be moving on?

'Yeah, I might just do that,' I reply.

I actually might...

## 8

It doesn't matter how far you've come, or how much you think you've matured, you are never too old to find yourself lying face down on your bed, thinking about your life choices.

When my phone dings, I lift up my head and stare at it suspiciously, as if it just did what it did of its own accord, and not because I told it to. I did tell it to, though, because desperate times call for desperate measures, and I really wasn't joking when I said I only know of one way to meet men.

When I found out I was sitting at the singles table at the wedding yesterday, I had hoped that it might actually be a good way to meet new people, to try to make myself comfortable with the idea of moving on (or to try to make Millsy jealous at the very least).

The singles table was positioned right at the back of the room – because aren't they always? – tucked away from civilised society. A place for us all to scheme, to try to find someone to team up with so that next time, if we're lucky, we get to sit with the others, instead of being banished to the undesirable corner with the undesirable people. Perhaps I'm being dramatic but, cut me some slack, I truly believed I would never be single again.

I am not, however, exaggerating when I say that the quality of single men at the singles table was not great. For starters, there were only two men – for the six women at the table – and names like Gary and Nigel don't exactly make your knickers drop, not without some serious personality or devastating good looks to back them up. It was somehow the flip, for both Gary and Nigel – devastating personalities and serious looks.

With Gary, I don't know why, but he was all about his moustache. It was one of those perfectly manicured ones, sitting somewhere between a classic Hercule Poirot and Salvador Dali (although, like one of Dali's clocks, it slowly drooped as the day went on). Gary seemed so certain that his 'tache made him irresistible to the opposite sex. Unfortunately, I'm sad to report it had more of an opposite effect – confidence is a huge turn-on, but arrogance is not. Also, it just looked like a part of his costume. The only other thing he talked about was his novelty sock collection and I really, really wish I was joking.

So that left Nigel, a self-professed geek, and the gatekeeper to all things nerdy apparently. You know me, I love a geeky type, I'm one myself. Except I'm not, apparently. Not according to Nigel, who seems to be of the opinion that women can't really be nerdy and anything they like – or pretend to like, which is a seriously poor take – is to impress men. I gave up trying to talk to Nigel when I told him I liked *Star Wars* too and he started grilling me with questions like 'What odds does C-3PO give Han for successfully navigating the asteroid field?' and 'Which actor plays Moff Gideon in *The Mandalorian*?' to test my knowledge of the franchise (the answers are 3,720 to 1, and the phenomenal Giancarlo Esposito, if you don't know and you're at all interested). Honestly, it was like the nerd equivalent of when men ask female football fans to explain the offside rule (I think women are starting to suspect men don't actually know the answer, given the number of times the question is asked).

Oh, and none of this made Millsy jealous, by the way. We hardly spoke to each other all evening – he was oh so busy chatting with Tally – and I didn't even catch him so much as sneaking a glance in my direction.

So, like I said, like I keep reminding myself, desperate times really do call for absolutely desperate measures, so I've done it. I've downloaded Matcher again.

The good news is that I've thought about it and pretty much everyone we know, who could come up for me on a dating app, is in a relationship, so if they do see me on there, they would do well to pretend they hadn't. The bad news is just that I'm doing this generally.

As I set up my profile, choosing photos and writing an admittedly half-hearted bio, I cast my mind back to the last time I used the infamous dating app, back in 2020. Things were desperate then, as I searched for a plus one to take to cousin Flora's wedding – because the last thing I wanted was to turn up alone, especially seeing as though she'd honoured my ex-boyfriend's invitation, even though we weren't on speaking terms. So I swiped, I chatted and I even went on a few dates. It's hard to say what I found the most depressing about the whole experience. Could it have been the guy who stood me up? I'll never know if he turned up, took one look at me and left. Could it be the fact that I eventually ran out of men to swipe through? So much to unpack there. But I think the worst thing might have been the actual dates. It's not really a good advert for a dating app, when the actually dating part is the worst bit, but I had some serious stinkers. Notable mention must go to Aaron, who must've been using photos from when he was my age because when he turned up, he was clearly old enough to be my dad, and then there's Felix, who looked awfully dapper (if not slightly overdressed) when he turned up for our date in a black suit, but then it turned out he'd left his dad's wake to meet me – a wake where he had drunk stag-do levels of alcohol.

The award for the worst date of all, though, has to go to Matt. I turned up to meet him at the address he gave me and the only thing more alarming than it being a house and not a date location was when a middle-aged woman, clearly all dolled up for a date, answered the door and greeted me like she knew me. I was briefly relieved when I realised I wasn't being catfished, that this was Matt's mum, but then things took a nosedive when I found out that she was going out on a date and Matt and I were looking after his young nephew while they were out. By the time Matt's mum arrived home, and handed Matt some money as she dragged her date up to the bedroom, I realised we'd been babysitting this whole time. For money. Still, ever the gentleman, Matt did offer me £10 for my trouble. No, I didn't see him again, and my God, why am I back here, swiping, hoping things will be better this time?

As I swipe and swipe, I can confirm that things aren't better. Somehow they're worse. Dating websites, before the apps came along, weren't that widely used. They were favoured by introverts and those who had trouble meeting people in real life. But when Tinder and Bumble and Matcher (oh, my!) came along in the teenies, things shifted. These apps weren't for the introverts, they were for everyone. Every single someone who was anyone was on at least one app. It was cool and fun, and for the worst types in society it was a really efficient way to bang their way through their local area, but now that I think about it, in 2020 Matcher was starting to feel like more of a hook-up app and now, God, I don't know how to describe it. It may have had a moment, in the teenies, but now it feels like it's done. Like well-picked bones, a thoroughly scraped barrel – I'm the last person to the buffet and all that's left are the bits and pieces no one wanted. And I suppose I'm one of them.

It's fine, you know? I swipe a few people right (to match), but even more people left (to reject). I'm heartened to see the trend of posing for photos with poor sedated tigers on holiday has ended, but miserable to learn that protein is (somehow) still a personality for some guys. The first real conversation I strike up is with a man called Owen who seems nice enough. We swap a few messages, ask each other the usual questions, and while nothing about this or him is even beginning to light a fire anywhere in my body, I don't suppose it's realistic to expect love at first swipe, or a powerful connection like I have with Millsy to just spring up out of nowhere. It's going to take time to find myself feeling that way about anyone – I need to give men like Owen a chance.

Owen: The worst thing about apps like this is working out who is serious and who is messing about.

Cara: Right? It's impossible to know who is here for a hook-up and who is looking for a relationship down the line – unless they tell you, but people seem to keep that to themselves for some reason.

Hmm, should I have said that? Should I have said that *like that*? I don't want to seem like I'm too keen – mostly because I'm not.

Owen: That too. But I was thinking more about how some people don't want to meet. They just want a pen pal. With that in mind, want to go for a drink tonight? Let's get the first meet out of the way, and set our stall out.

Cara: *Cara is typing...*

I type and delete a reply a bunch of times, never pressing send, because I don't know what to say. I write something different each time – the only thing all the messages have in common is that I delete them before I send them. What do I do? Do I want to meet Owen? I know, meeting men is the whole point of using the app, but I didn't think I'd be getting back on the horse so quickly. On the one hand, I'm all for meeting up, seeing if there's a spark, and then working out where we go from there. On the other hand, I wouldn't mind being pen pals for a little longer.

I hear a knock on my bedroom door. I sit up straight and, for some reason – maybe because I'm embarrassed – I hold my phone close to my chest.

'Hello?' I call out.

'It's Millsy, have you got a minute?' he replies.

I pull myself to my feet and greet him at the bedroom door. It's so strange that he's knocking. I was going to say that it's our bedroom, but he owns the place, so it's his bedroom in a couple of ways.

'Hi,' I say, trying to sound casual, not that he could possibly know what I'm up to on my phone.

'Hi,' he replies with a smile. 'Are you hungry?'

I feel a flutter in my chest. It's music to my ears, hearing him say something he's said a thousand times before. We were always popping out into the city, trying new places, or visiting old favourites, whether we were going out for dinner or we just had a craving for a particular kind of food.

'Oh, you know me, I'm always hungry,' I reply.

Millsy laughs.

'Tally and I have been working all day, we're starving, we were going to grab something,' he explains. 'Can I bring you anything back?'

Oh. Right, of course he wasn't asking me out, he's going out with Tally.

Not that you should ever do anything for the wrong reason, but sometimes it's just the push you need. I remove my phone from where I'm holding it, squashed against my chest, and my face unlocks it to reveal the message from Owen, asking me to go for a drink.

'That's very thoughtful of you,' I tell Millsy. 'But I have a date tonight.'

I deliver this line with a smile although, judging by the look on Millsy's face, it's the last thing he expected me to say.

'I hope you're not going in your pyjamas,' he jokes.

'Cut out the middleman,' I quip back – which in hindsight doesn't mean what I thought it was going to suggest in my head.

He smiles.

'Okay, well, have fun,' he tells me.

'You too,' I call after him.

I thought that was going to feel good. That the jealousy was going to eat him alive. That I was going to feel like I didn't want him or need him.

None of that happened, though. Ah well, it is what it is. I guess I need to get ready for my date. And I'm not looking forward to it at all.

Cara: Sure. I can be ready in an hour.

# 9

I sit perched on my high barstool, lightly swaying my dangling feet – almost as though I'm treading water – and swirling the colourful concoction in my glass with my paper straw that is nearing the end of its short life. My cocktail is a vibrant pink drink, full of fresh fruit, with a sparkly sugared rim, and it's the only interesting thing about this evening so far. Owen is sitting across from me. He is clad in a perfectly tailored suit, his hair slicked back to the point where it almost doesn't resemble hair any more, and his meticulously trimmed beard looks like it required a ruler to get to where it is. It isn't just his suit that is tailored, it's like Owen himself has been carefully crafted (by himself, obviously), every little detail thought of, no part of his look for no reason. He told me very vaguely that his occupation is 'entrepreneur' – I think it was supposed to explain the suit or... I don't know. I didn't like to ask because it's awkward enough, meeting up with someone in real life for the first time, trying to spot them in a crowded place, hoping they look enough like their photo to be recognisable (and to not be trying to deceive you in some way).

I was relieved when he turned up, looking like himself (or the version he's consistently presented to me, at least) – that is until we sat down and started trying to have a conversation.

The energy in the bar is fantastic – probably because everyone is slowly allowing themselves to edge closer to getting into the festive spirit. A symphony of clinking glasses, laughter, animated conversations and ambient music serves as the soundtrack to our date. Warm hues from the dimmed lights cast a soft glow, creating a sort of casual intimacy for a first date, the spotlight above our little table shining down on us, creating our own little private zone. But unfortunately, within our little private zone, the atmosphere of the bar around us seems to be missing. Inside our vacuum, our conversation feels forced, lacking the natural ebb and flow that you hope for on a date – the only real sign I know of that means things are going well. It's as if the lively energy of the bar dissipates when it reaches our orbit.

We're currently trying (in vain, without a shadow of a doubt) to find something, *anything*, that we have in common.

'What do you like to do in your free time?' I ask.

'Ah, well, being an entrepreneur means that my free time is quite limited, but when I do have a moment, I like to network and attend business conferences. It's all about expanding your professional network in this biz, you know?'

I really don't know.

'I see,' I reply, trying to hide the fact that I was expecting him to reply with 'bowling' or something like that.

'What about you?' he asks, swigging his drink as he glances around the room.

'I love games,' I reply. 'Escape rooms, boardgames, videogames, emotional warfare.'

'I thought that was just your job?' he replies, completely missing my joke.

I don't point out to him that the answer he gave me was basically his job.

'It is my job, but playing games of all descriptions is one of my main hobbies,' I explain.

Oh, the look on his face, like he's just realised he's sitting opposite a nerd and he's worried it might be airborne.

'It is my job,' I confirm. 'But I'm still a big fan of games.'

'I see,' he says simply.

'What sort of music do you listen to?' I ask.

'I'm not some sort of weirdo,' he insists – which, to me, is the biggest indicator of someone who is in fact some sort of weirdo. 'I can appreciate the value that music holds in society. I'm just not really one for listening to it. I find silence more enjoyable – less distracting when I'm working, leaving more room in my brain for coming up with incredible concepts.'

I'm still not sure what he actually does.

'Do you like to travel?' I ask.

'I *have* to travel,' he replies, like I'm stupid.

'But do you like to?' I persist. 'Just... for fun, to see new places, new cultures, try new foods...'

'I find it difficult to justify the time away from my work,' he points out. 'So the only travelling I do is for work.'

As *fun*, *friendly*, and *interesting* as Owen is coming across, this just isn't working.

'We don't have much in common, do we?' I point out with a friendly smile.

'No, it appears that way. Thank you for being honest,' he replies, very business-like. 'I appreciate your maturity. The way I see dating, especially through Matcher – it's a numbers game. I'm all for efficiency, so run potential dates through... well, to explain to someone who potentially isn't as savvy, I have a spreadsheet.'

I blink at him.

'It's good for figuring out compatibility, etcetera,' he continues. 'And scheduling multiple dates – particularly useful if they're on the same day. It's called date stacking.'

Owen says this as though it's the most normal thing in the world.

'Oh, yes, of course, if you have multiple dates in the same day,' I reply, not doing all that much to mask my sarcasm.

'Someone gets it,' he says with a clap of his hands, smiling as though we might just be compatible after all. 'Listen, I feel like I can be real with you. I've got another date lined up, in case this one wasn't going well, and it's not, is it? Let's not waste one another's time.'

For a moment, I just stare at him. Is he serious? He *is* serious.

'You're absolutely right,' I say, keen to nip this in the bud. 'Go for it.'

'Good luck finding someone,' he says, offering me a hand to shake.

'And good luck with your... spreadsheet dates.'

'Yeah, thanks,' he says, his eyes already on his next date and, wow, she is right over there.

As Owen takes a seat with date number – who knows? – I slump back in my chair and drain the last of my drink.

Am I impressed or horrified? Perhaps Owen's approach is the new way to be. Well, he's right, sometimes there's nothing you can do, you'll never fit two jigsaw pieces together if they're not meant to fit, so why waste time trying? But we're people, not puzzle pieces, we're adaptable, and we're caring, and maybe spreadsheet dating is the way forward, but it isn't for me. I would say that I don't know what is for me, but I do, it's Millsy, but it's starting to feel less like that can happen.

# 10

The little gate at the bottom of my gran's garden has stuck for as long as I can remember. It's old and tired (like my gran will claim she is, despite being ninety years old, and yet having a more active social life than the rest of us), but my grandad made it, so I can see why she's reluctant to have it replaced, even ten years after his passing – she never wanted to look for a replacement for him either.

My gran and grandad's love story might just be my favourite. My gran was seeing someone else, someone she wasn't really happy with, and then my grandad came to town. He was visiting Haworth with some friends, on a walking holiday, when he bumped into her on Main Street. They chatted, as they walked up the cobbles, and by the time they reached the top, she had agreed to go on a date with him. The rest, as they say, is history. They tied the knot after just six months and then they stayed together forever. I can't begin to imagine how terribly it would go for me, if I tried to meet a man in the street, although I imagine getting arrested at some point. But for Gran and Grandad they fell in love, it stuck, and it never budged an inch. Kind of like this gate.

I'm thankful for my long legs on days like today, when I'm running late and I can just step over it. It's not often you'll hear me being grateful for my above-average height because usually all it means is that I'm lucky if a shop carries a size 8 shoe, and often I can turn any trousers into the pedal pushers that were cool in the nineties. I didn't realise that being 5'7 made me officially tall until I learned that the average height for a woman is somewhere between 5'3 and 5'4, and while it's nice to be considered above average for once, it also feels neither here nor there.

What is interesting, though, is the average height of men. It's certainly a thing, especially within the world of app dating, that men 'need' to be a certain height – either because some women believe they do, or because men on the shorter side believe that the only possible reason a woman isn't interested in them is because of their height. I do think it's funny, when men complain about women not wanting to date short guys, when often men have a tick-list the length of their arm, with all sorts of requirements on there. God forbid you won't go on another date with a guy under six foot, but to have the audacity to have a waist thicker than your neck – tut tut. What is interesting in all of this is that the average height for men isn't as tall as most people think, it's about 5'9. I don't know why men, and women, have decided that men need to be over six foot and women need to be under 5'5. It's a very strange time for those of us stuck in the middle.

After hopping the gate and hurrying up the garden path, I head into my gran's house, into the heart of what will surely be a circus. The mission today: plan our family Christmas (my family, Gran, and Auntie Mary's branches of the family tree), which we're having before actual Christmas, because my lot are heading to Scotland to spend actual Christmas with Millsy and his family. It was supposed to be so special, our first Christmas where our families were merging together for the big day, and typically it's the first Christmas right after we break up. That's why we're putting a brave face on it. And speaking of brave faces...

With a deep breath, I brace myself and step inside.

Gran is in the lounge, with Flora's energetic children, one either side of her. She smiles warmly when she sees me, her eyes twinkling.

'Hi, Gran. Sorry I'm late,' I say. 'Everyone has the Christmas crazies.'

'Good things come to those who wait,' she says. 'I'd ask you if you wanted a cuppa but I think they're waiting for you in the dining room.'

'And you're babysitting, hmm?' I reply, raising my eyebrows. I know my gran is a young ninety, but Flora's boys are wild.

'Yes, and they're running me ragged, but I wouldn't have it any other way,' she says. 'It keeps me young.'

'Meanwhile, I'm about to walk into another room that will surely age me,' I joke. 'Are you sure you don't want to join us?'

'Oh, no, no, you go ahead,' she says with a cheeky smile. 'I'm more than happy here.'

My gran knows what's up, keeping out of it. I wish I could keep out of it myself, but I know my mum will need the backing.

Walking into the dining room, I can't help but feel like I'm walking into a board meeting, one with hostile vibes. Flora and Auntie Mary are seated on one side of the table and my mum Annie on the other, a seat waiting next to her for me. An invisible tension hanging in the air, as usual. I quickly take my seat next to Mum, ready to get involved.

'Sorry, sorry, festive delays,' I explain.

'That's okay,' Mum says with a smile. She looks relieved that I'm here.

'Fashionably late, Cara?' Flora teases. 'You always like to make an entrance, don't you?'

I really don't.

'She finally decides to grace us with her presence,' Auntie Mary adds, getting her snide remarks in before I've even made myself comfortable. 'I was beginning to think we'd have to start without you.'

'We have started without her,' Mum adds. 'But you're here now, darling, so let's bring you up to speed.'

'We're talking about where to host,' Flora tells me.

'And I was saying we have a dining room that can comfortably seat everyone, so I'm happy to host,' Mum adds. 'Me, Ted, Cara, Oliver, Millsy – oh, and Tally, is it? Then Mum, Mary, Paddy, Flora, Tommy and the kids.'

My mum, unsurprisingly, snapped into hosting mode when she heard Tally would be with us for Christmas. Well, she has no reason to think anything strange might be going on, and she hates the thought of anyone not having a good Christmas.

'Always so quick to show off,' Mary says with a click of her tongue.

'Oh, you know the whole point of that room was so we had somewhere for our ever-increasing family to be able to gather,' Mum says, smiling, ignoring the negativity. 'Mary, if you want to host, that's absolutely fine with me.'

'I'm not saying that,' Mary quickly adds. 'I'm happy for you to host – and to cook.'

'You're cooking?' I say to Mum, unable to hide my glee. 'Oh, I can't wait.'

'Yes, and I think I've got something for everyone,' Mum says, tapping her way through her notebook with her pen as she checks the details. 'Traditional with all the trimmings, and then a vegetarian option, and a gluten-free dish for Auntie Mary.'

Auntie Mary has that stern expression on her face that seems to be a permanent fixture. Her neat curls frame her grumpy face, and she's wearing one of her usual conservative outfits consisting of a navy-blue blouse and a knee-length skirt. Her glasses sit on the bridge of her nose, and as she peers at you through them, it feels like she quite literally looks down her nose at you.

Flora bears a striking resemblance to her mum. Even though she straightens her curls, there is no denying their similar facial features. Flora, however, has a slightly more relaxed and cheerful demeanour, although I can't help but notice she's getting spicier as she's getting older, turning into her mum a little more each day. She used to dress in vibrant colours, before she had kids, but these days she says she tends to opt for comfort over style, in items that she doesn't mind getting dirty, and that are easy to breastfeed through – and for some reason it usually feels like a dig at me when she points this out. I'm sorry I don't need to wear clothes with quick access to my breasts. Although I suppose now I'm back on Matcher, it might actually help.

'We'll bring the drink,' Auntie Mary says. 'As we all know Paddy is a wine expert.'

Well, he likes to think he is.

'Ooh, I can bring dessert if you like?' I suggest.

'Oh, yeah, Cara, just bring dessert and make us all look bad,' Flora whines. 'I have two kids to look after, you know?'

'That's why I don't mind bringing it,' I point out.

'Flora has a point. It wouldn't be fair,' Auntie Mary says, nodding.

'But...'

'It's fine, it's fine,' Mum interrupts. 'I'll sort the desserts when I sort the food.'

Mum knocks my leg lightly with hers under the table, a secret code between the two of us.

'Annie the amazing,' Auntie Mary says sarcastically.

'It's okay, Mum, you don't want to saddle yourself with that,' Flora reassures her.

I feel like I'm at some kind of bizarre boxing match, between Mum and Auntie Mary, and like Flora and I are the corner-women, supporting our respective fighters.

Just as things are starting to get a little too uncomfortable, Gran joins us.

'Flora, love, do you have a spare shirt in your bag for Vince?' Gran asks. 'He's poured his drink all down himself.'

'Honestly, Mum, you can't look after two kids for five minutes without one of them needing a bath,' Mary almost snaps, frustration in her voice.

'Erm, all right, you complain about free babysitting,' I point out, trying to lighten the mood.

'The kid poured it down himself, *for fun*,' Gran tells her. 'He's a kid – kids do that. Even you had fun, when you were a kid.'

I laugh. I swear, my gran only gets cheekier with age.

'I'll go sort him,' Flora says before leaving the room.

'And are we sorted in here?' Gran asks.

'I think so,' Mum says. 'It's going to be good.'

It's going to be horrible. I don't know why we spend time with these people. What's the point in keeping the peace in a family that isn't peaceful?

'How's Millsy doing with his work?' Gran asks me.

'It's going good,' I tell her. 'He's hard at it with his dialect coach.'

Why, oh why did I use those words?

'The reason we're going to have a stranger at our Christmas dinner,' Mary points out, annoyed.

'Tally isn't a stranger,' I insist. 'She's just a person doing her job, and Millsy is doing his job, and as his family we need to do our jobs and support that.'

'Well, I think it's inappropriate,' Auntie Mary persists. 'But I suppose we'll have to make peace with it this year. But mark my words, I won't be bending over backwards to accommodate strangers every year.'

Bending over backwards? She's hardly moving a muscle.

'It's going to be a Christmas to remember,' Gran says with enthusiasm. 'Now, who fancies a cup of tea?'

Normally a Christmas to remember would be a good thing but, this year, I'm worried it's going to be for all the wrong reasons. I can't believe I'm saying this but I'm with Mary on this one. I don't want Tally there either.

Still, with plenty of other unwanted guests at the table, I'll just have to suck it up. You would think I would be an expert at spending time with people I didn't like by now.

## 11

I take a deep breath of the chilly winter air and adjust the hem of my dress, a mixture of nerves and curiosity as I wonder what I'm getting myself into today.

I would say that I'm a glass-half-empty kind of girl, and it's not because I'm not a bright and happy person, it's more because – these days especially – I feel like I'm living in this constant anxious state, waiting to see what's going to go wrong next. You can't let things get the better of you, though, can you, and even though I don't really want to date right now, you've got to fake it till you make it sometimes, right? Well, you definitely do with Matcher.

As I wait at our arranged meeting place, I try to be optimistic, but I can't help but reminisce about my disastrous date with Spreadsheet Owen. I cringe whenever I think about it, and it hasn't made me all that keen to try another date with someone else, but I'm going to give today's date a shot. I can't judge everyone by Owen's standards.

Lenny, the guy I'm meeting today, seems promising. He's local, he loves pizza *and* dogs (which are two of my favourite things too), and he's a firefighter. I mean, how bad can it be when your date's job is to protect people, right? Plus, it's arguably one of the sexiest jobs a man can have – although I'm starting to think strippers and calendars may have perpetuated that myth.

I spot a familiar face approaching (it's always a huge relief when they look like their photos) and I can't help but be momentarily taken aback by Lenny's dapper appearance. With his messy brown hair swept back and a well-fitted blue suit, he reminds me a bit of Jack Grealish, the footballer, in the get-up you see players wearing when they get off the bus on match days. It's a good look on him.

'Well, hello there, look at you,' he says with a smile.

'And look at you,' I reply as he gives me a friendly hug.

'I love the blue dress,' he says. 'We're coordinated.'

'Oh, this old thing?' I say playfully, lifting my skirt slightly on one side, attempting a bit of a curtsey.

One of the things I liked about Lenny, as we chatted in the app, was how fun he came across. A joke never seemed far away, no matter what we were talking about.

'Anyway, shall we head inside?' he says, nodding towards the hotel next to us.

I laugh but then I quickly realise from the look on his face that he's serious.

My heart skips a beat. The Bancroft Hotel is a magnificent Grade II listed building. The very picture of Victorian elegance, and I'm pretty sure it's a five-star establishment, but even so! I find myself momentarily frozen. A hotel? What on earth is Lenny thinking? I can only think of one thing he could be thinking, and I am not on the same page at all.

As Lenny notices the panic on my face, his expression changes, and he looks mortified.

'Oh, God, wait, no, sorry,' he babbles. 'Yep, I'm feeling you, this looks bad. Sorry, I didn't even think of that, sorry.'

I've no idea what he's talking about, but he doesn't sound like someone who was expecting me to go to a room with him on our first date.

'I should have told you what the plan was, but I stupidly thought the surprise might be cool,' he explains. 'There's actually a wedding going on in the function room. I'm invited with a plus one. I thought it could be a fun first date – who doesn't love a wedding? – even if it's a bit unusual. Unusual is fun, right?'

'Unusual is fun,' I agree with a cautiously optimistic smile.

With a mischievous glint in his eyes, Lenny playfully gets down on one knee.

'Cara,' he says, exhaling deeply, feigning nerves. 'Will you watch someone get married with me?'

I can't help but burst out laughing, which must look like an incredibly off reaction to any passers-by, noticing him seemingly proposing to me and me cackling in his face.

'Yes,' I say, in a sultry, breathy voice. 'Yes, yes, yes.'

Lenny climbs back to his feet.

'You've made me the happiest man on earth,' he replies. 'And you'll be pleased to hear the ceremony has already taken place, so we're only here for the free food, the open bar, and the general partying.'

'My favourite part,' I say with a grin. 'Let's do it.'

The hotel's interior is just as opulent, with chandeliers casting a warm glow across the hall, and the most flowers I've ever seen in one place in the middle of December. The function room is decked out for the reception, with flowers and balloons at every turn, and a room full to the brim with excited guests. You really can't beat the joy of a wedding, can you? Even I feel optimistic at weddings.

As we navigate through the bustling crowd, Lenny introduces me to his friends with a sense of pride. Ally and Dec, a couple with infectious energy, greet us warmly. Theresa and Marty, another excitable couple, join the circle of conversation. It's a lively group, and I find myself immediately drawn into their banter. It's unusual, to get to meet a guy's friends on a first date, but it says a lot about him that, not only does he have friends, which is a very good sign, but that they seem like such a lovely group.

'Everyone, this is Cara,' Lenny says, making the introductions. 'Cara, meet Ally and Dec, and Theresa and Marty.'

'Nice to meet you, Cara,' Ally says warmly. 'Lenny has been talking about you non-stop.'

I smile. I'm sure she's just trying to be nice, and that Lenny hasn't actually been hyping me to his friends.

'It's nice to meet you all too,' I say with a smile.

Dec, with his mischievous grin, takes the opportunity to tease Lenny.

'Lenny, you actually made it to the wedding. I'm impressed!' Dec jokes, making me wonder if being frequently late might be another thing that Lenny and I have in common, but that obviously neither of us has disclosed to the other yet.

'Oh, you know me, always around for the important stuff,' Lenny replies.

Ally nudges me playfully, sensing my ease with the group.

'He's a good one, isn't he?' she says.

'Oh, absolutely,' I reply politely, although he does seem so far so good, and his friends are giving him glowing references. 'I'm the late person in my social circles, but I always manage to make it on time for weddings.'

'I always say weddings have magical, time-shifting powers,' Theresa joins in. 'When we got married, despite multiple hitches on the day, everything ran right on time – and yet somehow the day was over in the blink of an eye.'

'I hardly remember a thing about my wedding day,' Ally adds.

It's starting to seem like Lenny might be the only one in his friendship group who isn't married and I know exactly what that feels like, especially with my old school friends.

'I think I just have this extra motivation to be on time on wedding days, to make sure I don't let anyone down,' I say. Right on cue, a waiter arrives with a silver tray loaded with glasses of champagne, so I dare to make a joke. 'Or perhaps it's for the free champagne.'

Everyone laughs and Lenny smiles at me, almost approvingly, like he's happy he invited me.

'You never really know what surprises await you at a wedding,' Marty adds. 'But that's half the fun.'

The light-hearted conversation continues, and I find it easy to relax into the warmth and laughter that comes from Lenny and his friends. It certainly eases the tension I felt earlier – both my unique brand of worry, and the usual kind that comes with first dates. Perhaps these sorts of things should always be done in groups. Not like *that*, obviously.

As the time to sit down for the meal approaches, I excuse myself for a quick trip to the loos. I navigate through the crowd, catching glimpses of the intricate decorations and elegant table settings along the way. Having never planned a wedding myself, I can't say I have the first clue about how much they cost, but having attended a bunch, I can certainly spot the expensive ones, and this one seems like it must have cost a fortune. It isn't an over-the-top display of wealth, it's subtle, but it's unmistakable. The quality of everything, the sheer volume of fresh flowers, the free-flowing champagne, the open bar. If you can afford it, why not?

Returning to the table, I find everyone engrossed in conversation, and as the smell of delicious food begins to fill the air, I realise it must be time to eat – great, I'm starving.

Lenny leans in closer to me.

'I really hope you're not a vegetarian,' he says. 'I ordered meat meals for myself and my "plus one" ages ago.'

Theresa must have been listening in because she chuckles.

'Oh, Lenny, you should know by now,' she playfully ticks him off.

'It's fine,' I say with a laugh. 'I'm not a vegetarian, and there's still plenty of time for us to learn so much more about one another.'

I don't want him to feel awkward, for not knowing everything about me yet.

'She's right, I suppose there always will be,' Ally adds with a friendly smile. 'The adventure never really ends.'

Dec, clearly not enjoying the mush, turns to Lenny.

'Lenny, how's business? Putting out fires and what have you?' he asks curiously.

I feel a strange sense of excitement as servers place pasta dishes down in front of us. There's something really fun about having no idea what's in it, but it smells amazing, and I can't wait to tuck in. Oh, and if you needed further proof that this is a fancy wedding, the portion size is so small I could probably fit it all in my mouth at once.

'Busy, as always. You know how it is,' Lenny replies. 'Never sure if busy is a good thing or a bad thing.'

'Busy is never a good thing if it puts you in harm's way,' Ally points out.

'Cara, do you worry about Lenny doing such a dangerous

job?' Theresa asks curiously. 'I'm always so relieved Marty works behind a desk.'

I've never really thought about it, given that I've only known him a matter of days, but I need to say something.

'I understand that Lenny does an important job,' I reply. 'It's admirable, really.'

'But you must have been worried sick when Lenny attended that big mill fire?' Ally adds.

I stare at her for a second. I haven't heard of any big mill fires, never mind Lenny attending one. It throws me off my game.

'She doesn't care,' Dec says, straight in there with a joke. 'Cold-hearted Cara.'

I know he's only joking but I don't like what he's suggesting. Not wanting the nickname to catch on, I quickly correct myself – even if I have no idea what they're talking about.

'Of course I care,' I quickly insist. 'It's just... scary, isn't it?'

Theresa nods thoughtfully. Ally gives her husband an elbow.

'You ignore him, Cara,' she insists. 'Of course you care about your boyfriend. Dec just thinks he's funny.'

My heart stops for the second time today. Boyfriend? Why does she think Lenny is my boyfriend?

I turn to Lenny, expecting him to correct her, but I can see something behind his smile.

'Shall we go grab some more drinks?' he suggests. 'And maybe when we get back we can talk about something other than me dying.'

Lenny says this in a jokey way.

'Give over, you love being the centre of attention,' Dec calls after us.

As we arrive at the bar, my gaze fixes on Lenny expectantly. He takes a deep breath, as though he's about to let me have it.

'I have a confession to make,' he tells me – as though I didn't already know that. 'June, the bride... she's my ex-girlfriend. And Dan, the groom, is one of our oldest friends.'

My eyes widened with horror. Well, that's awkward.

'The thought of coming to their wedding alone filled me with dread, which is why I invited you in the first place, but then while you were in the toilets, Dec made a joke about me picking you up off the street and I panicked – I told them you were my girlfriend. I know it seems silly but I just didn't want to appear foolish, or seem like I was still hung up on June, because that would make things so awkward. So, yes, sorry, I lied and said you were my girlfriend. I know it was wrong of me. It's just been really difficult for me to move on and accept seeing her with someone else. I feel like an arsehole for lying, and for dragging you into it. Sorry – again. I'll go tell them the truth.'

Lenny sighs deeply and I feel my heart softening. Well, it's not like I can't sympathise, lately I'm getting a taste of what it feels like when your relationship comes to an end, but you have to keep seeing that person. It hurts. And I hate seeing Millsy with Tally, even though I don't really know what's going on, but the thought of watching him marry someone else makes me want to throw up. Can I say that I wouldn't be doing the same thing if I were in Lenny's situation because, if I'm being honest, it seems like exactly the kind of thing I would do.

'I see where you're coming from,' I tell him. 'Are you really just doing this so that people believe you've moved on?'

'*Yes*,' he says with extra emphasis. 'But I know it's wrong, and daft, and if I put it right, I hope you can still stay and enjoy the wedding – although I totally understand if you would like to leave.'

'It might sound crazy, but I do have some idea of what you're going through,' I tell him. 'And I like to think that, were I in the same position, someone would step up and help me keep a brave face on it so, okay, I'll pretend to be your girlfriend.'

Lenny looks like he can't quite believe his luck.

'Really?' he practically squeaks.

'Really,' I reply.

'Barman, two shots of tequila, please?' he says, turning around to face the bar. Then he turns back to me. 'I owe you a drink.'

'Oh, not for me, thanks, I'll stick with my fizz,' I say.

'Okay, well, no point wasting it,' he says before he knocks back one, then the other. 'Thanks again for doing this. I thought everyone was going to spend the day giving me pitying looks. Perhaps now I can actually enjoy myself.'

I smile to myself. It feels nice, to do something good for someone.

Back at our table, I notice that our empty pasta plates have been replaced by the world's smallest roast dinner. A bite-sized portion of lamb, skinny carrots, a small cluster of peas and one roast potato – yes, *one* roast potato. When my mum makes a Sunday dinner, I eat more than one roast potato while she's still serving it.

'We were beginning to think you two had snuck off,' Dec says with a wink.

'No, we weren't,' Ally says, elbowing him again. I wonder what hurts most, Ally's elbow or Dec's upper arm, because a big part of her day seems to be dedicated to giving him a tactful nudge to shut up.

'So, how did you two meet?' Theresa asks. 'Lenny never said.'

I stifle a chuckle, amazed to be in the thick of it so quickly, but thankfully Lenny is in there like a shot with a reply.

'I actually saved Cara from a burning building,' he tells them.

Did I say thankfully? I take that back.

I feel my eyes widen in surprise. Of all the things he could've said!

'Really?' Ally replies, her jaw on the floor.

'Really,' Lenny says.

'Yeah, because meeting on a dating app or in a bar has been done to death,' I joke. 'Our meet-cute was in a fire.'

I'm talking almost sarcastically, really only for Lenny's benefit, because surely keeping it simple is the smartest thing to do? I suppose it's encouraging, that he clearly doesn't do this kind of thing all the time, and also mildly alarming that I seem to consider myself some sort of expert.

'Oh, my goodness, Cara, what happened?' Ally asks me.

Why did she have to ask me?

'Well, the building I was in caught fire,' I explain, like they hadn't already guessed that part. 'I was stuck in the building, on the top floor, actually, and Lenny came to my rescue.'

Ally's face lights up, as though she's standing in front of a fire herself, captivated by the romantic notion.

'The flames were raging, some of the biggest I've ever seen, and Cara was trapped in probably the most dangerous part of the building,' Lenny explains. 'But I didn't think twice about throwing on my gear, charging through the smoke-filled corridors to find her, throwing her over my shoulder, and carrying her out to safety.'

I think it's really interesting that, rather than Lenny's tale sounding like it comes from a professional firefighter, it sounds more like something you would read in a romance novel you found on your mum's bedside table.

Ah well, I may as well lean into it.

'I was terrified but then Lenny emerged from the smoke and I knew it was all going to be okay,' I say with a smile.

'Did the building collapse behind you in slow motion, while

"Up Where We Belong" played in the background?' Dec asks cheekily.

I haven't seen the movie but I think everyone knows the Joe Cocker and Jennifer Warnes song from *An Officer and a Gentleman*.

'Oh, absolutely,' I joke. 'The choreography was perfectly timed – the building did a great job.'

'And I bet you both emerged unscathed, without a hair out of place,' Dec adds.

'What can I say?' Lenny replies through a cheeky smile. 'I'm that good.'

Lenny and I exchange a subtle look, both pleased with our work, and I must admit, this is a lot of fun.

We all continue to chat, making short work of our tiny meal and our dessert, having a genuinely lovely time. The food might be in short supply but the alcohol certainly isn't. The boys are taking it in turns, making trips to the bar, coming back with trays of drinks and shots. I suppose a wedding is a good excuse to drink too much during the day – and I suppose it is Christmas time, after all.

'There's a photo thing,' Dec announces as he sets a tray of drinks down.

'A photo thing?' Ally repeats back to him.

'Yeah, a camera and a screen, like school photos, where you go pose and they stick it in the wedding book or summat,' Dec explains.

Lenny knocks back a shot of whatever the clear liquid in the shot glasses is.

'Come on, Caz, let's do it,' he says – I don't think anyone has ever called me Caz before, to the point where my brain freezes while it tries to work out if he's talking to me.

'Yeah, okay,' I say.

'And we'll be right behind you,' Ally tells me. 'We could get a photo, just us girls.'

I follow Lenny, whose alcohol consumption shows in his steps, to the space where the photographer is waiting. Eventually, it's our turn.

'Okay, I take one photo,' the photographer tells us. 'You get one to take home and the other goes in the memory book for the happy couple.'

'Great,' Lenny says. 'Let's do this.'

I take my position next to him and strike a pose.

'Hang on, let's give them something to talk about,' he whispers to me. 'Show them that I've really moved on.'

As the photographer counts down from three, Lenny grabs me. He practically scoops me up by the bum and the weight of the top half of my body throws me off balance, sending me down towards him, my chest pressing firmly against his face. I'm expecting a mess of blur to come out of the printer but instead, it looks like some sexually charged display of lust on both our parts – almost literally. I'm so busy stuffing the copy the photographer gave me into my clutch bag that it's too late to stop him from gluing the other into the memory book and then handing Lenny a pen.

'Wishing you as much happiness as us,' Lenny says out loud as he writes.

He's obviously joking – but then I glance over to look what he's really writing and it's exactly what he said. Suddenly I'm relieved he's signed my name as Caz, it gives me plausible deniability.

'Let's go congratulate the happy couple in person,' Lenny suggests hyperactively.

Hell no! So he can dry hump me in front of them?

'I'll catch you up,' I tell him. 'I told Ally and Theresa I would take a photo with them.'

'Okay, but hurry up,' he insists.

The more Lenny has to drink, the more the vibe changes. Suddenly I don't quite feel like I'm doing him a favour, it's more like aiding and abetting.

After my photo with the girls, I'm annoyed with myself, for feeling like Lenny is my problem, but I suppose he is.

As I glance around the room, my eyes land on the gift table, stacked high with beautifully wrapped presents. Then I realise Lenny is standing there, a mischievous grin on his face as he surveys the table in front of him.

'So, what did we get the happy couple?' I ask him with a friendly smile.

Lenny chuckles softly, his eyes on fire with amusement.

'At this point, who knows?' he says through a snort.

I've no idea what he means, and I don't think I would've believed him if he told me, but it's obvious, seeing it for myself.

'Lenny, why are you swapping all the gift tags around?' I ask in disbelief.

Lenny's grin widens, and he leans in closer, lowering his voice as he explains.

'Just imagine the chaos when they start opening their presents and then write the thank you notes. It will be absolutely hilarious, when they get everything wrong, they're going to look so ungrateful.'

I stare at him in disbelief.

'I'm not sure anyone will appreciate that,' I point out.

'Oh, come on, Caz!' he slurs. 'It's all in good fun. It'll give them a good laugh once they realise their mistake.'

I sigh.

'Come on, let's get back to our table,' I tell him, dragging him back into the heart of the room.

Lenny is reluctant at first, until he hears the DJ announce that it's time for the first dance.

'Yes, let's get back to partying,' he agrees with a mischievous smile.

June – Lenny's ex – and Dan, her new husband, take to the floor to dance to Lewis Capaldi's 'Pointless'. It's a beautiful song and you can tell they've taken dance lessons to perfect their performance.

I sit down on a chair at the edge of the dancefloor, my feet starting to ache in my heels now I'm darting around after Lenny.

He offers me a hand.

'Dance with me,' he says.

'You're supposed to wait until you're invited to join them,' I tell him. 'Just the couple dance first.'

'Nah, come on, let's join them now,' he insists as he tries to pull me up by the hand.

'No,' I tell him, snatching my hand back.

'Come on,' he whines. 'It's easy.'

Lenny starts dancing around me and, even though I'm not joining in, it looks like he's giving me a lap dance.

Thankfully it's not long after when the DJ announces everyone can join in with the dancing and as everyone moves, it hides whatever the hell it is Lenny is doing.

Now, I don't think I'm reading too much into things, I think I'm bang on in my assessment that Lenny is in no way, shape or form over his ex. And it's not that he's just down in the dumps about it, I think he might actually be trying to actively ruin their wedding, and I think he genuinely believes I'm going to help him.

I watch Lenny stagger over to the DJ. He chats with him for a moment – it almost looks like he's negotiating – and whatever he says works because the DJ hands him a microphone.

'Gadies and lentlemen, hello, my name is Lenny, I'm a *friend* of the *happy* couple,' he starts, putting sarcastic emphasis on certain words. 'And as one of my gifts – I don't know if you know this, but I have a very beautiful voice – one of my gifts is to sing them a song. This one is dedicated to June and it will be sung by me, Lenny, and my beautiful girlfriend, Caz. Caz, where are you?'

I sink into my chair as he shouts to me down the mic.

'No Caz?' he says. 'No worries. I'll do it alone. Hit it.'

Lenny does not have a beautiful voice – not when he's drunk, anyway. At least he's doing a crowd-pleasing song, I suppose, with everyone up and dancing. But then the realisation hits, rolling across the room like the tide, and everyone realises what he's singing.

'Maneater', by Hall and Oats, is actually quite a mean song to dedicate to someone – especially your ex-girlfriend – when you stop and think about it.

I grab my bag and head for the door, certain there must be some sort of lesson to learn here, but in no way willing to be part of it.

Actually, I do know what the lesson is: don't try to make yourself move on until you're good and ready – not that figuring it out matters. I'm running for the door regardless.

## 12

It's a truly surreal sight, walking up to the front entrance of a garden centre, only to be greeted by a doorman – and a doorman wearing antlers, no less.

'Name?' he asks us.

'Cara Brooks,' I say.

'Joe Mills,' Millsy adds.

'I've got Cara Brooks plus one,' the doorman replies.

'That will be it,' I say with a sigh and a smile.

Classic Flora, putting Millsy down as my plus one, and not by his name. I am delighted to report that it is just Cara Brooks plus one today, though – yes, we've managed to give Tally the slip. Well, not the slip, she's got a Zoom meeting, but I'm just so delighted that she isn't here with us, at the social event of the year – Flora's son Sal's first birthday party.

The doorman crosses off our names with exaggerated importance, as though we were vying to enter an exclusive club rather than a child's birthday party at a garden centre.

Flora has gone all out for this. She has been raving about the grandeur of the party for months now, hyping the epic celebration, which is being hosted here in the Winter Wonderland area at the local garden centre – Flora and Tommy have actually hired the whole area and the restaurant for the party, hence the guestlist, but I'm not sure it isn't all a bit over the top for a one-year-old, not that he doesn't deserve it, but my earliest memories are from maybe three or four years old, so anything anyone did for me when I was one was probably a waste of time. That said, we have brought Sal a present big enough to need its own seat in the car, so who am I to talk?

'After you, Cara Brooks,' Millsy jokes. 'I'm just the plus one.'

'And I only invited you to carry the big gift,' I tease.

Our relationship has always been an amusing blend of banter, wit, and undeniable chemistry. And yet we could go from playfully teasing each other one minute to having a heart-to-heart the next. Whatever the situation called for, whatever problems we had, we could always talk. I suppose with me being here and Millsy being in LA, and both of us being so busy, that line of communication was taken away from us, and that's when things went wrong. Today, just the two of us, little bits of the old us shine through the clouds like sunshine, but otherwise it's almost as though we're on a first date, awkwardly making small talk to fill the silence.

An unspoken awkwardness hangs in the air as we walk through the garden centre to get to the Winter Wonderland.

'How's the accent coming along?' I ask him in an attempt to fill the silence that has surrounded us again.

'You hear bits and pieces of my lessons,' he says. 'How do you think it's coming along?'

Things are weird at home. Millsy and I are like roommates, not interacting all that much, and Tally doesn't react or try to engage with me so I'm guessing she knows Millsy and I aren't together any more. I can't help but wonder why but, more importantly than that, I just hope she doesn't give the game away. Christmas is counting on it.

'I'm glad you're not doing it today,' I tell him honestly.

'Well, I'm supposed to be, so don't tell Tally,' he replies, as though it's our little secret.

'Don't worry, your secret is safe with me,' I reassure him.

'I don't doubt that,' he says with a laugh. 'I know too many of yours.'

I smile, and shrug, my body language betraying me when I'm trying to come across as cool and aloof. The nerves I'm feeling right now are so confusing, it really is like we're on a first date – although I didn't feel like this on either of the first dates I've been on recently.

'Well... I hope you get the hang of it soon,' I continue.

'Thank you, ma'am,' he replies, breaking out his terrible accent for a brief moment.

I look down at my feet and laugh. What do I say now? Our conversations used to flow effortlessly, now it feels so stilted and forced.

We continue to walk in silence for a few moments, heading into the section with fish tanks and caged birds, and as we approach a large tank in the middle of the room, we briefly separate, one of us walking on each side. I glance through the water and the fish to see him on the other side, stealing a glance, like our very own *Romeo + Juliet* moment. Millsy looks at me briefly, then back in the direction he's walking in. His eyes seemed distant, lost in thought. Is he feeling the same awkwardness as I am? Is he struggling to find the right words too? We can't go on like this, I need to say something.

'Millsy, wait, before we go in,' I say as our paths join again. I place an arm out to stop him, forcing him to put the brakes on.

'Whoa, watch out,' a voice calls out from behind him.

Millsy tries to move out of the way, to stop the man from colliding with him, and to stop the enormous present smashing into the fish tank, but as he quickly turns around, he swipes the man with the large gift he is carrying, knocking him to the floor.

'Oh, God, I'm so sorry!' Millsy exclaims, his voice filled with genuine concern and a little bit of embarrassment in there for good mix.

I know it was just an accident, but I feel like it was my fault.

We both hurry to the man's aid – and we're both equally taken aback when we realise what we're looking at. Red, red everywhere, but it isn't blood, thankfully.

There, sprawled on the floor, is Santa Claus, groaning in pain. My heart skips a beat. We've just assaulted Santa Claus. Then, as if things can't get any stranger, an elf comes running to help him, dropping to the floor, fussing him.

'Keith, are you okay?' she asks him.

She pulls his beard down and removes his hat.

Okay, so it's not *the* Santa Claus, just a man dressed as him, but that doesn't exactly make things better.

'It's my ankle,' he says. 'And I've taken a bit of a knock to the head.'

'I'm so sorry,' Millsy says, getting down on the floor to help.

'We're taking you to A&E,' the elf insists.

'Carol, I'm fine,' Santa replies. 'We can't let the kids down.'

'Right, but equally problematic would be allowing them to see an injured Santa Claus blacking out in front of them,' the elf responds.

'I can't let the kids down,' he says again. 'I... oh, I feel sick.'

'Are you here for the kids' party?' I check.

'Yes,' he replies.

'It's my cousin who booked you, but don't worry, we'll take

care of it, you go to the hospital,' I tell him. 'It's going to be fine, but best you get looked over.'

'You two can take care of it?' he asks.

Millsy and I look at one another for a second.

'Yeah, of course,' I reassure him.

'Brilliant, thanks,' he replies. 'I hate letting kids down. Can you help me to the car, lad?'

'Yes,' Millsy says, taking his arm as he helps him to his feet.

'I'll take the present through to the café,' I suggest. 'And let Flora know what's going on.'

'Yes, get that thing out of the way,' Carol the elf demands.

I grab the large gift we brought with us and carry it carefully through to the café where the party is taking place. The Winter Wonderland, and Santa's Grotto, are outside, so I suppose people are only going out there to see Santa... or they were at least, before we assaulted him. If anything was going to land you on the naughty list, this is it.

As I step inside, I'm immediately greeted by a riotous scene of screaming children running around in all directions. The air is thick with excitement, laced with the unmistakable scent of freshly brewed coffee and that uniquely distinct aroma of a traditional British buffet.

I must admit, it does look beautiful in here. Twinkling fairy lights hang from the ceiling, casting a warm glow over the festive scene, and the paper snowflakes dangling from the walls look beautiful. Everything about this room is calming and relaxing – apart from the party going on inside it, obviously.

A large Christmas tree dominates one corner of the room, decked with lights and colourful baubles. I notice the ever-growing present pile beneath it, so I decide to drop off my gift before I find Flora, to break the bad news to her about Old St Nick.

I'm only halfway across the room when I hear Flora's voice.

'Cara,' she calls out. I stop in my tracks.

'Oh, hi,' I say, turning to face Flora and Tommy, my voice very much in that 'fancy seeing you here' tone which makes no sense and is completely suspicious.

'You're late,' she tells me. 'Again. Where is Joe?'

I hold the large present in front of me like a shield.

'He's just helping someone out,' I tell her.

'Typical, on Sal's day,' she replies.

Good old Flora. You've got to love her mentality, which is basically: let's not make this not about me.

'Cara,' Tommy says by way of a hello.

'Tommy,' I repeat back to him.

That's pretty much the extent of our interactions and I'm happy to keep it that way. Oliver and I realised, quite early on, that our politics and Tommy's politics did not align – and by that I mean he's every -phobic and -ist you can think of, and then some. Uncle Paddy has totally backward views but thinks he's a good person. Tommy is different, he knows he's in the wrong (although obviously thinks he's in the right). He's an outwardly vile human. One of the strongest cases for me sticking around the particular branch of the family tree that he is on would be to make sure that his kids don't grow up with only his point of view and his politics. Anyway, I might have to be in a room with him at family events, but I don't have to talk to him. I do what I always do, and imagine a screen in front of him, essentially removing him from existence.

'Listen, Flora, there's been an accident,' I start softly, moving things along.

'What is it?' she asks quickly. 'Is Gran okay?'

I scrunch up my face.

'She's literally less than ten metres away from us eating a scone,' I point out.

'Well, what?' she pushes me.

'It's Santa,' I say, lowering my voice when I say the big man's name. 'He's hurt. That's who Millsy is helping out.'

'How did he get hurt?' she asks me. 'Were you there?'

'We... collided,' I explain.

'How did you...' Her voice tapers off as she locks her sights on the large gift I'm holding in front of me. 'That?'

'It was an accident,' I tell her.

'What the heck even is that?' she asks.

'Sal's present,' I say.

'But what the bloody hell is inside it?' she persists. 'It's comically big.'

'It's a Bentley,' I say, suddenly realising how stupid that sounds, my voice losing confidence with each word.

'A Bentley?' she repeats back to me. 'For a one-year-old?'

'Not an actual Bentley, obviously,' I add quickly. 'It's a pushchair version, meant for kids his age. You said he liked cars.'

'He's one,' she replies, pure crazy in her voice. 'He doesn't know what he likes.'

It doesn't seem worth mentioning that you could make that case about every single part of today.

'I can return it,' I say.

'Don't be daft,' Tommy chimes him. 'Here, I'll take it.'

I hand it over. Funny how he can find words to say to me when it benefits him. He seems the most excited about it, as he carries it off, unwrapping it as he goes. Arsehole.

'Santa is due in the grotto soon,' Flora says. 'What's going on?'

'The thing is, he's hurt his ankle, and he's taken a knock to the head, so his wife has taken him to hospital,' I say, wincing, ready for a hurricane of anger.

'Cara, are you serious right now?' she replies. 'Tell me this is just one of your pranks?'

Once again, I involuntarily scrunch my face in response to her words. One of my pranks? I never prank people. And if I did, this certainly wouldn't be one of my ideas.

'Oh, my mum is going to kill you, you know that, right? She thinks you're always trying to ruin things for me,' she rants.

That's because she's a pantomime villain of a woman.

'Joe, tell me she's joking,' Flora says, addressing Millsy as he joins us.

'It's all going to be okay,' he reassures him. 'We promised Santa it would be fine and he told us what we need to do to help.'

'Yeah?' she replies. 'Because, honestly, it's like the main part of the whole day.'

'Absolutely,' he tells her. 'Leave it to us.'

Flora goes off in a huff. There is no way she isn't telling Auntie Mary about this.

'Any bright ideas?' I ask him, kind of casually, but I guess it feels like we do this sort of thing often.

'None myself, but Santa had one,' he tells me. 'I think he got the wrong idea, when you told him we would sort it, because after I helped him into his car he handed me a bag, told me everything we needed was inside.'

Millsy holds a bag out in front of him, opening it just enough for me to peer inside.

'No...' I say. 'No, no, no.'

'I think we already agreed to it,' Millsy says. Then he smiles. 'Come on, it might be fun.'

'Me and you?' I blurt. 'Santa and elf?'

'Well, elf and Santa,' he replies. 'I'm twice your size, it might confuse the kids.'

'Do we really have to do this?' I whine.

'It is kind of our fault,' Millsy reasons. 'And we don't want to let the kids down.'

He's right. He's almost always right.

'Okay, that's true,' I say. 'And I guess it gets out of socialising – with the adults, at least.'

'That's the spirit,' he says with a laugh. 'Come on, a staff member told me we can change in the break room.'

I puff air from my cheeks.

'Let's do it.'

As we enter the staff break room, I feel a mixture of excitement and awkwardness. I have to admit, it does feel good, getting into one of our trademark scrapes together, yet again, and having to figure out a way out of it together.

Millsy throws me my costume and stands with his in his hands for a moment.

'I didn't realise it was only one room,' he says. 'I'll step out for a minute.'

'Don't be daft,' I insist. 'We've seen each other naked a million times. Well, I mean, I don't mind if you don't, anyway.'

What started out as confident and casual fast turned into a confusing mess of a sentence.

'Okay,' he replies with a smile.

Millsy removes his jacket and begins to undo his belt. I go to undo my jeans, my fingers lingering on the button for a moment. The palpable chemistry that still exists between us is undeniable. Obviously getting undressed in the same room as him triggers memories, but it's not just that. Trying to maintain a platonic and mature demeanour, I discreetly steal a glance at Millsy as he begins to unbutton his shirt. My eyes involuntarily wander over his muscular frame, a reminder of why I found him so attractive in the first place, and my heart races as he bares his toned chest.

Dangerous is the only way I can describe being here with him like this. I don't know why but that's the first word that springs to my mind.

His muscles ripple beneath his skin as he steps into the red trousers. He has a movie star body, that's for sure, carefully crafted. There is nothing careful or crafted about me, as I almost fall stepping into the red and white striped leggings.

'Oops,' I say, finding my feet again, drawing attention to myself, which is not what you want to do when you're standing around in candy cane leggings and a pink lacy bra.

Millsy's gaze meets mine, and I can see the spark of recognition in his eyes, almost as though we're both remembering the nights we spent together, the fiery chemistry and passion that once consumed us. Well, at least I think that's what I can see, perhaps it's just wishful thinking on my part? Perhaps I'm alone in this dance of restraint. Every movement, every subtle adjustment of fabric, feels charged. Every inch of his body reminds me of the things we did together when things were good.

Ugh, I need to knock this off. I avert my gaze, trying to regain my composure, because a kids' party is hardly the time or the place for such thoughts, especially not when you're dressing up as Santa Claus and his faithful elf. I suppose it's only normal though that, deep down, I still find him irresistibly attractive. Yes, even with an elasticated beard.

Standing side by side in front of a full-length mirror, we finally take in our new togs. I glance at Millsy, my eyes drawn to his bright red ensemble. The fluffy white beard frames his face, accentuating his rugged features. Any mum taking her kid to see this Santa would surely know there was a hunk of a man underneath the costume, it's impossible to hide, and a sight that stirs something deep within me, which is something I never thought I would say.

'You look cute,' he tells me.

'Is it my green, tattered mini skirt?' I ask jokily.

'No, I think it's the hat and the pointy ears,' he replies. 'Although I like your outfit more than mine. Still, at least I have the lead role.'

'You do,' I say. 'Do you need any help with the accent?'

'Ouch,' he says with a laugh. 'Come on, let's do this.'

'After you, Santa,' I say – flirtatiously for some reason, because apparently all it takes is a man unbuttoning his shirt in front of me to get my knickers in a twist.

I follow Millsy's lead, ready to take on the role of a lifetime – well, for me, at least.

Santa's Grotto sits inside a cute little (thankfully heated) log cabin tucked away in the corner of the outdoor Winter Wonderland area. As we step into the waiting room, the air becomes infused with the scent of freshly baked cookies and hints of cinnamon, which must be coming from some sort of air freshener, but it's a really nice touch. This room has lights, animatronic penguins, the faint sound of a cold wind blowing around – were Santa's Grottos anywhere near this sophisticated when I was a kid? I remember them being quite rubbish, and that's through the eyes of a child. I wonder how much the process has advanced. Can you email Santa Claus now? That seems far more efficient, and better for the environment. Unless, of course, your child Googles the origin of Santa Claus while they're online.

The entrance to the next room – Santa's room – is adorned with twinkling fairy lights and a sign that reads 'Santa's Magical Workshop'. We step inside, and the room unfolds before us like a scene from a festive storybook. It really is magical – and such a shame it's going to be ruined by completely inexperienced actors playing the main characters.

'How do we do this?' I ask him.

'I guess, when it's time, you greet the kids in the waiting room, one at a time, and then bring them in to see me?' he suggests. 'Do kids still sit on Santa's lap? I don't want to sound like a square, but I'm not sure I'd encourage our kids to sit on a stranger's knee.'

Millsy freezes on the spot as he realises what he just said.

Oh, boy. Do I say something? What do I say? I should probably say something.

'Perhaps that's what the little stool is for?' he suggests, changing the subject before I have chance to say a word. 'Maybe the kids just sit there?'

'Makes sense to me,' I reply.

Marriage, kids – stuff like that – are things Millsy and I used to talk about. We knew we wanted to get married and as far as kids went, we both had a similar attitude, we were happy to wait and see where life took us, and figure out what we wanted when we got there, but it was never something we ruled out, and we would often have fun talking about baby names and which of our individual traits our potential kids might inherit. Something about the way he delivered that line, so effortlessly, so casually, so happily... I feel like my heart is breaking.

'It sounds like it's showtime,' I tell him, hearing the chatter of parents and excited kids in the waiting room. 'Are you ready?'

'How hard can it be?' he says with a shrug.

I step into the waiting room and understandably Flora is waiting there with Sal, the birthday boy, and Vince, his brother.

Flora stands there, disbelief etched across her face, as she clocks me in my elf get-up.

'Come on through, boys,' I say. 'Santa is waiting for you.'

Flora follows me into the main room of the grotto. I take Vince by the hand and lead him to the stool. Flora glances at the stool next to Santa and frowns.

'Is Santa not going to let the kids sit on his lap?' she asks in that high-pitched voice people use around children.

'I didn't think it was appropriate,' Millsy tells her quietly. 'But of course I'll hold the birthday boy, he's family.'

'Family?' she replies through gritted teeth as she places Sal in Millsy's arms. 'You can't say that in here, they might ask questions.'

Sal, being a one-year-old, is blissfully unaware of the conversation, giggling as he grabs at Santa's beard curiously. Meanwhile, Vince, the two-year-old, is thoroughly engaged in a staring contest with a model snowman nearby.

'Vince, come on, sit on Santa's lap and tell him what you want for Christmas,' Flora instructs.

Vince, without breaking eye contact with the snowman, simply says, 'No.'

'Kids,' I say with a laugh. 'Hey, Vince, why don't you hop on Santa's lap, and tell him what you want for Christmas?'

Vince is indifferent but easy to steer.

'Ho, ho, ho! Well, hello there, little Sal! Have you been a good little boy this year?' Millsy asks.

'He's one-year-old, Santa. I'm pretty sure he hasn't been plotting any mischief,' Flora replies.

'I don't know, he looks smart,' Millsy reasons. 'Sal might be running a secret baby mafia behind our backs.'

'Especially with a name like Sal,' I dare to joke.

Flora gives me a glare as I place Vince on Millsy's lap. Millsy, embracing his role as Santa, turns his attention to Vince.

'And what about you, young man? What would you like for Christmas?'

'I want a dog,' Vince says. At least I'm pretty sure that's what he says. Kids his age talk like drunks, babbling in their own language.

'A dog?' Millsy replies cheerily. He looks at Flora, who shakes her head.

'I have a dog?' Vince says, reaching out to try to put a finger in Millsy's nose.

'You like dogs?' Millsy says, trying to change the conversation slightly.

'I have a dog?' Vince says again.

'I have an idea,' I interrupt. 'Why don't we take your picture with Santa?'

'Yes, let's try to get something out of this,' Flora says. 'I'll take it.'

I step aside so Flora can take the photo, figuring she'll say something if she wants me in the snap, but she doesn't.

'Well, I'll leave you two to your shift,' she says through a smirky smile. 'Have fun.'

'Always,' I say with a smile.

I head to the waiting room to retrieve the next child.

'Okay, Santa, this is Sophia, she's five,' I say, making the introductions. 'Sophia, this is Santa, if you want to sit on the stool next to him.'

Sophia is a spirited five-year-old who bounces into the grotto with tonnes of enthusiasm and boundless energy.

'Santa, Santa! I have a very important request!' she says.

'And what's that, Sophia?' Millsy replies.

'I want a bike, but with rockets, so I can go really, really fast,' she tells him, almost gasping for breath.

'Rockets?' Millsy replies. 'Well, you know, we don't actually make rockets at the North Pole, because they're quite dangerous, so we leave rockets to the professionals. But we do make bikes,

awesome ones, that go really fast without rockets. How does that
sound?'

Sophia thinks.

'Can they be blue?' she asks.

'They can be any colour you want,' he tells her. 'But only if
you've been a good girl this year.'

'I have,' she says. 'I promise.'

'Is that true?' Millsy asks her mum.

'It certainly is,' the mum replies, all doe-eyed. See, what did I
tell you, women just know when they're dealing with a dream-
boat, even if he's hidden inside a costume. 'I've been a good girl
too.'

Oh, that is not subtle at all.

'Well, then, maybe your mum can have a bike too,' Millsy
tells Sophia, ever the professional.

Hilariously, I feel a pang of jealousy.

Next up is Alex, who must be at least ten years old.

'Hello, Alex,' Millsy says.

'Hello, Santa,' Alex replies seriously. 'Listen, to get to the
point, I've been really good this year. Really good. I made *you* a
list.'

'You made me a list?' Millsy repeats back to him.

'Yes, it's a list of everything I've done well, and why you
should give me all the presents I want,' Alex explains. 'You can
take it back to the North Pole with you.'

'I'll take that for you,' I tell him. 'I'll put it somewhere safe.'

As I take the piece of paper from Alex, I notice a few things
on the list:

*Kept my books in alphabetical order.*
*Looked after the goldfish.*
*Dealt with my mum and dad's divorce.*

Okay, wow. That's... wow.

I bring kid after kid in to meet Santa, and we may not be the best or the most professional, but we're, y'know, here, and we're doing an okay job, I think.

There is just one kid left and, honestly, I'm knackered. I know I've only been walking back and forth across a room, but this is such a draining gig.

'And last but not least, Santa, we have Richie,' I say, leading a small boy with bright blue hands and lips over towards Millsy.

His mum must notice me staring curiously.

'We're not sure if it's from a cupcake or a pen,' she says with a laugh – then she spots Millsy. 'Oh, hello, Santa!'

Richie stands in front of Millsy and within a second, he is projectile vomiting all down Millsy's Santa costume. As I hurry forward to help, Richie turns to me and throws up on me too. So much for me thinking this was going well.

'Oh, okay, we'd better get you to the toilets,' his mum says. 'Thanks anyway.'

And with that they leave, and now it's just the two of us, covered in blue puke.

'Oh... my... God, that smells so bad,' I blurt.

'Really, really bad,' Millsy replies. 'Does this thing have a staff bathroom or anything?'

We head into the waiting room but all of the doors in there only lead to cupboards.

'I can't... I'm going to be sick myself, if I don't get this off,' Millsy says as he whips off the top part of his costume.

I'm way ahead of him, stripping down to my bra and leggings once again, because whatever it is that makes sick blue is just unbearable.

I notice a bolt on the inside of the door, so I lock it.

'I can get someone to bring us our clothes,' I tell him. 'But in the meantime, best I lock this, in case any more kids walk in.'

'Yeah, your cousin would not be happy with that,' Millsy laughs.

'Well, she's never happy with anything,' I point out.

'That's true,' he says, walking over to me. 'Vomit aside – which wasn't actually our fault – I feel like we did a really good job.'

'You know what, me too,' I reply. 'Who knew we were good with kids?'

'I've always known you would be good with kids,' Millsy replies. 'Which reminds me... sorry if I made things weird before, talking about us having kids, it's just... old habits.'

'Oh, I didn't think a thing of it,' I lie. I'm actually thinking about it more than I was, now that he's said he always thought I would be good with kids. 'For what it's worth, I think you would make an incredible dad.'

Millsy smiles, ever so slightly, but I can tell that he's thinking about something and it's clearly distracting him.

Once again, the sexual tension feels overwhelming, the air is thick with it, so much so that I swear it's getting rid of the smell of sick – although that could be because we took our tops off, which is only turning up the sexual tension. Wow, what a mess.

Suddenly things feel quite intense. We're staring at each other, looking into one another's eyes, and I have no idea what is going through Millsy's mind, but I know exactly what I'm thinking: I want him, and feeling like I can't have him just makes me want him more.

At first, I think my senses are betraying me, that I'm imagining Millsy slowly moving closer to me, and that I'm slowly moving closer to him, but it's not in my head, it's happening, we're gravitating towards one another.

It's so subtle until it isn't. We've both done this dance a thousand times before and so without much thought or a word spoken, we snap together like magnets (opposite poles, obviously).

As Millsy scoops me up into his arms, I wrap my legs around his waist, tugging his fake beard away so that our lips can meet. The feeling of his stubbly beard on my skin, his lips on mine, the gentle flick of his tongue – I've missed this. I've missed him.

As Millsy carries me back through into the grotto, I feel one of his hands slowly walking up my back, where he removes my bra in one easy movement. There's something so, so sexy about a man who can undo a bra, and few things more awkward in the moment than having to offer to do it yourself – and that doesn't exclusively relate to the removal of bras, but Millsy has never had any trouble in any other departments either.

Our kissing pauses briefly as Millsy looks for somewhere for us to land. He spies some beanbags and so we fall down onto them. We start kissing again until we feel a shift. Not beanbags, plastic bags, full of fake polystyrene snow that spills out everywhere. We laugh and it feels like old times. Serious, steamy sex is great and all, but once you've found that special someone, that person of your dreams, the one who makes you laugh like no one else can, you realise just how sexy it is to laugh in the bedroom – or wherever else you may be.

We cackle with glee as we roll out of the pile of polystyrene balls together, to dry land, where Millsy presses his body down on top of mine. I don't think I've wanted him more. We've got the best of both worlds. We're like a well-oiled machine, both of us knowing how this goes, knowing exactly what the other person likes, what works time and time again. But then at the same time, we're not together any more. This isn't part of the script. It's like all the heat of a random hook-up without the risks that come with a stranger.

I know that we should stop and think about this, but screw it. All I want to do is get lost in the moment.

\* \* \*

As we lie on the floor together, I rest my head on Millsy's chest. I notice one of the little polystyrene balls on his stomach, so I flick it off before resting my hand where it was.

I snuggle closer. I can feel the steady rhythm of his heartbeat, thumping in his chest. This all feels so familiar and so comforting, our bodies intertwined, keeping one another warm. I really miss this.

When things were good, they were great, but when things got bad, we fell apart. I never thought that would happen. And now here we are, stuck in this liminal space, teetering between wanting each other and the harsh reality of our situation.

The familiarity of his touch, the scent of his skin, and the softness of the way he's holding me now are all things I have been desperately trying to keep out of my mind. I don't want this with anyone else, ever again, Millsy is my person. Surely we can figure this out?

'I think we're definitely on the naughty list now,' I say, breaking the silence.

'Oh, definitely,' Millsy replies. 'I'm sure almost all of that is outlawed in the North Pole.'

'Well, Santa would probably have a heart attack,' I point out.

'And the elves surely don't have the core strength,' he adds.

'*I* don't have the core strength,' I say with a laugh. 'You have the core strength for both of us – that's our secret to success.'

'Well, whatever our secret, we make a good team,' he reasons. 'In and out of the grotto.'

'We should probably get out of here,' I say, pulling myself to my feet. 'Before we get caught. We'll just say a kid burst that bag or something.'

'Yeah, and I'm sure you'll come up with some other reason why it's all in your hair,' he teases as he searches for his clothes.

'I'll flag someone down from outside, see if they can bring us our clean clothes, I'll explain the vomit situation to them,' I tell him, my bra firmly back in place as I head for the door.

'It's the perfect cover story, for us taking our clothes off,' Millsy chuckles.

I'm hoping I can poke just my head out and spot a member of staff to flag down from the door (not someone from the party, because I can't imagine that going down well) – I'm sure someone who works here will know that this sort of thing happens all the time. Never work with kids or animals, that's what they say, and while the animatronic penguins were no bother, I'm sure kids throw up all the time. I don't know how often they projectile vomit bright blue, though.

I unbolt the door but, as I try to open it, it won't budge. It's as though it's locked from the middle, but there's no mechanism on the inside for key to go in – take it from someone who knows locks, this door only locks properly from the outside, and this door is absolutely, most definitely locked from the outside.

'Shit,' I blurt quietly.

'What?' Millsy asks as he joins me.

He looks so sexy, wandering around in his Santa trousers and boots, like something straight off a sexy Christmas calendar.

'They must've assumed we weren't in here any more and they've locked us in,' I confess.

'Let me try,' he says, reaching for the handle.

He tries the door and of course it doesn't open.

'Feel better for that?' I say.

'Anything is worth a try,' he replies. 'We're stuck in here, we don't have our phone, they might close up for the day before anyone even realises we're here.'

'Shit,' I say again. 'Shit, shit, shit.'

'Let's not panic,' Millsy suggests. 'Come on, there's a party full of people just across the outdoor area – there's bound to be someone in there who cares enough about us to come looking for us?'

With my family, I'm not so sure.

'Joey?' we hear a voice call out. 'Joey, is that you?'

'Is that...'

'Tally?' Millsy calls out. 'Oh my God, Tally, you came.'

'I thought you said she wasn't coming?' I blurt, which I know, sounds childish, but whatever.

'I told her to come, if she finished work early, and thank God she did,' he says quietly. Then he raises his voice. 'Tally, they've locked us in, can you go get someone to get us out?'

'Oh, my goodness, yes, sure,' she replies.

'And ask them to bring towels or something,' he adds with a laugh. 'We're covered in kid puke.'

'Wow,' Tally blurts. 'I'm right on it.'

'You're our hero,' he calls after her. Then he turns his attention back to me. 'Shit, okay, we need to make sure none of this looks suspicious.'

He seems worried. He wasn't worried a few minutes ago. He must notice the look on my face.

'What?' he asks.

'Nothing,' I say with a shrug.

'Your words and your body are saying different things,' he

speculates, checking himself for polystyrene balls, brushing a couple out of my hair. I duck out of his way.

'Cara, come on, what's going on?' he asks.

'Nothing,' I say again. 'I just... wasn't expecting Tally to be here, and you're clearly freaking out, and maybe this was a mistake.'

Millsy tips his head curiously.

'It sounds like you're the one freaking out,' he points out. Then he thinks for a moment. 'You're right, sorry, this was a mistake, we've moved on, it was inappropriate.'

'We've moved on,' I repeat back to him, almost as though I'm confirming it for myself. 'So, you don't mind me dating? You're fine with it?'

'Cara, you have my blessing, what more do you want me to say?' he replies, his patience wearing thin. 'Go on all the dates you want, and let's just forget about today.'

Wow. Perhaps this was a mistake, giving in to the moment for old time's sake, but nothing that could come close to fixing things between us.

'Our little secret,' I say to him as I hear someone fumbling with the lock on the other side of the door.

Shit, I feel so stupid. He's moved on, of course he has. He's Millsy, I'm sure this is what he does – it sounds like it's what he used to do. Done with one girl, on to the next. And I know we were together for years, and that's a big deal, but if I'm defaulting back to my old methods, then perhaps he is too? Either way, this was most definitely a mistake, and one that I need to make sure I don't repeat.

Even though I really want to.

**13**

Christmas is a joyous occasion, a time to spend with your family – what I want to know is how it can possibly be both?

Don't get me wrong, I love spending time with my parents, and with Oliver, and my gran may just be my favourite person on the planet. But the rest of them. Oh, the rest of them.

The annual festive ladies' afternoon tea at my gran's house has always been a cherished Christmas tradition in our family. We all gather in her cosy dining room, which is always lovingly adorned with twinkling fairy lights for the occasion, and the scents of cinnamon candles and freshly baked scones and tea fills the air. The table is always set out with her best china teacups – delicate little things that, even as an adult, I'm terrified to touch – and a platter of delectable treats. My gran and my mum always slave for days to prepare everything.

The only thing about the day that isn't ideal is that it isn't just me, Mum and Gran – and it's not so much the extended family members who turn up (the ones we only really see at this, weddings and funerals), it's Auntie Mary and Flora's presence that puts a dampener on the day, they're that one bulb that's out in the string of Christmas lights, the one that ruins the whole set.

Still, I turned up, as I always do, and I have my phone to keep me sane. Well, as much as chatting to Matcher dates can keep anyone sane. Actually, I say that, but I've been messaging with a familiar face all day.

Liam, the guy I've been chatting with, is actually someone I spoke to the last time I was on Matcher. I remember him well, he was studying to be a doctor, really funny, and charming, the kind of guy who would happily chat with no pressure to meet up. I assumed him being a doctor made him instantly trustworthy (although I have since learned my lesson with Lenny the fire-fighter) and beyond that, he seemed genuinely kind and refreshingly normal – a rare find in the digital dating world. We never managed to meet before he found someone and left the app, which was a shame for me, but I thought it was admirable that he was willing to give up on the dating game for a shot at something real – it actually gave me hope, that I might find someone for me. Ha! And now here we are, both back on Matcher, like it hasn't been a day. I'm happy to report that he is still funny, and charming, and messaging him is a nice break from the party.

Today is going as expected. We're all chatting, occasionally mixing up the conversation groups – which roughly translates as me moving around the room to avoid talking to my auntie, but Auntie Mary isn't happy unless she's making people miserable, which is evident as she saunters over to me with a sly grin, her eyes gleaming mischievously.

'So, where is the lovely Tally?' she asks, her voice dripping with suggestive undertones.

Her blatant attempt to wind me up is as transparent as glass. I've already suspected that there might be something brewing between Millsy and Tally, so the idea is nothing new. It's as if

Auntie Mary's bullets bounce off me, deflected by an invisible shield. I've definitely grown immune to the meaning behind Auntie Mary's words over the years but what still manages to piss me off is the intention behind them. She wants to upset me. What a villain.

I respond with a nonchalant shrug and a casual smile.

'She's with Millsy,' I tell her.

'But this is supposed to be a celebration for the ladies in the family,' she responds.

'She's not in the family,' I remind her, still smiling. 'She's here to work so that's where she is.'

'With Joe,' Auntie Mary concludes.

'Working,' I add.

I keep my tone light, devoid of any hint of concern or jealousy. I refuse to give Auntie Mary the satisfaction of seeing me flustered over this.

Auntie Mary's eyebrows shoot up, clearly disappointed by my unflappable demeanour. I watch the cogs turning in her brain before she tries a different tactic.

'Well, you know, Cara, sometimes things aren't as they seem,' she says, feigning innocence. 'People can surprise you.'

Her words are laden with hidden implications and normally I wouldn't let it rattle me but it's just occurred to me why it's different. Ordinarily, when Auntie Mary takes her little swipes, it's just shots in the dark to try to wound me. She's aiming, sure, but she doesn't really know at what, or why, but it's different now because her aim is bang on. Something is going on with me and Millsy and she doesn't even know it but she's twisting the knife in the open wound. I wonder, if she knew we were separated, if she would say things like this. Perhaps this is just her brand, the thing that she believes makes her different, and that she isn't the villain she seems. Then again, perhaps she would enjoy it, seeing me going through a bad time. Whatever it is that is wrong with her must come from some insecurity somewhere inside her. I keep the peace for my gran, and usually I just feel sorry for Mary, but the thought of her having a front-row seat to my break-up really rattles me. I don't know what to say.

'Hello?' I hear Millsy call out.

'Ah, hello,' my gran says, hugging him. 'The only boy allowed in.'

I love the way my gran looks at Millsy, with genuine love in her eyes. She once told me that she loved him, not just because of how amazing he was, but because of the way he loved me – she said it was something special. When you break up with someone you never stop to think about how other people will take the news – just about how it will ruin Christmas, apparently.

Millsy walks over to me and kisses me on the cheek, saving me from my auntie, somehow knowing I needed him, and getting here right on time. I wasn't even expecting him.

'What are you doing here?' I ask him.

'I thought I'd surprise you,' he says with a smile.

I glance at Auntie Mary, as if to confirm that she's right, people can surprise you.

'Consider me surprised,' I reply.

'Well, I figured you'd be winding things down about now,' he says as he wraps an arm around me. 'And I didn't want you getting the train home, not when it's so busy, so I thought I would come and pick you up.'

'Aww, isn't that lovely?' I say.

'It is,' my mum calls over. 'You've got yourself a good one there.'

'She has,' my gran adds. 'In fact, we were about to have a

toast, you've just given us the perfect thing to toast to. Mary, open the Prosecco, you can have a sip, can't you, Millsy?'

'I can have a sip,' he says with a smile.

'A big strong man like you, I'll bet you could handle a bottle,' my gran's niece Leslie calls out from across the room, practically fanning herself as she looks Millsy up and down.

Auntie Mary returns with a mix of different glasses, all filled with varying levels of Prosecco. She hands Millsy and me a glass each and I notice that they're my gran's commemorative glasses for Prince Charles and Princess Diana's wedding. A suppressed giggle escapes my lips, because there's no way Auntie Mary hasn't done this on purpose.

'Charles and Di,' I say to Millsy with a playful smile.

'How lovely,' he replies through a grin.

Gran takes one of the glasses, holding it up high for everyone to see.

'To Cara and Millsy,' she proclaims, her voice brimming with affection. 'The sweetest couple I know.'

'To Cara and Millsy,' (almost) everyone echoes.

I raise my glass, meeting Millsy's gaze briefly before taking a sip. He smiles at me, his eyes filled with a mix of nostalgia and resignation. It feels like a moment frozen in time, a reminder of how things would have been if we hadn't broken up. At times like this, when we're together, I can't think of a single reason why we shouldn't be together.

'Thanks for coming to save me,' I tell him.

'Anytime,' he replies.

Not long after the toast, we say our goodbyes, and I walk along the garden path with a real spring in my step, but then I look up and spot Tally in the car.

'Oh, Tally is here,' I blurt.

'Yeah, well, I told her I wanted to pick you up, so she suggested we take our lesson on the road,' he replies.

'You shouldn't have put yourself out,' I reply, I'll admit, a little ungratefully.

'I figured that's what I would usually do,' he replies. 'I thought it might seem strange if I didn't.'

Ah, so that's what this is, all just part of the act.

I take my phone from my bag and see that I have a message from Liam.

Liam: Okay, Cara, it's been four years in the making. Why don't we finally have that date tonight?

Cara: Sounds great. What's the plan?

Well, I'm just playing my part, right? Going through the motions. It's what Millsy wants, so I'll give it to him.

## 14

Another day, another date, another chance for disaster.

I'm at our designated meeting spot – first, as always – in Leeds centre, feeling a mix of nerves and cautious excitement. So far, I've been on two dates and both of them have been nothing short of awful. I'm really hoping that Liam will be different, and I'm curious to meet him after 'knowing' him for so long. At least with Liam I have the advantage of having chatted to him for weeks – albeit years ago – so I know a little more about him.

And there he is, strolling towards me, his arms weighed down with bags of shopping. He's definitely him, he still looks like his photo, and he doesn't look like he's going to take me to his ex-girlfriend's wedding – that makes him a regular Prince Charming in my book.

Liam flashes a charming smile, his eyes filled with warmth, as though he's just as surprised as I am to be meeting someone who looks like they do in their photos.

'Hey, Cara! Sorry I'm a bit late,' he greets me. 'I just had a few things to grab.'

'Just a few?' I joke, nodding towards his well-stuffed shopping bags.

'Well, after hearing about the day you've had, I thought you might appreciate being spoilt,' he explains. 'So I thought I'd cook for you. How does that sound?'

'Oh, er, cooking sounds nice, but you shouldn't put yourself out,' I insist.

'If you would rather go out, that's absolutely fine,' he quickly says. 'But, after what you've told me about your stressful family party, I thought you might appreciate a bit of chill time, someone to complain to, and someone who – I think, at least – is a pretty decent chef.'

It's sweet of him, to want to cook for me, and to have been paying attention when I told him I was at a family party earlier and that it was stressing me out. You have to trust someone, sometime, right? Not every single man on this planet is a freak, surely?

'Okay,' I say. 'Sounds good.'

'Perfect,' he replies. 'Well, this is my building, let's head up.'

I follow Liam into the lift and watch curiously as he presses the button for the top floor. The penthouses are usually at the top, right?

As we step into Liam's apartment, I can't help but feel my jaw drop in awe. The place is absolutely stunning, a penthouse nestled high in the sky, boasting breathtaking views of the city below – one I know so well, but haven't even seen from this angle before. The floor-to-ceiling windows probably bathe the space in natural light during the daytime, accentuating the modern decor and sleek furnishings, but at night it just gives everything this super sleek, high-end vibe. I absolutely love it.

It's an open-plan layout, with the living room seamlessly flowing into a stylish kitchen with what looks like top-of-the-line appliances. The polished wooden floors gleam under the slightly dimmed lights above us. Everything about this place screams luxury and sophistication. Liam is clearly a man with excellent taste and I'm not sure what kind of doctor he is, but it must be one that pays really well. I wonder if he's a cosmetic surgeon, or in a private practice somewhere. Either way, good for him.

Liam sets his bags down on the island next to the shiny black hob. He turns on the oven before unloading his shopping, getting all of his ingredients in order.

'I'm thinking steak, chips, onion rings and fried mushrooms,' he says.

'Sounds great,' I reply.

Well, everything but the mushrooms does. I'm not really a fan of those, but it's nothing to ruin a first date over.

At first Liam looks a little flustered, as he searches for everything he needs, but once he has all his tools in front of him, he's in his element. I'm actually quite excited about the food.

'Take a seat,' he says, nodding towards the sofa. 'I'll put the chips in, then we can chat for a bit, before I cook our steaks. I hope you're not one of those people who likes it practically burned.'

'Oh, no, I'm a medium-rare girl,' I tell him as I sit down. 'I can't stand it well done.'

'That's what I like to hear,' he says.

Eventually Liam joins me over by the sofa.

'What's wrong?' he asks me. 'Are you hurt?'

'Oh, no, I'm fine,' I insist. 'I tripped the other day and I think I've twinged a muscle of something. I keep getting this crampy feeling in my calf but it's nothing.'

'Can I see?' he asks.

'Erm, sure,' I reply. 'Sorry, I'm not just here for the medical assessment.'

'Don't worry, I know,' he says with a laugh. 'Let's see what we've got.'

Liam gets down on his knees in front of me and carefully lifts up my leg, stretching it out, placing my foot on the coffee table behind him. He looks at my calf, then he pushes it in particular places to see what happens.

'It's fine, honestly,' I tell him. 'It's just a bit of cramp, it's probably nothing to do with me tripping.'

'Does that feel better?' he asks me as he massages my calf.

'It does,' I reply with a sigh.

'What about this?' he asks, his hand running up my leg.

Erm...

'Or this,' he continues.

As he attempts to run his hand up the inside of my thigh, I quickly shut my legs. I'm about to shout at him, to tell him that I'm not here for that, that I'm not interested in that, when a man in a suit walks in through the front door. The first thing I notice is that he's carrying an iPad. The second thing I notice is the young couple standing behind him. Everyone looks horrified.

Confusion furrows my brow as I turn my attention to the crowd we seem to have drawn.

Their presence immediately raises my suspicion, no doubt about it, it's just that this is clearly a new level of disturbing, so much so that I can't even guess what is going on.

'Mr and Mrs Powel, if you could please wait downstairs for me, I'll get this all smoothed out,' the man in the suit says. He waits for the couple to go before turning his attention back to Liam.

'Liam, what the hell are you doing here?'

His voice is laced with authority, his eyes fixed on Liam. It's clear that something is amiss, and that Liam has done something wrong. Something else, anyway.

Liam doesn't say anything, so the man in the suit turns his attention to me.

My heart starts to race and I feel a knot forming in the pit of my stomach. Whatever is going on here, it isn't good.

'Did Liam tell you this was his apartment?' the man asks me.

I nod my head.

'Well, this isn't Liam's apartment,' the man informs me. 'Liam is a letting agent – one who has been told before about taking keys home at night so that he can try to woo girls by pretending he's something other than a fuck-up who dropped out of med school and now he can't even be trusted to show people around flats.'

My jaw is on the floor. They're all the same. My God, they are all the bloody same. Every single (and not single, if we're being real) man on Matcher is an absolute freak.

Without wasting another moment – or saying a word – I grab my things, anger coursing through my veins as I head for the lift. Liam doesn't try to stop me – what would he say, if he did? What could possibly make this all okay?

I press the button to go down and the second the doors close, I grab my phone from my bag, find Matcher on my home screen and delete the app.

It's gone from my phone before I'm back down on the earth.

I think that's quite enough of that, don't you?

'...so it makes sense to use the train station as a location,' Charlie says.

'Right,' I reply.

'We'll just use the city side,' he continues.

'Okay,' I say.

'Or we have people walk along the tracks,' he adds.

'Good idea,' I tell him but then I realise what he's just said. 'Wait, what?'

'Oh, so you are listening,' he says with a laugh. 'Look, we're done for the day, you look tired. Go home, get some rest, have that fella of yours cook something for you.'

His words take me by surprise. It's not that he's said anything inappropriate, it's just, well, I don't have a fella to cook for me, unless letting agents count. Charlie must notice the look on my face.

'Cara, is everything okay?' he asks me. 'You don't quite seem yourself at the moment, and I thought it might be work stress, but I'm so brilliant at my job it's all going without a hiccup.'

I laugh at his joke.

'Work is great,' I tell him. 'It's the only thing that's great.'

'I thought you'd be happy, with Millsy being home,' he replies.

I sigh.

'It's not worth getting into the ins and outs of why but, just between us, Millsy and I broke up, a while ago actually, but it's not proving all that easy to deal with because we're actually still pretending we're together, so we don't ruin Christmas, and I'm trying to make myself move on, but all of my Matcher dates so far have been nothing short of a nightmare – some of them documentary worthy – it's just so bloody completely horrendous and I've had e-fucking-nough.'

I stop, if only to breathe.

'That's a lot,' he points out. 'A lot to take in, a lot going on.'

'Tell me about it,' I say. 'Sorry for blurting it all out at you.'

'You're technically paying me,' he jokes. 'Listen, I sense that you don't want to talk about your break-up, so I won't, but can I give you a bit of advice about Matcher?'

'Sure,' I reply.

'Don't use it,' he insists. 'It's not good, for anyone involved, unless you're after a hook-up or something specialist.'

I laugh.

'No, neither of those things,' I tell him. 'I already deleted the app from my phone.'

'Good,' he says. 'If you're going to use anything, there's a website I'm using at the moment, called Love @ First Site.'

'Seriously uncool name,' I point out.

'Well, if you want to find love, you can't be afraid to be uncool,' he replies. 'It promises – as you would guess – that your true love will be the first person they match you with. I know it sounds cheesy, but trust me, I've heard some success stories. It goes a lot deeper than Matcher, to find the right person for you. Worth a try maybe?'

'I'll look into it,' I say sceptically, but with a smile. 'Thanks.'

My stomach growls so loud we both hear it.

'Do you want to go grab some food?' he asks me. 'I feel like a dick about my dinner comment now.'

'You're not busy?' I reply.

'I'm a nerd,' he replies. 'What am I ever busy with that doesn't have a pause button?'

I laugh.

'I would love to, in that case,' I say. 'What do you fancy?'

'What's that place you always talk about?' he asks.

'Thin Aire?' I reply. 'You want to go there?'

Thin Aire is mine and Millsy's place. A contemporary bar and restaurant and an iconic piece of the Leeds skyline. It's the place we met so it means a lot to us and I couldn't tell you the last time I went there with anyone other than Millsy. I suppose going there with Charlie could be good, I could get the first time without Millsy over with – I imagine I'm going to have a lot of first times without Millsy and it's going to take a lot of getting used to.

'Yeah, let's do it,' he says.

'Okay, let's go,' I reply.

Thin Aire, a rooftop bar with breathtaking views of the River Aire, perches atop an astonishing eighty-metre-tall office building. It's made almost entirely of glass, with floor-to-ceiling windows encircling the bar, allowing an uninterrupted panoramic view of the city – I don't think there's anything you can't see from up here.

It's the kind of place where the lights are low and the prices are high, a place where everyone thinks they're cool, although I'm not actually sure it's all that exclusive these days. 'Cool' is very much one of those things that only matters if you buy into the idea. Still, they make amazing arancini, and that's cool in my book.

'Table for two?' the hostess greets us.

'Yes, please,' I reply.

'I think I can squeeze you in,' she tells us. 'Follow me.'

She guides us through the busy room, so I guess she really is squeezing us in, but as she leads us to our table, I spot something that knocks me sick.

There, at the table just a few metres away, is Millsy. And next to him is Tally, leaning in close as they laugh together. They seem so at ease, so comfortable in each other's presence. I feel hurt, not just because they look so cosy, but because this is supposed to be our place, mine and Millsy's, and here he is with someone else. I suppose I'm doing the same – or am I? They really do look close…

I can't bear the thought of them noticing me, of seeing the hurt etched across my face, so I scurry past them to our table, which is thankfully out of their eyeline.

As I settle into my chair, my eyes fixed on the menu, I try to distract myself.

'Are you okay?' Charlie asks, noticing something is up.

'Yeah, no, I mean… I think I need the loo,' I reply. 'I'll be right back.'

'No worries,' he says.

Thankfully the toilets are nowhere near Millsy and Tally, so I can walk there like a normal person, not leaning forward, going as fast as I can, with my hand over my face.

I sit in the cubicle for a moment, just having a moment on my own, reminding myself to suck it up. It's just a restaurant, just a dinner, and I'm doing the same thing. Just dinner with a colleague. *I'm doing the same thing.*

I wash my hands and head for the door, only for it to open for me. I step aside, to let the person who opened it through, and it had to be Tally, didn't it?

She stops me with a knowing look, one that suggests she knows what a complicated situation we're all in.

'Oh, hi,' I say.

'Hey,' she replies. 'I thought I spotted you. Are you on a date?'

'Oh, no, no, not at all,' I babble. 'I'm here with Charlie, from work.'

'Relax,' she reassures me. The corners of her mouth turn up as she leans in and lowers her voice. 'I know you guys are separated. I also know it's a secret but, don't worry, I'll play my part.'

Her words hit me like a punch to the stomach. Millsy has told her the truth, and I can see the blossoming connection between them, and while I'm not exactly sure what is going on, I don't have a good feeling about it. I force a polite smile and head back out into the restaurant.

Gosh, what a mess. But hang on a minute, why am I skulking around in the shadows, embarrassed, when Millsy clearly isn't feeling the same? He's here, unashamedly, sitting at a table where everyone can see him. Why do I feel so differently? Is it because he's over me, and I'm not over him? How has he done this so quickly, I don't understand. I'm trying my best to make moves to move on, hoping that if I try at some point it might start to feel normal, but it doesn't. I hate it. I absolutely hate it.

I suppose there's always Love @ First Site – the website, not the idea that some rando man is going to take one glance at me and fall head over heels in love.

My mind darts back to the night Millsy and I met, here in this bar, when I was stood up by a Matcher date and found myself sitting all alone at that table over there. For some reason, I caught Millsy's eye. He came over, chatted to me, helped me come to the gentle realisation that I had been stood up by my app date. And then for some reason he stuck by me, he invited me out with him and his friends, took me under his wing and then... well, you know what happens next.

It's like that old corny chat-up line: do you believe in love at first sight, or should I walk by again? Perhaps that's what I need to do, I need to catch his attention again, and I could start here, tonight, by walking past him right now, sashaying like I don't have a care in the world.

Hmm, except I do have lots of cares in the world, and I'm not sure I know how to sashay but perhaps that's what I need to do. I need to show Millsy why he loved me in the first place. Wow, why did he ever love me in the first place? What exactly is it about this awkward nerd – who is once again scurrying through the bar with her hand over her face – that he ever found all that attractive to begin with?

Perhaps figuring that out is the key, but not tonight. Tonight is for hiding and eating arancini. And then tomorrow, well, tomorrow is family Christmas. And won't that be fun.

## 16

Family Christmas Dinner Day is here – Merry Christmas to all who celebrate.

Kind of like with my gran's festive afternoon tea party, there are pros and cons, the pros being spending time with the family I like and the food, and the cons being Auntie Mary et al. Actually, today is going to be worse than the afternoon tea party, because today we'll not only have Millsy and Tally here, but all of the boys from Auntie Mary's side of the family. I can handle the babies, Vince and Sal, because they're on my wavelength, but Uncle Paddy and Tommy do my head in.

At least it's just pre-Christmas, not the real thing, so when it inevitably goes tits-up for some stupid reason (because, let's face it, it will) then at least it won't feel like the day is ruined. It's almost like a practise Christmas, in extreme circumstances, with guests that can stress-test the best of us.

I arrived earlier today, here to help my mum with the cooking, and I like to think I've been doing a good job – I couldn't imagine cooking Christmas dinner without my mummy, though. Long may her cooking every meal for everyone continue.

Festive spirit is filling the air already, mingling with the yummy scents of roasting turkey, cinnamon-spiced cranberry sauce, and the freshly baked mince pies Mum made this morning. The kitchen itself is a cosy chaos of pots and pans – but it's a chaos that we have fully under control. Mum has even put fairy lights on the pan rack, and given me and Oliver matching festive aprons, which feel like lovely extra touches.

My mum, the family master chef, is like a conductor in the kitchen, giving me and Oliver jobs to do – except she's like a conductor who plays most of the instruments in the orchestra too, because I don't feel like I'm doing all that much, and Oliver is doing even less. Most of his tasks seem to involve tasting things. Mum effortlessly glides between the cooker and the island, so gracefully, and without a drop of anything on her snowman apron. I, on the other hand, had spilt a cup of tea down mine before the cooking even started.

While we're all busy in here, my dad has managed to turn the seemingly simple task of lighting the dining room fire into a two-hour affair. My mum shakes her head every time she looks out of the window and sees that he's still in the garden.

'I wonder if he's lovingly carved each piece of firewood by hand instead of simply chopping it with the axe,' she says in amusement, a twinkle of exasperation in her eyes.

The thought of my dad meticulously shaping firewood brings a smile to my face. That man will do anything to get out of doing what you want him to, even if it's harder work.

'You know, it's blatant sexism,' Oliver says through a mouthful of carrots – it's hard to tell if he's joking when he's eating. 'The woman is cooking, the man is chopping wood.'

'So insightful, sitting on there on the worktop, eating the carrot your mummy cut for you,' I tease him.

'Is that why you're not helping?' Mum asks through a laugh as she sets the turkey down to rest next to him.

'Oh, no, not at all,' he quickly insists. 'I'm not not helping because I'm a man. I'm not helping because I'm just a baby.'

He says this in a silly, baby voice.

'A baby in his mid-twenties,' I point out with a smile. 'But, little baby brother, have you ever thought that maybe you could help to break the system by lending a hand with the food?'

'Ah, but we do actually want it to be good,' Mum teases. 'You didn't have to eat the food tech concoctions he brought home with him. He's safest as a taste tester.'

'I make a mean beans on toast,' he says to himself, shrugging casually, as he pops another carrot in his mouth.

Amazingly, as the clock strikes the hour, everyone seems to pull up outside at once. Gran is already here, Mum picked her up earlier, but now we've got Millsy and Tally in one car, Auntie Mary and Uncle Paddy in theirs, and finally, there's Flora, Tommy and the kids.

Oliver, keen to show he can be helpful, goes to greet Flora as she steps out of her car, burdened by a mountain of bags filled with the baby essentials she takes everywhere she goes – I'm sure I can't even name half of the things she has in those bags. He takes charge, relieving her of the bags, not that he's all that strong himself. You can see the weight of them making his eyes go bloodshot.

I go to greet Millsy and Tally, only for Uncle Paddy to call out to us before I get to open my mouth.

'Joe, come here, carry this wine for your future uncle,' he says. He directs Millsy to the large box of wine he brought, nodding towards the back seat of his car. 'Make sure you take the seatbelt off.'

'Duty calls,' Millsy tells us with a sigh.

'You can just stick the box in the utility room,' I tell him. 'Go in through the side door, you know what this lot are like for taking twenty minutes to walk from a car to a building.'

'I remember losing a restaurant booking over it,' he says with a laugh. 'Back in a minute.'

'Hi,' I say to Tally.

'Hey,' she replies.

'Are you looking forward to your first Christmas dinner?' I ask.

She pulls a face at me.

'Cara, you know we celebrate Christmas in the US, don't you?'

Oh, wonderful, she thinks I'm an idiot.

'I know that,' I say, without a hint of emotion. 'I meant your first of the year. It was supposed to be a joke.'

'Right,' she says, confirming that she doesn't find me funny. 'I guess I am looking forward to my first British Christmas dinner.'

'Traditional British food isn't exactly known for its surprises,' Auntie Mary chimes in. 'Don't expect to be impressed.'

I scowl at the back of her head. My God, she is so rude.

'It's not right, having Christmas dinner on a day other than Christmas,' Uncle Paddy moans. 'It's just another thing "the left" are trying to ruin.'

My eyebrows shoot up.

Tommy, as expected, is the first one to agree.

'Too right, Paddy. They're always messing with traditions.'

Oh, the pesky left.

'The left what?' Flora asks no one in particular, but her question is left hanging in the air. It's not worth getting into.

The dining room door swings open, and my mum enters with a warm smile, ready to welcome her guests. She greets each family member with a hug and a pre-emptive Merry Christmas.

When she approaches Auntie Mary, her outstretched arms are met with a hesitant embrace, one that doesn't last all that long. It's sad but Oliver and I always joke that hugging Auntie Mary is like riding a mechanical bull – points if you can hang on for longer than a second.

Mary pulls away, straightening her cardigan with a disapproving look on her face.

Intimacy. Ew.

'Are we eating right away, as requested?' she asks my mum impatiently.

'We are indeed,' Mum replies, her smile still firmly in place.

Honestly, you'd never believe we were doing all this for fun.

'Let's all take our seats,' Mum adds.

As the rest of the family finds their seats at the dining table, my mum assigns me and Oliver tasks to keep everything running smoothly.

'Oliver, if you can help me carry the food,' Mum instructs. 'Cara, if you can help Millsy with the drinks.'

'See, this is why I always say it's harder, being an only child, because you don't have siblings to help you,' Flora practically moans.

'Is that why you keep having more kids?' my dad dares to joke.

Flora is very much an only child, it shows in so many ways – but if it doesn't, she tells you. She's very proud of the fact for some reason.

I make my way through the kitchen, navigating my way past Mum and Oliver as they carry plates of food through to the dining room, and head towards the utility room where Millsy should be. I push the door open and I stop in my tracks when I catch sight of what appears to be blood stains on his shirt.

'Oh, God,' I exclaim, my voice trembling with concern. 'Are you hurt? What the hell happened?'

'It's okay, the good news is I'm not hurt,' he's very quick to reassure me. 'But the bad news is that someone left an axe on the floor by the side door, and I tripped over it, smashing every bottle of wine in the process.'

I'm relieved for a second but then, of course, it hits me that we still have one very big problem.

'Oh, God,' I blurt.

'There were three bottles of red and three bottles of white,' he explains. 'And it's total shit that white wine brings out red wine stains because I have both on my shirt right now.'

I rummage around in the clean washing pile for something for Millsy to change into. It's a huge relief when I find one of my dad's white shirts in there – I'm also really lucky that my dad is a giant, or there's no way his clothes would fit Millsy's muscular frame.

'We need an idea,' I tell him.

'And fast,' he replies as he takes his shirt off.

I quickly look away. I'm not going to come up with anything staring at his pecs.

'I've got it,' I say, turning back to face him as he buttons his fresh shirt up. 'Run to the corner shop, grab some replacement bottles, any kind, just three red, three white – there's no way Uncle Paddy will be able to tell the difference.'

'Right, okay,' Millsy replies. 'But we can't pour them into the old bottles, they're all smashed.'

'I'll find something to pour them into,' I tell him. 'And stand guard until you get back.'

'I'll run,' he says. 'It can't take more than ten minutes.'

I head into the kitchen and find a couple of wine carafes in the cupboard, then I take point at the utility room door, just in case someone comes in. I don't know what my excuse will be, but I'll come up with something.

Mum sticks her head into the kitchen.

'Beer for Paddy, Tommy and Oliver, and lemonades for Flora and your gran,' she tells me. 'Wine for everyone else.'

'Okay,' I reply. 'Millsy is just opening it.'

'Lovely,' she says before disappearing as fast as she appeared.

I wait, it can't be more than a few minutes, but it feels like a lifetime, until Millsy returns.

'I've got three of each but they're all different kinds,' he tells me breathlessly.

'Oh, that lot will never tell,' I insist. 'Here, pour it into these carafes, I'll get the other drinks sorted.'

With everything sorted, we *carefully* carry the drinks through, Millsy carrying the two carafes, one with red wine and one with white wine.

'So, my next role, after Billy, is one that I can't talk about yet,' Millsy starts telling the room. 'But the character in question is a sommelier, so I'll be serving the wine, all night, if that's okay with everyone? If you want anything, just ask.'

Oh, good work, Millsy. That's seriously quick and incredibly smart thinking.

'Well, you're already doing a bad job by decanting the white,' Uncle Paddy scoffs.

I glance at my mum, sensing her eyes are already on me.

She subtly mouths at me: 'That one is a vase.'

I don't know whether to laugh or cry. Instead I just nod, to show her that I know. I did have my suspicions about the unconventional decanter when I spotted it in the cupboard, but in times like these, beggars can't be choosers.

With crisis averted for now, we all tuck into our food, and I allow myself to relax a little. It's all going fine, until Auntie Mary pipes up.

'So, your plans for your real Christmas,' she starts. I think it's a question, or a prompt at least.

'It's the first year we'll be getting our families together,' I say. 'I'm looking forward to it, all of us, in beautiful Scotland.'

'Not all your family,' Auntie Mary points out. 'And Tally will be with you.'

'You bet Tally will be there with us,' Millsy adds. He always stays in character when Tally is in the room.

'Millsy, I thought your normal voice was irritating enough but that accent is like nails on a chalkboard,' Tommy complains, trying to make it sound like it's just banter, but isn't that what they all say? 'I can't imagine lowering myself to doing that, by playing the fool like that. No job is worth it.'

'Tommy, if you saw what they're paying me, you'd soon change your tune,' Millsy replies.

Millsy is never one to brag but, sort of like me, he knows there's only one way to handle this lot sometimes, and that's to fight fire with even more fire.

'Joe, I will have you know that Tommy makes a very respectable living as a plumber,' Flora chimes in, defending her man in an argument that he started.

'Yeah, and it's honest work – real work,' Tommy insists. 'I'm not afraid to get my hands dirty.'

I'm sure there's an easy joke to make there, with Tommy putting his hands in toilets on the regular, but that's not my style.

'Oh, it's going to be a sorry, quiet New Year's Eve with all of you being away in Scotland,' Auntie Mary persists. 'And taking my mum away from me too.'

The look on my gran's face is priceless.

'Well, Mary, you did spend last year's New Year's Eve in

Iceland with Paddy's family,' my gran dares to remind her. 'I think you'll be okay.'

'Yes, but that was only because Paddy's family paid for it,' Auntie Mary replies defensively.

Okay, well, if it was free that's fine then, obviously.

'Ah, it's no big deal,' Uncle Paddy chimes in. 'I once spent Christmas without my family, when I was a kid.'

'Really?' Tally blurts.

Wow, I never knew that.

'Yeah, well, I actually wasn't supposed to,' Paddy says. 'It was this one year when we were supposed to be going on holiday.'

Tally is gripped. So am I until… oh, for God's sake.

'But they actually left without me,' he continues. 'It wouldn't have been so bad, but there was quite a bit of crime in the area at the time. Still, I held my own, and did a good job looking after myself.'

He's doing *Home Alone*. He's actually doing *Home Alone*. It's festive, I suppose. Millsy and I exchange a sneaky side-eye. We always think it's so funny that Uncle Paddy tries to pass well-known movies off as his own personal anecdotes.

I get the feeling that Auntie Mary is angling for an invitation to join us in Scotland for New Year's Eve and, as easy as it would be to invite them all, I just can't face it. It's going to be hard enough, with everything Millsy and I have going on, and our families essentially taking their first trip together. Imagine throwing Auntie Mary, Uncle Paddy, Flora, Tommy and the kids into the mix. It would be a nightmare. I keep my mouth shut.

'Joe, more wine, if you please,' Paddy demands, waggling his empty glass in Millsy's direction.

I look to my mum and she gives me a look that suggests she can tell Auntie Mary is angling for an invitation too. God, I can't even think about that right now.

I'll say one thing, the food is amazing, Mum has done a really good job. Everyone is getting stuck in, clearing their plates, and then going in for even more.

'Is everyone enjoying the wine?' Uncle Paddy asks.

Everyone who is drinking it replies politely to say yes.

'Can you tell anything different about it, though?' he asks.

My heart races. Does he know? How could he know? I glance at Millsy and we exchange a brief look of recognition. I don't think either of us were expecting him to say that.

'Erm, no,' my mum replies. 'It's very lovely, though.'

'Let me tell you something about this wine,' Paddy starts, pausing suspensefully. 'It's special, my friend sells it, and what's special about it is that it is completely alcohol-free.'

Millsy almost chokes on the sip of water he was taking, his eyes widening in astonishment.

'Alcohol-free?' I repeat back to him.

'Alcohol-free,' Paddy confirms proudly. 'Which means no hangovers and that I can drive home later without a worry.'

Millsy and I exchange another glance. Oh, God, this is bad.

'That's funny,' my mum says. 'It must be a placebo effect or something, because I've actually been feeling a buzz from it.'

I mean, of course she has, Millsy has been serving her real wine this whole time.

'Garçon,' Paddy calls out to Millsy, and he certainly sounds like he's had as much wine as he has had. 'Top me up, will you, garçon.'

'Yep, coming right up,' Millsy says.

Well, there's no point in stopping now, is there? The damage is already done. Uncle Paddy thinks he's safe to drive home, and will probably be wanting to leave soon after dessert, and he's got to be way over the limit by now.

We're just going to have to think of something, some way to

stop him driving, otherwise we're going to have to come clean and, after everything we've been through, I can't face the bollocking today.

'I'm going to get another drink,' I say, standing up, following Millsy into the kitchen.

We'll just have to come up with something, that's all. Something, anything...

Oh, God.

## 17

It turns out that, when you're an actor, you can get away with just about anything if you say you're preparing for a role. Oh, and it didn't hurt that Uncle Paddy and Auntie Mary were so drunk that they would have believed just about anything, including the tall tale that the sommelier Millsy is supposedly going to be playing is also a part-time limo driver, so could he please, please give them a lift home – all for the sake of the role.

It was quite funny really, watching him running around, opening doors for them, fully committed to the bit, and now it's just me and him, in the car alone together, about to head back to my mum's house to collect Tally.

'Do you fancy a Maccies milkshake?' he asks me.

I wasn't expecting him to say that.

'I would love one,' I reply.

'Quick detour then,' he says, turning the car around.

There's a McDonald's in town, not too far away, so a cheeky drive-thru won't add long to our journey. Anyway, I left Tally chatting away with my dad, trying to teach him how to smooth some of the Yorkshire out of his accent. Good luck to her – even his sneezes have a Yorkshire twang.

'Vanilla?' Millsy checks.

'Yes, please,' I reply.

He orders our drinks. A vanilla milkshake for me and a strawberry one for him. Then we head back on our way.

'Today was fun,' he says simply.

'They're always fun,' I reply. 'We just create our own chaotic brand of fun wherever we go, don't we?'

I say this almost sarcastically.

'We really do,' he replies. 'Personal highlight?'

'I mean, having sex in a Christmas grotto made for children while we're dressed as Santa Claus and an elf has to be a new low,' I point out. 'But, as for a high, hmm. I really loved seeing you throw together a gender reveal balloon with nothing but a white balloon, a black marker pen and the air from your lungs.'

Something he only had to do because I let the actual baby-blue helium-filled gender reveal balloon out of the box early, thinking it was the cake.

'A classic,' he chuckles. 'For me, and I mean this honestly when I said I found it genuinely impressive, was the time I set my gran's kitchen on fire and accidentally let her dog out, only for him to swim to the island in the loch. The way you managed to open that boathouse padlock without knowing the code – I still don't understand how you did it.'

'It's my job,' I say with a laugh. 'Aww, Dougie, bless him. I miss him.'

'Me too,' Millsy says. 'It's going to be strange, going to my gran's this year, and him not being there for the first time.'

We fall silent for a second, as a sad mood takes over, and I don't think it's just because of Dougie the dog passing away (thankfully peacefully, after a long and happy life), but because he's not the only thing we're going to miss. Chatting about our scrapes, about the good old days, it only reminds me of what I'm not going to have any more. Sure, the scrapes are exhausting, but it's our thing. Who am I without them? Without Millsy?

Millsy exhales heavily as we pull up at some traffic lights.

'You know, they say on a clear night, if you look in the right direction, you can see Iceland from here,' he tells me.

I furrow my brow.

'Really?' I squeak.

'Yep, there you go,' he says, pointing down the road, towards the supermarket.

'Oh, har-har,' I reply, smiling again.

'Just thought I'd lighten the mood,' he says before slurping his drink. 'Listen, whatever we have going on, we always get away with it, right?'

'Right,' I reply.

Although this time, pretending we're not together any more, I don't know. I don't really want to get away with this one.

## 18

The air at the Christmas market is so thick with festive cheer it's almost impossible to take it all in.

A net of vibrant twinkling lights hangs above where I'm walking, casting a warm glow over everything below. Festive smells like cinnamon and roasted chestnuts waft through the air, enveloping everyone around, giving us all that same seasonal high. For me, though, it's not quite hitting, not like it usually does.

I find myself drawn to the carousel, its beautiful colourful horses spinning in calming circles, bringing joy to the children (actually, it looks like mostly adults) riding atop them. Laughter echoes in my ears, making me feel happy and sad at the same time. I usually love it here, with the array of charming stalls, offering handmade crafts, sparkling ornaments, and irresistible sweet treats. Visiting all the Christmas markets in the area is something we do every year, it usually makes me so happy. But that's the problem, it's something *we* do every year, Millsy and me. Doing it alone just doesn't feel right.

Amidst the sea of smiling faces, families hand in hand, and couples lost in each other's company, I can't help but feel a pang of emptiness, even though I'm not going to be here alone.

I know what you're thinking: will I ever learn? Well, I'm trying to, but I would be crazy to give up on dating altogether, just because Matcher turned out to be a shitshow *again*. I am trying to remain hopeful, and open, and not resign myself to sobbing over romcom movies while I eat a whole tub of ice-cream and think about how single I am – there's plenty of time to do that later.

No more Matcher, though, I promise. Instead I took Charlie's advice and set myself up on Love @ First Site – a cringe-worthy name if ever I heard one, but perhaps cringe is what I need, instead of another hook-up app with a contemporary name.

Love @ First Site reckons that, if you fill in one of their lengthy quizzes, with all the details you can think of, that they can set you up with your perfect match. So I filled the thing in, with as much information about myself as possible, and despite it saying that sometimes it can take time to find a perfect match, it came up with one for me almost right away. Too good to be true or just the thing I need right now? Well, when it threw me in an anonymous chat with my supposed Mr Right, I thought screw it, let's do this. I could sit and chat with an avatar for God knows how long, only to be disappointed at a later date, or we could just get this over with, meet up, see if this site is legit or just another gimmick.

If I stop being cynical for a second, he does seem great. We have lots of things in common, both live in Leeds, and it was a conversation about our shared love of churros that sparked the idea for our IRL meet-cute. So here I am, walking through the Christmas market, heading for the churro food truck where the man of my dreams should already be waiting for me, a churro in each hand.

As I near the food truck, I notice a man taking two fresh churros from the counter. I stare at the back of his head for a moment, waiting for him to turn around, like this is some sort of dating scratch card. Is it weird that I feel like I know him already? Maybe this website is decent after all.

He turns around and our eyes meet across the crowded market. Oh, screw you, Love @ First Site, you total pile of crap. Suddenly it seems so obvious and I feel so stupid. In hindsight, it was obvious who it was going to match me with: Charlie. Well, how many escape room enthusiasts do you think there are in Leeds who both happen to be using this website? I only know of two, so it makes sense that it matched us.

I watch as the realisation hits Charlie and he practically winces – at least I know he didn't set this whole thing up because he's secretly in love with me.

'Fancy seeing you here,' I joke as I approach him. 'Is that for me?'

'I suppose it is,' he says with a laugh and a shake of his head. 'Unbelievable.'

'Does it make you wonder what's wrong with you?' I ask playfully. 'That your dream woman is me.'

I hold my arms out in a ta-da kind of way, careful not to drop my churro. At least one good thing has come out of this trip.

'I think it's a sign that perhaps the things that make us who we are are possibly not the things that we will have in common with other people,' he replies tactfully. 'I feel so guilty, that I convinced you to sign up, and all you got was me, someone you already know.'

'I think it's time I gave up on trying to date again, you know,' I confess. 'My heart isn't really in it.'

'Listen, you don't need to rush yourself back out there,' he tells me. 'I don't want to sound corny, but you need to grieve.'

I sigh.

'Yeah, I guess... I suppose I don't want to,' I admit.

Charlie wraps an arm around me and gives me a squeeze.

'Give it time,' he tells me. 'Can I walk you home?'

'Oh, you don't have to do that,' I insist. 'I feel bad enough that I catfished you – even though I didn't.'

'I feel like I catfished you,' he replies with a laugh. 'Come on, it's no trouble. If you got murdered on the walk home, I'd probably feel even worse.'

'Well, we can't have that,' I conclude. 'Go on then.'

As Charlie and I stroll through the chilly city, I laugh to myself about this whole situation. So Charlie is my dream guy, huh? I don't suppose I've ever looked at him in that way. Well, I was loved up with Millsy when Charlie and I met, and we may be friends now, but this started out as a work relationship. I've never had reason to look at him in that way. He's good-looking, there's no denying that, and he's smart, he's funny, he's kind – he could be any girl's dream guy. For me, though, he's just a friend, a good one, one too good to waste. I mean, look at Millsy. He and I were friends, before we were a couple, and look how that turned out.

'Here we are,' I say as we arrive outside my building.

'Wait, are you not going to invite me up?' he jokes. 'After such an incredible date – and with your algorithm-determined soulmate, no less.'

I laugh but then I realise something.

'Oh, actually, do you want to pop up for a minute?' I say. 'I've still got the T-shirt you let me borrow.'

'I had completely forgotten about that,' he replies. 'Sure.'

We continue our small talk as we enter the building, lowering our voices as the sound of our footsteps echo in the empty hallway. It's so sweet of Charlie, to walk me home. I almost wish I could see him romantically.

Inside the flat, sure enough, we find Millsy and Tally in the middle of a session – a work session, that is, although I have my suspicions.

Millsy's accent is improving, although still not great. Tally's annoyingly adorable laugh echoes through the hallway.

'I reckon we're gonna have ourselves a mighty fine time,' Millsy says enthusiastically – presumably a line of dialogue but, once again, I have my suspicions.

'Come on, again,' Tally says enthusiastically. 'I know you can get this, come on.'

'I reckon we're gonna have ourselves a mighty fine time,' Millsy says again. 'A mi— a mighty fine – a mighty fine time.'

'Does this not drive you mad?' Charlie whispers.

'In so many ways,' I reply. 'Come on, if we're quiet, we might make it to my room unseen.'

'Cara, hey!' Tally calls out.

I sigh.

'Hello,' I say brightly, turning on the smile. 'Sounds like you guys are making progress.'

'Getting there,' she insists. 'And you've brought...'

'Charlie,' he says.

'Charlie again,' she replies. 'Things must be going well.'

'Oh, work is going great,' I reply, purposefully misunderstanding her.

I look over at Millsy. He seems... odd. There's a look on his face, a mix of curiosity and guarded interest. Does he think something is going on between me and Charlie?

For a moment, we freeze, our gaze locked, and in this brief moment, I can see a flicker of something in Millsy's eyes – jealousy, perhaps, masked by a façade of indifference. His facial muscles tighten ever so slightly, a subtle hint of tension betraying whatever reaction he's trying to put out, not exactly masking his emotions simmering beneath the surface.

I feel a pang of guilt, a rush of conflicted emotions bouncing around in my brain. But as quickly as his fleeting expression appears, Millsy's familiar charm and light-heartedness takes over once again. He flashes a playful grin, pushing out nonchalant vibes, as if the sight of me with another man is of no consequence. With a casual shrug and a drum of his hands on the table, he redirects his attention back to Tally, as if to assure himself that he is unaffected by the sight of me and another man.

'It's just through here,' I tell Charlie, getting back to the task at hand.

'Oh, I forgot, I need to ask Cara something,' I overhear Millsy tell Tally. 'One sec.'

'I'll be with you in a minute,' I tell Charlie. 'But your top is on the chair, if you want to grab it.'

I turn around, hovering just outside my room, waiting to see what it is he wants to ask me.

'You're dating Charlie?' he asks me in hushed tones. 'The Charlie you work with.'

'I'm not dating Charlie,' I reply.

'Tally said she'd seen you at Thin Aire, in the toilets, and that you were on a date,' he says before I have a chance to explain. 'I thought it sounded like Charlie, and now here he is.'

'Cara?' I hear Charlie call out. 'Come on, Cara.'

'I need to go,' I tell Millsy. 'And you need to practise.'

I close my bedroom door behind me.

'Erm, you called?' I say with a laugh.

'I did,' Charlie replies, a knowing smirk spreading across his face. 'And, listen, I know I told you that you need to grieve, but now that I've seen it first hand – Cara, Millsy is jealous. So jealous. He looked out of his mind.'

'Do you really think so?' I say.

'Absolutely,' Charlie confirms. 'And I heard him just now. He thinks we're a thing and, honestly, he sounds gutted.'

Charlie leans in closer, his voice dropping to a conspiratorial whisper.

'You know, you could use this to your advantage,' he suggests. 'Let him think we're dating. It'll drive him crazy with jealousy.'

I arch an eyebrow as I consider Charlie's suggestion. On the one hand, I'm supposed to be a grown-up, above playing games, but, on the other hand, I quite like the idea of playing with fire, and we all know games are my jam.

'Do you think it will work?' I say.

'I think, either way, it will tell you everything you need to know,' he concludes. 'Trust me, it's a tried and tested method. There's nothing quite as effective as a good old dose of jealousy to make someone realise what they've lost. And, hey, if it doesn't work, I will temporarily deactivate my Love @ First Site account so that you can get a genuine match. I need to get you off there too – I can't believe my perfect match was wasted on Cara from work.'

I snort.

'All right, all right, I get the picture,' I say. 'So, what's the plan?'

'Let's make one now,' he suggests. 'Because I guarantee even just the two of us being in here alone will be driving him crazy.'

I know, I know, it's low of me to resort to these tactics, but if it works, if it shows Millsy what he is missing, perhaps we can find our way back to one another.

'In that case, make yourself at home,' I say with a cheeky smile.

It's worth a try.

## 19

This evening we are in Birmingham for one of the events my brilliant brother hosts as part of his PhD. He teams up with other academics and they screen films, music videos, documentaries – all sorts – and then host panels where they talk about what the audience just saw before taking questions. No, I am in no way smart enough to always fully understand what they are talking about but, yes, I am incredibly proud of him, and Millsy and I always go with him to these things, just to give him support, and an extra couple of bums on seats.

And speaking of bums on seats we, of course, have the lovely Tally with us *wherever we go* which is just *so great*. So, as jazzed as I was to be selling extra tickets for Oliver, I couldn't stand the idea of being stuck on a train with Millsy and Tally, the two of them practically flirting in their Southern drawl as they read romantic lines together. I suppose I should just be relieved that she's booked her own hotel room, and that she isn't staying in ours, but I'm worried enough about it being just the two of us. Obviously we were still together when we booked it, and it would seem weird if we didn't share a room, if Oliver realised somehow, but it's going to be odd, just the two of us, in a room, alone. At least, it will be odd, if my plan doesn't go, well, to plan.

Getting the train after them was step one. Step two was arranging for Charlie to come with me. You know, this is why we work so well together, because not only do we have an entirely platonic relationship, but we're both so good at games, and he jumped at the chance to help me make Millsy jealous.

So, the event has finished, and Oliver absolutely smashed it. Now he's gone out for a drink with his smart friends, leaving me to get the ball rolling on the next part of the plan.

'So, Millsy has no idea I'm here?' Charlie asks me.

'No, not unless he turned round and spotted us during the screening,' I reply. 'But he and Tally should be there somewhere.'

I glance around the foyer.

'Oh, there they are,' I say, smiling widely as I catch their attention. Millsy's face falls when he realises I've got Charlie with me.

'Wow, this is really working,' Charlie says under his breath. 'That fella is clearly still head over heels in love with you.'

I sigh. God, I hope so.

'Erm, hi,' Millsy says. 'Charlie, hello.'

'Hey,' Tally greets us both.

'Hello,' I greet them jointly, all smiles still. 'Wasn't he great?'

'Your brother is very smart,' Tally replies – I'd swear, almost reluctantly.

'And Charlie came,' Millsy says. 'Charlie from work.'

'Well, you've got Tally from work with you,' I say almost play-fully. 'I've got Charlie from work with me. Which reminds me, we're actually going to get a little bit of work done this evening, so I'll catch up with you in our room later – did you get me a spare keycard?'

'Erm, yes,' Millsy says, a little taken aback, as he searches his wallet for the spare keycard. 'You know it's already eleven o'clock, right?'

'I know, I'll try not to wake you,' I promise him. 'See you soon.'

It simultaneously feels awful, being so aloof with him, but kind of great to see that it's working. I just need to be careful, to not overcook this one, or it might backfire.

'Right, let's grab a Maccies,' I say to Charlie once we're out of earshot. 'We can eat it in your room and then by the time I get to my room...'

'...he'll be so jealous, everything will fall back into place,' Charlie continues. 'Hopefully.'

I hold belief in the plan as we walk to McDonald's and then to our hotel. We head to Charlie's room to eat our food.

The room is a mixture of modern comfort and understated elegance. As you step inside, you are greeted by a warm ambience that comes from the earthy colour pallet and the delicious smell of whatever diffuser is lurking somewhere. Whatever it is, I like it.

It's so spacious, with a comfortable king-size bed taking centre stage, adorned with crisp white sheets and plump-looking pillows. I hope mine and Millsy's room is this nice too.

I start unbagging our food at the two-seater table over by the window.

'Let's see what's in here, shall we?' Charlie suggests as he gets down on his knees to check out the mini bar. 'Fancy a cocktail?'

'Only if you don't need a bank loan to afford one,' I call back.

'Ah, if you can't buy your boss a drink from your mini bar at Christmas time, then when can you?' he jokes as he removes several cans from the fridge.

He places them all down in front of me, giving me options.

'I mean, I'm not really your boss-boss, right?' I say, suddenly self-conscious. 'We're more like... collaborators.'

'Sure,' he replies. 'Whatever you say, boss.'

'Oi,' I warn through a laugh. 'Enough of...'

My voice trails off as I examine one of the cans.

'Lovers' kit?' I read out loud. 'Charlie, this one isn't a drink.'

'What?' he says, taking it from me. As the realisation hits him, his face comes alive. 'Oh my God, Cara, it's some kind of sex... thing!'

'I'd worked out that much,' I reply through a smile, amazed that something spicy in the mini bar has turned him into a teenage boy. 'It hasn't been that long.'

'Let's crack her open,' he suggests. 'There might be something you can use.'

He pours the contents out on to the table.

'Or something you can put on your Flurry,' I suggest, holding up a small bottle of something called 'strawberry dick-lick'.

'Sounds yummy,' he practically cackles.

'If it's all the same, I'll have the can of vodka and orange,' I tell him.

'Open one for me too, please,' he says, still engrossed in the 'Lovers' kit'.

I take a big gulp of my drink as I try not to worry about heading back to my own room. It's fine, it's all going to be fine.

'Oh, Cara, this is it, this is what you need,' Charlie says excitedly. 'You want to walk up to him, slip him this pineapple-flavoured condom, and say "take me to paradise".'

Charlie pushes the condom into my shirt pocket, with a sort of OTT faux seduction. I laugh. I really appreciate him making me smile right now.

'I don't think fruit-based seduction is what I need,' I insist. 'I think I need Dutch courage and to suck it up – not like that.'

I have to quickly add that last part, for the dirty minds in the room.

'Fair enough,' Charlie says. 'Well, let's eat, drink, and then send you on your way.'

'Perfect,' I reply.

'And in the meantime, I'm going to go through the rest of this kit,' he says.

I eat my food and then move to sit on the sofa instead. It's a plush green material, so inviting, the perfect spot to sit and finish my drink while Charlie tries to spank himself with a mini whip.

I roll my shoulders, trying to relax myself a little. It's going to be fine, it's going to be fine, it's...

Oh, fuck. Fuck, fuck, fuck. It's morning. It's fucking morning. What happened? Did I fall asleep? Obviously I feel asleep, or it wouldn't suddenly be half seven in the bastard a.m.

I pull myself up from the sofa, carefully stepping over Charlie who must've fallen asleep on the floor. Then I grab my bag and sneak out, practising being quiet, because the plan when I do get to my own room is to try to sneak in without waking Millsy.

I place my key card in the slot and then slowly open the door, pushing it a millimetre at a time, being as quiet as I can.

There's a dim light on – perhaps he left it on for me? I tiptoe past the bathroom, around the corner to where the bed must be, but instead of finding Millsy fast asleep, I find him fully clothed, sitting in the chair.

'Morning,' I say softly.

What a fucking idiot I am.

'Morning,' he replies. 'Good night?'

'Not really,' I say. 'I fell asleep on Charlie's sofa.'

'I see,' Millsy says simply, pulling himself to his feet. 'I figured you'd spent the night with Charlie.'

'Yeah, well, like, in his room,' I say, absolutely sounding like I'm lying, even though I'm not. 'But not *with* him.'

'Then why are you sneaking around?' he asks.

I approach him, my hands up to show him I mean him no harm, as I try to explain myself.

'Just because it's early,' I tell him. 'And...'

I notice Millsy's eyes fix on my chest for a moment. Then he reaches out and, as I follow his hand, I realise he's reaching for the small foil packet in the pocket. As he pulls out the pineapple-flavoured condom, he just holds it between us for a moment. The two of us stare at it.

'That's not mine,' I tell him. 'It's Charlie's. Well, no, it's not Charlie's, it's from his mini bar. He was just... he was having a laugh with it. Just messing around with it.'

I sigh. Everything sounds so bad.

'We've got the Christmas party tonight,' he reminds me. 'So I've arranged for me and Tally to get an early train back, so we can get some work done.'

'Wait, don't rush off,' I insist.

'It's fine, Cara,' he says – quite firmly for Millsy, actually. 'Get some sleep, you seem like you need it.'

Millsy grabs his already packed overnight bag and heads for the door.

'Can we talk about this?' I call after him.

'Later,' he replies. 'I've got to go.'

Oh, boy. I should have known I would stuff this one up.

## 20

Everyone is dressed in their best, stomachs are lined, the emergency services are on standby, it can only mean one thing – it's a night out in Leeds in the week before Christmas.

I suppose I should be grateful that we're doing our night out on a Thursday this year, because last year we went out on Mad Friday (the last working Friday before Christmas). The notorious Friday night has earned its various nicknames over the years, with Black Eye Friday being the first one that springs to mind. It is a night where office Christmas parties are in full swing – because for some reason the craziest night of the year seems like a good idea for that – and others fancying a wild festive-themed night of chaos flood the streets, ready to indulge in all the night has to offer, to see how much chaos they can cause.

That's why I'm out tonight, on a work night out, but no, it isn't my work, because that would be just me and Charlie sitting here. Thankfully it isn't Millsy's current work night out either, because that would be just me, him and Tally and, my God, can you think of anything more awkward? We're actually on the Christmas night out for one of Millsy's old jobs, and it's one that I am glad we're still invited out on, because I look forward to it each year. Oh, and just because we're doing it on a Thursday this year, it doesn't mean it will be any less wild.

Before Millsy started trying to make it as an actor on the big screen, and before he was working as body double to the stars, he was just a regular guy, doing bits in plays here and there around working in a coffee shop, but he did have one regular sort-of acting job: he was the Leeds Lions mascot. Well, he himself wasn't the mascot, he was the man inside the Leo the Lion costume, who used to breakdance on the side-lines and wave to the kids at rugby league games. Millsy said that his dad – a diehard Leeds Lions supporter – wanted him to be a player, and started him playing rugby when he was a kid, but no matter how hard Millsy tried, no matter how big he got, he just always lacked the aggression needed to play. He's this tall, broad, muscular giant of a man, he's got all the ingredients he needs, except the little voice in his head telling him that it's okay to tackle people to the ground and potentially injure them. Isn't there just something so, so attractive about that? He could plough through players like a hot knife through butter, but his soul is just too gentle. It's one of the things I love about him the most. Anyway, his dad wanted him to play for the Lions, Millsy wanted to be an actor, so in the end he decided that being the man inside the mascot – an honorary player – was a good compromise. I don't think his dad thought so but, even now, after most of the players have been and gone since Millsy's time in the lion, they have always treated him like part of the team so, here we are, at the Leeds Lions Christmas do.

It's nice, hanging out with the team, everyone feeling like a family. Players are from all over the world, many of the Aussies and Pacific Islanders whose families couldn't be further away, but with their annual Boxing Day friendly in less than a week, they're all here for Christmas. It's nice, that we all get to do this together, and I can't say that I hate hanging out with rugby players, even if I can only drink about 10 per cent of the amount they can.

After a delicious meal in the Japanese restaurant downstairs, while some have chosen to go home, or somewhere swankier, a bunch of us have decided to go upstairs, to the karaoke bar. It isn't technically supposed to be a late night, with the boys having training tomorrow, but when did that ever stop professional sportsmen from having a good time, huh? It seems to me that the rule is basically 'it's fine, so long as no one finds out' which is a rule I often live my life by, so I can't really say anything.

Things are wild in the main room of the karaoke bar, so we decide to hire one of the private booths, upstairs, which are basically little rooms with big screens, squishy sofas, and lots and lots of lights. It's probably for the best we're tucked away from the public. The last thing the players need is to wind up on TikTok if someone films them off their heads, screaming down a microphone, the night before training.

There are six of us in here – but with four of the six being rugby players, and Millsy being an absolute unit, it actually makes the space feel much smaller. Still, it's nice to feel like the shortest, smallest person in the room for once.

It's also nice – and I know it makes me sound like a cow for saying so – that Tally decided to go back to her hotel after the meal. It's just not the same when she's around. Millsy doesn't quite seem himself, and he has to do his accent which is just so bizarre, and she just stands next to him for every second of everything and I feel like I don't get near him. Without her, we feel a bit more like us again.

So there's me, Millsy, Kai who is from Australia, Laki who is from Papua New Guinea, Anjelo from Tonga (yes, *the* Angelo Aholelei, the Leeds Lions' star player), and Josh, who is from Wigan.

'I'm first,' Josh insists, grabbing a mic before tapping away on the touch screen that sits on the round table in the centre of the room.

'Surely there are only so many songs you can do with that accent,' Millsy teases him as he removes his suit jacket and loosens his tie.

'What do you mean?' Josh replies, offended, in the strongest Wigan accent I've ever heard.

'Oasis, maybe,' Millsy persists.

'Piss off,' Josh replies. 'I'll pick my own song, tar.'

'He can't sing, so it doesn't really matter,' Kai says with a shrug.

Kai must be at least 6'4, with one impressive pair of shoulders. He takes off his jacket which, without his body for context, looks enormous. He's got his black shirt unbuttoned to close to his tummy button and no matter where he sits, stands, or even slouches, he looks like a statue of a Greek god. He leans over Josh, towering above him, as he peeps to see what songs he's choosing.

'Right, sit down, watch how it's done,' Josh insists.

The song he's chosen is 'Shotgun' by George Ezra and perhaps it's because George almost speaks the lyrics in the original, but as Josh tries to copy his style, his Wigan accent couldn't be coming across more powerfully. Still, it's one of those songs that just sets a room on fire with joy – it's almost impossible not to enjoy George Ezra's infectious music – so we're all up and dancing. Millsy and I gravitate towards one another. He grabs my hands as we twist together and he only let go so I can turn around and playfully back up to him, sliding up and down him like a bear trying to itch its back on a tree – and yes, I know that doesn't sound very sexy, but I've had a fair bit to drink this evening, so it probably isn't sexy at all. Anjelo, ever the joker, and probably the drunkest person in the room, grabs me, locking his arms around my waist as he practically throws me up and down to the beat of the music. Honestly, I cannot stress this enough, if you ever feel like you might not be as petite as society wants you to be, spend a bit of time with rugby players being effortlessly thrown around like a ragdoll because it reminds you that there will always be people bigger than you, and smaller than you, and none of it matters. It does wonders for your self-confidence.

Kai is up on the table, pretending to surf, only lasting about five seconds before he rips open the remaining buttons on his shirt and removes the thing entirely.

Released from Anjelo's arms, I find myself naturally gravitating back towards Millsy, and I don't think it's part of the act, it's just us and the rugby boys, there's no one here to pretend for, really. I think it's more that this, us, here, with our friends, having our one wild night out of the year (one is about all I can manage now I'm in my thirties, which I never thought would be true, and it's not because I feel old physically, it's because I have big granny energy, with a love for being cosy, drinking tea, and wearing jumpers – hilariously, both mine and Millsy's grans are less of a granny than me).

'Are we going to do a song next?' he asks me.

'Oh, go on then,' I reply. 'I don't remember the last time we sang a duet. Oh, wait, yes I do, this time last year.'

'This place has never heard a "Love Shack" like ours,' Millsy says with a smile, the memory (or what pieces we have of it, at least) coming back to him.

'What song shall we do this time?' I ask him as I look at the screen. There's a section for duets so I load it up. 'Laki, pick a duet for us.'

'Anything?' he replies.

'Anything,' I say.

Laki scans the list as Josh winds down his performance.

'Let's have a look,' Josh says. 'Oh, mate, perfect.'

I raise my eyebrows expectantly.

'"A Star Is Born",' Josh cackles. 'That's what we've been calling Millsy, with his new accent.'

'You've seen "*A Star Is Born*?"' I say in disbelief.

'Well, no, I haven't, but my missus has,' Josh replies. 'I've seen enough – and everyone has heard the song, right? "Shallow", right?'

'Erm, yeah, that's the one, but I'm not sure my mouth has the audacity to open for it,' I insist. 'Do you think *I* can sing like Lady Gaga?'

'There's only one way to find out,' Josh says.

'There's actually two ways, I've heard you sing in the shower,' Millsy says, leaning into my ear to whisper, resting his hand on the small of my back as he talks to me.

I feel the hairs on the back of my neck stand on end.

'You did say anything,' Laki reminds me. 'Come on. You can pick one for me next.'

'Fine, fine,' I say, giving in with a smile on my face.

Millsy and I take our microphones and then our positions in front of the big screen. The lighting seems to match the songs as the lights dim slightly and the disco ball switches from all the colours of the rainbow to a simple warm white.

This isn't a song I listen to, and I haven't seen the film, but with pop culture and the internet, it's easy to know everything these days, so I basically know how it goes. I also know that it takes some serious pipes and I don't have them.

I grab my cocktail – my God knows how many-th of the night – and take a big swig as Millsy sings his verse first.

My eyes widen and my grin is nothing but impressed as I hear him sing. He's always had a good voice – or a confident one, anyway – but he had a bunch of singing lessons earlier in the year to refine his voice for the Billy Gill role. Now he's got the accent just about in the bag too, wow, he really sounds the part. My heart is swirling with pride and, oh, it's my turn to sing now.

I'm okay at first, the verse isn't so bad, and less is more – the softer I sing, the easier it is to hold a tune. Ah, but then the chorus comes, and with no choice but to screech it, I know that I have to let go of my inhibitions and let the cocktails do the work for me. You know, it feels almost therapeutic, just belting something out at full volume, without a care in the world. The boys let me have my moment, for what it's worth, before they all join in too. Anjelo plays air guitar while Kai moshes next to him – not something I've ever seen done to a ballad, but there we go. By the time the song is finished, we're all falling about laughing.

'I'm picking you a song, Laki,' I tell him.

'And I'm off for a piss,' Josh announces.

I tap the screen, scanning the list. Millsy comes up behind me and wraps his arms around my waist.

'Give him a Britney Spears song,' he whispers into my ear. 'He once – just once – quoted "Baby One More Time" in a training session and everyone called him Britney for months.'

I laugh.

'Okay, I like the way you think,' I reply. '"Toxic", what do you reckon?'

'Perfect,' Millsy replies, kissing me on the cheek before darting off to give Laki the mic.

I take in a sharp breath. My God, I miss him. I miss us.

As the intro plays, Laki laughs and rolls his eyes, instantly getting the reference.

'Joke's on you guys, I love this song,' he says with a smile.

I cackle at his commitment to the bit. He sings, he dances, he does really seem like he's loving it.

'I'm going to the toilet,' Anjelo tells us as he stumbles towards the door.

Millsy, Kai and I carry on watching Laki until Anjelo catches all of our attention.

'Guys, the door won't open,' he says. 'It's like it's locked.'

Anjelo pushes the door, then he pulls it, then he pushes it again. Wow, it won't move an inch.

'Could Josh have locked it?' I ask.

'Why would he?' Kai replies.

The music keeps playing as we all take it in turns to push and pull at the door.

'Cara, locks are your thing, anything you can do?' Millsy says.

'There's no lock,' I reply. 'Not that I can see. Do you want to see if there's a metal nail file in my bag? Maybe I can use it to feel if anything might be stuck around the latch or... something.'

I'm not even sure I know what I'm talking about.

Millsy grabs my clutch and I remember a split second too late what's in there. I haven't used this bag since the wedding, the one I went to with Lenny, and the photo of him all up close and personal with me is in there. I make a play for my bag, to get in there first, but the photo is already in Millsy's hand.

'Weddings,' I say with a shrug, offering no further explanation.

'And no nail file,' he says simply.

'Well, there's only one thing for it, boys,' Kai announces. 'Scrum! Let's break the door down.'

'Let's not break the door down,' I say, sobering up suddenly. 'As much as I would love to see you all do that.'

Wow, imagine!

'Yeah, no one needs to take out a loadbearing wall today,' Millsy adds.

'I'll just give it a bit of a barge then,' Kai suggests. 'Just to see if it budges.'

I wince. Is this really the best we've got?

'What do you think?' I ask Millsy in hushed tones.

'I was hoping you would have an idea,' he replies.

'Why is there always a crisis everywhere we go?' I ask no one in particular.

'Right, I'm doing it,' Kai says, taking as much of a run-up as he can.

Of course, the second he gets to the door, Josh walks back through it, and we all realise the only reason it hasn't been opening is because it is, in fact, a sliding door. With nothing to charge into, Kai essentially runs through the open door and tackles Josh to the floor.

Laki whistles with his fingers and shouts, 'High tackle!'

'What the hell?' Josh asks as he climbs to his feet. 'Save it for tomorrow, pal.'

'And, speaking of tomorrow, I hate to be a bore but maybe we should call it a night,' Millsy suggests. 'I promised I'd get you all home safe and sound – and in a state where you would be fine for training tomorrow. Two out of three isn't a bad job.'

'Anjelo has gone,' Laki announces. 'He said he was tired.'

I glance around and, sure enough, in the chaos he left.

'But isn't that his phone on the table?' I point out.

'Yes, I think so,' Laki replies.

'We'll go after him,' Millsy tells me. Then he turns to the others. 'Meet us outside.'

I grab Anjelo's phone and we head down to the street.

'Where is he?' I say. 'He's so drunk, he can't have got far.'

'Oh, there he is,' Millsy says. 'Getting into that taxi.'

'Oh, God,' I blurt. 'That's not a real taxi, is it?'

We watch as a man bundles Anjelo into a bright pink taxi – or what looks like a taxi – but Millsy and I both know what it is.

'Tell me that's not a Taxxxi,' Millsy blurts.

'It looks like it,' I reply.

Everyone in Leeds knows what a Taxxxi is – well, everyone but a drunk Anjelo apparently. It's essentially a pretend taxi, owned by an adult channel that's based in Leeds somewhere, that picks up drunk people on a night out and gives them a chance to win money by answering seriously personal questions asked by a woman without a top on. Super classy stuff, sure, but absolutely not something you want your star player to be caught going along with in the run-up to Christmas.

'We need to get him out of there,' Millsy says.

'I'll grab us a taxi,' I reply.

I run up to the nearest cab and, thankfully, there's no one in it.

'Can you follow that car?' I ask him, pointing out the pink cab.

'Oh, I've always wanted someone to say that to me,' the driver replies excitedly. 'Get in.'

I hop in the front seat, to help keep eyes on the pink taxi. Millsy is no sooner in the back when Laki, Kai and Josh all pile in too – thankfully it's a taxi big enough for all of us.

'Where are we off now?' Josh asks.

'Home,' Millsy insists, not telling them the full truth.

The driver, over the moon to be involved in a real-life car chase, takes a few liberties with his driving – it is actually quite impressive – until the bright pink taxi stops at some traffic lights.

'I'll grab him,' I tell Millsy. 'You wrangle these three out and pay the driver. Definitely a big tip.'

'The pleasure was all mine,' I hear the driver say as I get out, running towards the pink taxi, flinging open the thankfully unlocked door where, sure enough, a dazed-looking Anjelo is staring wide-eyed as blonde woman holds a microphone in front of him.

'Come, Anjelo, we're going home,' I tell him.

Anjelo shrugs before doing as he's told.

'Hang on a minute, we're filming,' the cameraman says, placing his camera down before getting out to confront me.

'Preying on people who have had too much to drink is awful,' I tell him. 'And Anjelo doesn't want to be part of it.'

'He did when he got in,' the cameraman replies.

'Did he sign a release?' I ask.

'Not yet,' the man replies. 'We do that after.'

'Then you can't use it, can you?' I reply smugly. 'Actually, can you delete it too, please?'

'I don't have to delete it,' the man replies.

'Listen, either you can delete it for me, or you can delete it for them.'

I point over to where Millsy, Kai, Laki and Josh are standing. I don't know what they're doing but right on cue, Laki knocks Josh down on his arse with the kind of force that would probably kill me – or this puny little cameraman.

'Okay, fine, it's gone,' he tells me, deleting the clip in front of me. 'Merry fucking Christmas.'

'Yeah and a happy new get a different job to you,' I call after him angrily as I escort Anjelo back over to the rest of the gang.

'You won't believe what was going on it that taxi,' he tells the boys, a distant look in his eye, like he's recalling something terrible he saw in a warzone.

Millsy takes me to one side.

'All okay?' he asks me.

'Oh, yeah, fine,' I blurt with a playful casualness. 'I just think it's really funny that we thought getting stuck in the room was the crisis, but it turned out not to be, and then I actually allowed myself to believe we might not have a crisis tonight. But here we are, at the real crisis. Gosh, crisis is a hard work to keep saying when you're drunk.'

'Well, crisis averted,' he tells me, stepping closer. 'But, it has to be said, you're great at them.'

'Causing them or solving them?' I ask.

'Both,' he says with a grin.

'You too,' I reply.

Millsy purses his lips for a second, as though he's thinking carefully about what to say next.

'You know, I've had a really good time tonight,' he tells me.

'Me too,' I reply. 'It felt like old times.'

'Oh, are they old times now?' he replies with a laugh. 'It's not even been a couple of months and you're calling them the old times and you're going to weddings with other boys.'

There's a playful, almost flirtatious tone to his voice, but then there's an inquisitive edge too, as though he's trying to work out what's going on.

'Ah, he's just a friend,' I say, moving my body closer towards him.

'Oh, really?' Millsy says, sneaking his arm around my waist as he places his other hand on my face.

'Yes,' I practically whisper.

Our faces slowly inch towards one another, our lips just about touching, when the sound of Anjelo vomiting at our feet ruins the moment.

'Incredible,' I blurt.

Millsy just laughs.

'Come on, let's get this lot home,' he says.

We wrangle the boys and attempt to flag down another taxi.

Okay, so we didn't kiss, but it's been a good night and, I don't know, it's like everything is still there, if we want it. I'm not quite sure how we get it but, wow, suddenly it feels like there's a chance.

## 21

It's Friday, 22 December and Christmas finally feels like it's coming. December is a weird one, because decorations go up and shops put out their festive offerings in November, and it feel like it goes on and on, like Christmas is never going to arrive. Then, all at once, boom, it's here, and the mad rush begins.

There is an extra step in our Christmas preparations this year: the small matter of travelling from Leeds to Pitlochry in Scotland, where Millsy's gran, Iona, lives.

The drive takes just under six hours under ideal conditions, with no traffic and no breaks, but you know what road trips are like with unforeseen delays and regular stops. I don't want to seem like I'm hating on Tally, but she is constantly asking to stop, either for a drink, or the toilet, and I can't help but think that if we didn't keep pausing for coffees, we wouldn't need to keep stopping for the loo. Tally is so LA, only drinking iced coffees, even in the freezing cold weather – and it's only getting colder as we get further up north.

It's strange, being in the car with them both. I offered to sit in the back, so that they could continue to work on Millsy's accent on the drive, but it feels bizarre, like I'm a kid in the back, watching my parents chat in the front seats, the two of them occasionally acting like they've forgotten I'm there.

Because the drive is so long, and because we're not ones to get up early, it always seems to be bedtime by the time we arrive in Pitlochry. Thankfully we're nearly there.

The last leg of the journey takes us into the heart of the Scottish Highlands, where Iona's big house – which she lives in all alone – sits on the edge of Loch Tummel. As we near our destination, the road becomes narrower, winding its way through thick foliage and towering trees. The darkness intensifies, enveloping the surroundings, and the complete lack of a light source (beyond the headlights, obviously) truly makes it feel like you're cutting yourself off from the rest of the world, like this is some sort of decontamination chamber, cleansing you of the city before you arrive in rural paradise.

We've done this trip so many times now, I can practically tell you where we are from the varying curves of the road, and what you could see, *if* you could see. It's all trees on the left – big, beautiful ones, the home to all sorts of wildlife. On the right I'd say we were passing Loch Faskally, before carrying on along the edge of the River Tummel to Iona's – and I really do mean along the edge. The first time we drove here, it was too dark to see anything apart from the road in front of us, and the incredible sight of deer running alongside our car, but the next day when we drove past it in the light and I saw just how close to the water we were, it sent me sick. Thankfully Millsy knows this road ever better than I do. He could probably drive it with his eyes closed.

For the last part of our journey, time has officially been called on work for the day, although Millsy does have to stay in character now, but I'm weirdly starting to get used to it. When I really stop and think about it, it's odd and kind of uncomfortable, how much Tally has fundamentally changed him. He no longer sounds like my Millsy doing a dodgy accent, his voice has changed, it's deeper – if I heard him on the phone, I wouldn't recognise him. Don't get me wrong, it's sexy, deep, and rugged, but it's not him... even though sexy, deep, and rugged are all words I would use to describe Millsy.

We've been listening to Tally's music. Her taste is very much what you would call 'good' on paper. Undeniably good, nice music. Cool stuff, like James Blake and Bon Iver.

'The Bluetooth is open, Cara, if you want to play anything for the last stretch,' Millsy says.

Things are... interesting between me and Millsy today. After our almost kiss last night, I felt so certain that something was going to happen, but then, after we got everyone home safe, we went back to our apartment and he simply wished me a good night and then went off to his room. And that was that. Absolutely no idea where I stand.

'Oh, yeah, okay,' I reply.

I skim through my Apple Music, looking for something to put on, well aware that there is probably nothing on here that can rival Tally's good taste. Hmm, then perhaps I shouldn't try – why should I start trying to be cool now?

I don't overthink it, I just hit play, on the most perfect song at the most perfect moment.

As the familiar gentle and rhythmic guitar strumming starts, its soft chords dancing around the breeze on a summer's day, I smile to myself.

'Is this Enrique Iglesias?' Tally blurts in disbelief, unable to hide the smirk of a girl at school who thinks she's cooler than you.

'It is Enrique Iglesias,' Millsy replies excitedly. 'It's "Escape", only the greatest song ever made!'

It was on this very road trip, not long after we met, when were just friends who agreed to be each other's plus one for the summer, that we dared to talk about guilty pleasures, and we couldn't believe what a coincidence it was when we realised that we had the same ultimate guilty pleasure song: "Escape" by Enrique Iglesias.

Millsy turns the music up, belting out the lyrics at the top of his voice, as he always does whenever he hears it. It soon levelled up from being our shared guilty pleasure song to *our* song, one we would joke about dancing to at our wedding. For the first time, I see Tally look at him like he might not be the coolest person in the room, he's breaking character, breaking free of his handsome movie star exterior to show the big, soft nerd underneath – the whole reason I fell for him in the first place.

I look at him in the rear-view mirror, and it might just be a closeup of his eyes, but I see a joy and a happiness in them that I haven't noticed for a while now. And then he looks at me, and I can only see his eyes, but through them I can tell that he's smiling at me. I smile back. Tally may be beautiful and intelligent, but she'll never be able to compete with years and years of happy memories, and all the weird and wonderful things we have in common that got us together in the first place.

I narrow my eyes, trying to figure out if the sparkles of light in the distance are from Iona's house, or whether my eyes are just playing tricks on me in the dark. As they get bigger and brighter, I realise we're at our destination.

Aside from the glow of light coming from the house, everything around it is in total darkness, a solitary figure, nestled amidst the tranquil beauty of the night. I think that, because I know what everything looks like in the daylight, the darkness here doesn't scare me. I'm so excited to see the place in the light tomorrow – the loch really is something stunning.

The gravel path crunches beneath the car wheels as we pull up outside.

'This is new,' I say.

'Ah, yes, the garage conversion,' Millsy says. He turns to Tally to explain. 'It's a bit of a tourist hotspot here, so my step-mum, Iona's daughter, convinced her she should convert the garage into a holiday rental. It's super swanky, with a self-check-in so my gran doesn't have to do anything, but the idea is the money from it can keep her in the big house. There's no way she would ever want to move.'

'I can't believe your grandma is eighty-eight and she lives alone,' Tally says. 'My grandma lives in a retirement centre.'

'My gran is ninety, and still living at home,' I point out.

'Except for right now,' Millsy adds. 'She, Cara's mum and dad, and Oliver are all staying in there. It's lovely in the main house too, don't worry. It looks like everyone might be in bed. I'll show you to your room and then introduce you to everyone tomorrow. Sound good?'

'Sounds great,' Tally replies.

Gosh, I love this house. It must be an absolute dream living here. The first thing you see when you step through the door is the staircase to upstairs on the right and the kitchen on the left. It's a massive, L-shaped kitchen that looks out over the driveway and the road. The next thing you come to is the large open-plan living and dining room space. It's a beautiful room, with a feature fireplace in the centre, and two walls that are entirely glass – you won't believe the views in the daytime.

There's another room, downstairs, which is probably my favourite room in the house. The party room – yes, this house has a party room – boasts a huge TV, a full-sized snooker table, and pretty much every board game you can think of. It is impossible to feel bored here.

Millsy returns from showing Tally to her room.

'We're in our usual,' he tells me.

Inside 'our usual', the familiar sight of the four-poster bed makes me smile. The frame is made from dark, twisted wood, with the same fairy lights that were beautifully wrapped around the frame the first time I came here. The piece of furniture commands the room and yet somehow doesn't detract from the large window it sits opposite – another window with a stunning view in the day, that looks like a painted black wall at night-time.

I close the curtains to keep the warmth in and turn around to look at the bed. If the dark red sheets didn't add to its grandeur, then the fact that you have to use a small footstool to get in and out of it surely does.

It's hard not to feel nostalgic. This room always makes me think of the first time we came here, when we were just friends, but we had to share the bed. I remember it like it was yesterday, Millsy adamant that he would go to sleep in the living room, leaving me with the bed to myself, but I very maturely pointed out that life wasn't like the movies, that two platonic adults could share a bed together and it mean absolutely nothing – who was I kidding? I was no sooner in bed with him, with the lights off, when I started musing about how it felt like being blindfolded, and then I started thinking about the stories he was telling me, about when he was in the Leo the Lion costume, and women would want to sleep with him because they couldn't see his face. I don't think I acknowledged it to myself then but, thinking back, I had already fallen head over heels for him.

'Are you getting déjà vu?' Millsy asks as he unpacks his bag.

I panic for a second, that he might be able to read my mind, but it would be weird if we weren't both thinking the same thing right now. The walls of this room are also ones that could tell a story or two if they could talk.

'Are you getting déjà vu?' Millsy says again, with a cheeky smile this time.

'Once again, it is me, you and a bed we're trying to figure out how to share,' I say with a sort of muted laugh. 'Whoever thought we'd be back to this?'

'I could always sleep on the sofa, you know,' he says. 'I would have last time and I will this time.'

'And I am once again reminding you that we're adults,' I reply. 'Only now I've seen you naked a whole bunch of times. This isn't like it was the first time, we'll be fine.'

'I just... with you and Charlie... I don't want to make things weird,' he says as I climb into bed.

'I only told Charlie a few days ago, and he doesn't know anyone who we know, so our secret is safe. And Tally knows, doesn't she?' I point out. 'Even though I thought we weren't telling anyone around us.'

'She's not going to tell anyone,' he says. 'I had to tell her, though, for obvious reasons.'

'I see,' I reply softly. 'I'm just going to the bathroom.'

I grab my pyjamas and my wash bag from my suitcase and take them to the bathroom with me. When I get in there, for the first minute or so, I just stare at myself in the mirror. What I'm wondering is, what on earth was I thinking when I told myself that Millsy and me pretending to still be a couple over Christmas would make this less awkward? This is a nightmare.

Ready for bed, I head back to the bedroom, where Millsy is hovering by the door, waiting for his turn in the bathroom.

'It's all yours,' I tell him as I pass him.

I'm only in bed for a couple of minutes when Millsy returns. He's wearing a pair of pyjama bottoms but no top. He's usually one of those guys who always sleeps naked, but makes an exception when he's in other people's houses. For some reason, seeing him in pyjama bottoms makes the fact that his chest is bare seem all the more apparent. I quickly look away, because it feels like I just accidentally looked at the sun – especially because, even though I'm not looking now, I can still see it.

I'm wearing a cropped vest and shorts – I would be much warmer in full, flannel bad boys but I need to look as sexy as possible, if I'm going to show him what he's missing. Ha! Who am I kidding? His words are still ringing in my ears, about how he had to tell Tally we were separated *for obvious reasons*. Is the obvious reason that the two of them are together? Am I being ridiculous? He hasn't told me they're together, and with what happened in the grotto...

'You're sure you don't mind sharing?' he checks, hovering by the bed.

'I'm sure,' I tell him.

'Do you want the light out?' he asks.

'Sure,' I reply. 'I'm shattered. I'll be asleep in seconds.'

The light goes out and I am right back to that night. I should do what I did that night, push the thought of him lying next to me from my mind, and try to sleep. But we all know that's not going to happen...

I wait a few minutes, giving it time, making it seem like I'm asleep. Then, without really thinking it through, and with the potential to make things so much more awkward, I take a chance, and I roll onto my side, facing away from Millsy, edging my body ever so slightly closer to him. It's supposed to be a subtle manoeuvre but I am me, so I somehow wind up with my butt pressed firmly against him, and I guess he was already lying on his side, facing me, because we're low-key spooning. I freeze, trying to style it out like something I've done involuntarily in my sleep, because while I did intend to edge over to his side of the bed, just a little, I hadn't planned on connecting our bodies like a jigsaw. I wait to see what he does – if he rolls away, pushes me back to my own side, or even gets up and goes to sleep in the living room – but he doesn't.

What happens surprises me more than any of that, though. I feel his hand lightly rest on my hip – and now I'm wondering if he has done this in his sleep. Fantastic.

I open my mouth, ready to ask if he's awake, but then I chicken out and close my eyes tightly. I just need to sleep. No sense in asking the question if I might not like the answer.

## 22

I wake up in the four-poster bed – which instantly reminds me where I am – the faint light that's sneaking in through the edges of the curtains illuminating the room just enough to see. Millsy and I have somehow drifted apart during the night – oh, how poetic. I allow myself a gentle stretch, careful not to wake Millsy up, before sitting up and feeling for the footstool with my toes.

Once I'm on the safety of the floor, I tiptoe to the bathroom. It's still early, too early for anyone to be up yet, and the bathroom door is directly across the hall from ours – perfectly fine for dashing across in my cropped vest and shorts. I'm no sooner out of the bathroom when my body sends me another signal, telling me I need a drink, and the house is in silence so it's not like I'll be walking my short-shorts past the breakfast table, flashing my cheeks to Millsy's entire family.

Still half asleep, I head towards the kitchen, my eyes adjusting to the upcoming brightness of the living room as I walk. I've just about got my senses in order when collide with something – a person – our bodies meeting with a loud clap.

I dart back, blinking to clear my eyes, trying to figure out what on earth just happened. My eyes focus again.

Ugh, it's Jay, Millsy's step-brother. Of all the people I could bump into, it had to be him. To say Jay and I had a history would be to afford it more airtime than it's worth, but back when Millsy and I were just friends, I thought Jay was a dream. Oh, how wrong I was. Memories come flooding back as I stare at him, his smug face smiling back at me. Jay, with his Hugh Grant accent, fancy job, and generally charming nature. What a con.

'Jay,' I mutter, practically through gritted teeth, a combination of surprise and disdain in my voice.

He smirks cheekily, almost as though he is revelling in the awkwardness of the situation.

'Well, well, well. Cara Brooks,' he replies. 'Fancy running into you like this.'

I resist the urge to roll my eyes at his corny line. Fancy indeed. I wonder for a second if I might be having a nightmare, my stressed-out brain cooking up an absolute corker of an awkward situation just to toy with me.

Millsy never liked Jay, and I never knew why, but it turned out it was for a good reason. It wasn't until Jay made a play for me (before Millsy and I were together, not that it makes the situation much better) that I realised, just in the nick of time, what a dirtbag Jay truly was. It came out that Millsy hated Jay because Jay had slept with Millsy's girlfriend. I can't even begin to imagine Oliver betraying me in that way – although that's probably because, right now, his PhD is his partner.

I cross my arms, studying him with a mix of caution and curiosity.

'Jay,' I say again, my tone laced with a mixture of sarcasm and contempt. 'Creeping around, in your boxers, in the middle of the night.'

'Erm, it's morning, for starters,' he points out. 'And you are also creeping around, in your underwear, so you're one to talk.'

Of all the people I could have bumped into – our nearly naked bodies literally colliding – in this house, it just had to be Jay, didn't it? Even Tally would've been less awkward.

'I didn't think you would be here,' I tell him. 'In this room right now or here for Christmas, in fact.'

Jay gasps, feigning shock.

'You think I would miss spending Christmas with my family?'

'Yes,' I reply, very matter-of-factly. I snort, finding it hard to believe that Jay could genuinely care about family ties after what he did. 'I'm sure someone said you had a girlfriend – I assumed you would be spending it with her.'

'You sound jealous,' he says.

'I don't sound anything,' I reply.

'No, no girlfriend,' he says. 'You must be thinking of Agatha, older woman I dated for a bit, she'd just come into a small fortune flogging her late mum's business, decided to try to relive her youth, get back on the club scene, get her hands dirty.'

'She sounds lovely,' I say sarcastically.

'Nah, she was a horrible old bag,' he informs me. 'Mean, dull, face like she had eaten a lemon with a wasp inside it – no taste in anything, except young men. I'm starting to think she was only with me for my body.'

Jay – for comedic effect, I imagine, rubs his abs with his hand. The only thing he's wearing is a pair of those tight boxer shorts, the ones that don't really have a leg, or leave anything to the imagination.

Oh, he has to be winding me up.

'As great as it is to hear about your, frankly, icky love life, I'm going to get a glass of water, and then I'm going back to bed,' I inform him. 'Wonderful to see you, though, can't wait to spend Christmas with you.'

He laughs at my almost aggressively sarcastic tone.

'Yeah, it's going to be great,' he replies. 'Except, once again, Millsy turns up with a random bird, and she gets my bed and I'm stuck on the sofa.'

'She isn't a random bird,' I say, pointlessly. Jay will know full well who Tally is and why she's here.

'You worried about her?' he asks me, raising an eyebrow, picking up on something in my tone that I hadn't intended to be there.

'Why would I be worried about her?' I reply. 'About her and Millsy?'

'Well, we all know what my brother has been like over the years, but you're solid, yeah?'

'Yeah,' I insist.

'Is that why I've been stuck out here listening to the two of you at it all night?' he persists.

'We haven't been at it all night,' I reply.

'The tell-tale fingerprint-shaped bruises on your hips beg to differ,' he replies.

'I do not have fingerprint-shaped bruises on my hips,' I reply through a cackle, with a roll of my eyes.

'Why not?' he asks, his tone purposefully sexy.

He tilts his head, a smug grin spreading across his face.

'Flirting with me,' I say. 'Classy.'

'I'm just being friendly,' he protests. 'You might not believe this, but I'm a changed man, I've turned over a new leaf.'

I fight the urge to laugh wildly in his face – only because I wouldn't want to wake anyone up.

'I'm sure you have,' I say. 'Good luck with that.'

'People change, Cara,' he persists. 'Maybe I'm looking for something more than I was three years ago.'

'You're not going to find it here,' I point out. 'Now can I please, please go?'

As soon as I learned what Jay was like, I joined Millsy in doing whatever I could to avoid him. Sometimes it would be unavoidable and we would be at the same family parties but we've never had much trouble keeping out of his way, and I don't think I've been in a room on my own with him since before Millsy and I got together.

'Sure, sorry,' he replies. 'The last thing I want is to get you into any trouble.'

Jay backs away, as if to show me that he's sincere, and I'm about to walk away when an almighty sound echoes through the house. It takes me a moment to realise what it is: Jay, sitting down on the keys of the piano.

We both freeze. That was loud – seriously loud – what are the chances no one heard it, in this big echoey house, with nothing else nearby that makes a sound?

Jay and I stare at one another, for a moment thinking it might be okay, but no such luck. Rod, Millsy's dad, runs downstairs with a small but heavy-looking ornamental bronze bust in his hands. His wife – Millsy's step-mum – Mhairi is following close behind him. Then, from the other direction, Millsy comes running from our room. Tally isn't far behind him from the same direction.

Amazing, brilliant, wonderful, fantastic. Almost everyone is here.

It's hard to say whose eyes are the widest – actually, scratch that, no it isn't. Millsy's eyes are definitely the widest. Then again, I suppose Jay being around any women he's had relationships with is always going to be a sore spot for him.

Rod and Mhairi look completely bewildered. How could they not, finding me and Jay standing here, in the dimly lit living room, wearing nothing but our underwear? It's a situation that couldn't scream 'illicit meeting' any louder if it tried. My heart sinks as I realise how this must look. All I wanted was a glass of water, not a double dose of embarrassment and awkwardness.

Jay, ever the smooth talker, quickly steps forward, attempting to defuse the situation.

'Oh, sorry everyone, nothing to worry about, false alarm,' he insists. 'It was just a minor mishap with the piano. Got a bit too close for comfort, you know.'

Millsy's eyes narrow suspiciously, his gaze darting between Jay and me.

'I just sat on it,' Jay says with a shrug.

'You sat on the piano?' Millsy replies.

I can feel my cheeks burning with embarrassment, and I rush to explain, my words tumbling out in a jumble.

'No, well, he didn't intend to,' I insist. 'We literally bumped into each other in the hallway, I was just going to get a drink, half asleep, wasn't looking where I was going – I didn't even know Jay was here.'

Tally, ever the perceptive one, smirks mischievously.

'I've heard that one before,' she jokes.

Rod raises an eyebrow, his voice laced with amusement.

'I think we've actually seen it before, with our Jay,' he adds.

Rod looks just like an older version of Millsy – one with his Yorkshire level turned up to full. He stands tall, his broad shoulders hinting at a strong build from his younger years, back when he played semi-pro rugby. His salt-and-pepper hair is neatly trimmed, which adds a touch of maturity to his appearance, but then his strong jawline and a neatly groomed beard give him that rugged look. I imagine this is exactly what Millsy is going to look like, when he's his dad's age. He doesn't act like him, though. Rod is an old-fashioned man's man, Millsy is more in tune with his feelings, and less of a lad. Rod's attitude couldn't be clearer right now, given how amused and charmed he seems by Jay's antics.

'This is the lovely Tally I've heard so much about?' Jay says, smiling over at her.

Tally is wearing a nightdress – one that looks like something one of the girls on *Love Island* would wear to party on an evening. She has a confidence and self-assurance that you can't buy, meaning she is completely unrattled by Jay, and clearly uninterested.

'I'm sorry you're having to spend so much time with my brother,' Jay continues.

'Step-brother,' Millsy corrects him.

Millsy always makes a point of making clear that Jay is his step-brother, and not his real brother, and he always refers to Mhairi as his step-mum – although I suppose he does already have a mum, living on the other side of the world. With Iona, though, he's different, he doesn't refer to Iona as his step-gran, she's just his gran. The two of them have such a sweet bond, a closeness that I've never seen between Jay and Iona.

Mhairi, trying to maintain some level of decorum, clears her throat and chimes in.

'All right, let's not jump to conclusions. It's obviously just an unfortunate accident. We're all up now – why don't I make us some breakfast? Mum is awake – I'll go tell her the coast is clear.'

Mhairi is an elegant and graceful woman who carries herself with a quiet confidence. She has shoulder-length auburn hair, which cascades in soft waves that frame her face. I don't think she thinks Jay can do a thing wrong, even though we all know he does lots of things wrong, but he'll always be her baby, I suppose. There's certainly a family resemblance between them, although their accents are very different – Mhairi grew up in Glasgow, but moved to London before she had Jay.

Jay nods eagerly – potentially laying it on a little too thick – seizing the opportunity to redirect the attention away from our half-naked encounter.

'Yes, exactly, just a random accident, nothing more,' he insists.

'I thought you were gold-digging some middle-aged woman in Leeds,' Millsy can't resist saying.

'Yeah, but I didn't like what I was having to dig through to get it,' Jay replies. 'Come on, I'm joking. And starving. If we're having breakfast, if you'll all vacate my non-bedroom briefly, I'll pop some clothes on.'

'Breakfast sounds great,' I say, keen to move this along. 'Let's get dressed.'

I look at Millsy and nod towards the bedroom. There's an unmistakable look of scepticism etched on his face.

Tally catches up to us, as we head for the bedroom, lightly pushing me out of the way to take Millsy by the arm.

'Joey, listen, I know that was kinda awkward and I'm sorry for whatever you guys have going on,' she says softly. 'But you gotta keep the accent up, okay? Especially in moments like that. It will definitely enrich your performance.'

I mentally shake my head.

'Right, sorry, okay,' he says in his own voice. Then he corrects himself. 'Okay.'

Millsy closes the bedroom door behind us.

'You didn't tell him anything, did you?' Millsy asks.

'Jay?' I squeak back in disbelief.

Millsy hurries on his clothes.

'Yes, Jay,' he replies. 'You didn't tell him about us?'

'Of course not,' I reply, low-key offended. 'Why would I tell him, of all people, when we said we wouldn't tell anyone?'

'Right, okay,' he says, breathing a sigh of relief.

'I'm not the one telling people,' I point out.

I instantly wish I hadn't said it. I suppose I'm just annoyed, that he thinks I would tell Jay, and the whole Tally thing is really under my skin.

Millsy doesn't say anything. He checks his hair in the mirror and then heads back out for breakfast.

I sigh, finish getting dressed, put on a little bit of make-up, and then head to join everyone.

'I'll make your family some fresh when they're up,' Mhairi tells me. 'No sense in waking them up early too.'

'Oh, thank you,' I reply.

'Hello, Cara, so good to see you, hen,' Iona calls out.

She's sitting on the sofa with Millsy, so I join them.

'Hi, how are you doing?' I ask her, leaning forward for a hug.

'I'm doing well, thank you,' she replies.

Iona never seems to age a day. She's a petite lady who always has a smile on her face and something she wants to do. Millsy and I often talk about how fortunate we are, to both have grans around the ninety mark, both still so healthy and active, both still happy in their own homes. It's a real blessing.

'Gran was just telling me how she's getting on with *The White Lotus*,' Millsy tells me, smiling, raising his eyebrows.

'Oh, I love it,' she tells me. 'I can't thank you both enough, for putting me on to it.'

I smile to myself. She's going to be over the moon, when she finds out we've got her a *Succession* boxset for Christmas. Iona's gift was one of the few we've had for ages, knowing ages ago that it would be perfect for her – a love of binge-watching TV series is one of the things she and Millsy have in common. That was it, though, it was the only one we had (apart from the gift I had already bought for Millsy), so we decided to take charge of buying our shared gifts for our own sides of the family. At least that's sorted.

'So delighted you decided to come, Jay,' Mhairi coos.

'We can actually have some fun now,' he replies.

'Like drinking out of a shoe or daring Tarquin to steal a traffic cone,' Millsy jokes under his breath.

'What was that, bro?' Jay asks from the table.

'Nothing, nothing,' Millsy replies, just as Tally walks into the room. He corrects himself. 'Nothin', nothin'.'

'Oh my God, I wondered if we would get to hear this famous accent,' Jay says, cackling. 'You sound like Woody in *Toy Story* when you pull his string.'

'Your voice is so much deeper,' Rod says. 'Say something else.'

'What do you want me to say?' Millsy replies.

'My God,' Rod says with a laugh. 'That's freaky.'

'It's so annoying,' Jay scoffs. 'Cara, it must be driving you mad.'

'It's very good,' Iona tells him. 'We're all so proud of you. I can't wait to watch your movie.'

'At least you can watch this one, Granny,' Jay tells her. 'Unlike his, ahem, earlier work.'

Jay is of course referring to when Millsy used to be a body double.

'That's not true,' Iona chimes in. 'I've seen his bum in *Bragadon Forest* – that was you, wasn't it, Millsy?'

'It sure was, Grandma,' Millsy says, in his new accent, with a cheeky smile.

With a mischievous glint in his eyes, Jay leans forward, looking around the room expectantly.

Mhairi places a plate of breakfast down in front of us all. The first thing I do is dip my toast in my fried eggs, until there is no yolk left, while Millsy goes straight for his mushrooms. Then, without saying a word, we swap plates.

'Oh, come on, you two make me sick,' Jay teases. 'You can't even eat breakfast without each other.'

'Shut up,' I reply. 'Millsy doesn't eat the yolks, I don't like mushrooms, we're just being efficient.'

I wonder if we're doing things like this because we always have, because it feels normal, or whether it's all an act now. It still feels so natural.

'Anyway, enough about that, it's putting me off my food. What are we doing for fun?' Jay asks.

'We thought maybe we could go for a wee walk, perhaps go to a café in town,' Mhairi says diplomatically.

'What?' Jay replies in disbelief. 'What about the traditions?'

Millsy, not one to hold back when it comes to Jay, echoes his word, a tinge of frustration in his voice.

'Traditions?' Millsy repeats back to him. 'You're never around...'

'I mean the old stuff,' Jay insists. 'When was the last time we had a pedal-boat race across the loch?'

'Never, while I've been around,' I point out.

'It's a blast,' Jay informs me. 'Are the boats and lifejackets still in the old shed?'

'They should be,' Iona says.

'It's not that cold today, come on, let's do it!' Jay urges, clearly excited about the prospect.

'Don't be daft,' Millsy retorts, his Yorkshire accent sounding oddly out of place in his newfound Southern tone.

'Is this because I beat you last time?' Jay taunts, a smug smile spreading across his face. 'And because you know I could beat you again?'

'If I remember right, there was some controversy last time, over who actually won,' Rod points out.

'And there wouldn't be a contest this time,' Millsy adds.

'So, let's do it,' Jay says. 'Come on, don't be a chicken. I'll even ride with Cara, if you like?'

I raise an eyebrow at his choice of words.

'Come on, Joe,' his dad chimes in, joining the persuasive effort. 'You could knock seven bells out of this one.'

I cock my head curiously.

'They're not fighting,' Mhairi quickly clarifies, sensing the tension.

'Thrash him,' Rod commands his son, adding fuel to the fire.

'He's too scared,' Jay taunts, goading Millsy further. 'And he's gutted Cara would rather be with me – in my boat.'

Millsy runs a hand through his hair.

'Do I need to beat you, in front of everyone, to get you to shut up?' Millsy asks.

'Not "beat",' Tally interjects. '*Whoop his ass.*'

'You want me to whoop your ass, boy, in front of all these people?' Millsy says again, fully embracing his newfound Southern charm.

My breath catches in my throat.

'That was really good,' I tell him.

'You bet it was,' Tally says through a big smile.

Bloody hell, don't tell me Jay is the secret to Millsy getting the hang of the accent.

'That's the spirit, cowboy,' Jay says excitedly. 'Cara, your brother is here, right? Do you think he would want to be on my team?'

'If I know my brother, and I think I do, he would rather

perish in the water than do anything considered exercise in it,' I reply, with a hint of amusement. 'And I'll pass on riding with you, thanks.'

'Okay, so Cara and Millsy,' Jay concludes, unbothered by my tone. 'Tally, come on, what do you think? Me and you putting the love birds down?'

Tally's smile widens, clearly up for the challenge.

'Sure, count me in,' she replies.

'After breakfast then,' Rod declares excitedly. 'Brother on brother.'

'And may the best brother win,' Jay adds, sounding way too enthusiastic for my liking.

Oh, this can't be good.

## 23

The crisp Scottish winter air nips at my cheeks as I stand by the side of the loch, surveying the scene before me. Lochs are deep, aren't they? I'm tempted to Google, to see how deep Loch Tummel actually is at its deepest point, but I don't think I'd like the answer.

'You know, in some places, the loch is pushing 150 foot deep,' Jay teases me, sensing my fear.

'Which is why we wear lifejackets,' Millsy reminds me reassuringly, handing me one.

We're all out here for just, you know, your classic family gathering, nothing weird at all, just two step-brothers who are constantly at odds using a boat race to settle old scores while everyone watches and cheers. Pretty standard stuff.

The pedal-boat race across the loch and back is about to commence, pitting brother against brother in an epic battle of... pedalling. It's Millsy and me, ready to take on Jay and Tally, on the wide-open loch that stretches far and wide in front of us.

The loch is stunning, I can never quite get over its mirror-like finish that perfectly reflects the land and then the sky, creating a view that is almost like an optical illusion. The water is so flat, and so still, it hardly looks real. Can't wait to ruin such a pretty scene with a couple of pedal boats thrashing around, and Millsy and Jay shouting obscenities at each other.

The temperature is just chilly enough to make you question your life choices, but not quite cold enough for anyone to stop and say: 'Hey, you know what, maybe this isn't such a great idea after all.' And so here we are.

Millsy looks over at the blue boat.

'Shall we take this one?' he suggests to me. 'If you're sure you're still up for it?'

If I'm being honest, I'm not really up for it at all but, as tragic as it sounds, craving even just a couple of minutes of alone time with Millsy is my only motivation. Well, that and beating Jay. Jay's legs are nothing special, there's no reason to think I'll be an especially good pedaller, but each of Millsy's legs are like two of Jay's pushed together – Millsy could probably win this thing on his own while I sit back and take in the view.

'Hang on, mate, the blue boat has always been mine,' Jay insists. 'Ever since I was a kid. It means a lot to me.'

Millsy, the most laid-back man I have ever met, shrugs his shoulders and flashes a carefree smile.

'Whatever you think will help you, *mate*,' he replies.

I watch the interaction between the brothers, almost amused by their contrasting attitudes. Millsy's easy-going nature seems to really get on Jay's nerves, and Jay's, well, general bad attitude drives Millsy mad. I know they're step-brothers, so they don't actually share any DNA, but honestly, there is just no love or understanding between these two at all. Then again, my mum and Auntie Mary are siblings by blood, and they couldn't be less alike either.

'Go on, thrash him,' Rod calls out aggressively, but with a smile on his face all the same.

As (supposedly) light-hearted banter and laughter echoes through the crisp air, we all settle into our boats.

'Okay, so, not that much in the way of rules, it's all straight-forward,' Rod says, and then he laughs to himself. 'And then straight back. First one back is the winner.'

'Good luck, brother,' Jay says with a cheeky smile.

'No luck needed,' Millsy replies.

The race begins, and Jay and Millsy instantly complete their transformations into competitive monsters, their eyes narrowed, nothing but victory on their minds. I can't tell if it's kinda hot or just terrifying.

Their determination is palpable as they push their legs against the resistance of the water, propelling their boats forward with everything they've got. Millsy is actually going so fast, the only thing I can do is keep my feet as far away from my pedals as possible – I'll only hold him back. The sound of his heavy breaths mixes with the rhythmic splashes of water. He sounds like a well-oiled machine and he pedals like one too.

I glance back at Jay and Tally (because of course they're behind us) and I can't help but laugh. It seems like Tally, like me, is only along for the ride too, both of us caught in a tornado of sibling rivalry. We exchange glances, silently acknowledging our shared hopes and prayers that this race doesn't end with either of us plunging to the bottom of the loch.

As the boats approach the other side of the loch, Millsy and I seem to have a significant lead over Jay and Tally. I can almost taste victory – suddenly I feel quite competitive myself – until I hear a loud cracking sound, and Millsy's previously lightning-fast legs grind to a sudden halt.

The pedals on both sides of our boat are jammed. Panic grips my heart, but I glance at Millsy, hoping for a solution. It's no surprise that he, as always, remains remarkably calm under pressure. With a swift motion, he retrieves the emergency oar from seemingly nowhere, ready to row us to safety.

Jay and Tally catch up to us, their boat gliding effortlessly through the water. Jay grins like a maniac, clearly over the moon to see that we're stuck. It's no real victory, is it, if you practically win by default?

'Oh, no, mate. Looks like someone forgot that the red boat has dodgy pedals that jam if you go too fast,' Jay calls over smugly.

Millsy holds his tongue. Tally erupts into laughter, finding the whole situation hilarious, as they pedal past us and then head back on their way towards the house, to easy victory. Meanwhile, all Millsy and I can do is row our way to the other side of the loch – the closest land to us right now – which is of course the opposite side to where Iona's house is.

I would say I'm disappointed, to have lost, but the relief I feel as Millsy helps me out of the boat and back onto dry land is something close to euphoria.

'I should have known he would cheat,' Millsy says, almost laughing to himself, annoyed that he didn't catch what Jay was up to when he insisted he take the blue boat.

'At least we made it here in one piece,' I reply. 'Sometimes that makes you the real winner.'

Millsy laughs.

'Come on, let's go figure out how to get home,' he replies. 'I'm pretty sure this castle is a B&B.'

I've always wondered about the castle across the loch from Iona's house. It's funny, it's in so many of my photos, but I know nothing about it – including the fact that it's a B&B.

We walk across the grass until we're on the driveway which leads up straight up to the castle doors, where reception is.

A very smiley lady greets us as we walk through the large wooden door.

'Hello, welcome to the Castle on the Tummel,' she says. 'Do you have a booking?'

'We don't,' Millsy replies.

'Not a problem, we have rooms free until right into the new year,' she replies. 'Is it just the two of you?'

My eyes widen at the idea of us getting a room. I mean, it's not like we aren't already sharing a room, and haven't already shared a room hundreds of times in the past, it's just... I don't know. The idea feels kind of sexy.

'Oh, no, we don't need a room,' Millsy insists. 'Our, erm, boat broke down on the loch, so we rowed to safety here.'

'You rowed?' she replies, and I could swear she stares at his biceps, which is fair enough.

'Yes, well, only for a few minutes,' he says modestly. 'We're from the house across the loch. We were in a pedal boat.'

'I see,' she says, stifling a laugh. 'Well, as I'm sure you know, if you want someone to come and pick you up, it does take some time to drive around the loch and back. The alternative would be that Peter should be back in a half hour or so, he can drive our motorboat, he can get you back to the other side.'

'Oh, that would be great,' Millsy replies. 'Thanks so much.'

'Not a problem,' she tells him. 'Would you both like to sit by the fire in the bar area in the meantime? I can bring you some hot chocolates, to warm you up.'

'That would be incredible,' Millsy says. 'Thank you so much.'

'Yes, thank you,' I add.

I have always wondered if people really are just so nice, or if they give Millsy special treatment because he's handsome and charming. Usually I decide it's a bit of both but, if you ask him, he will always insist that being kind and courteous to everyone is the thing that makes people fall over themselves to help you, and he always reminds me that it's hard for people to be mean to you if you're kind and smiley towards them. I have an auntie who could beg to differ, but it does seem to work with the rest of the world.

The bar in the castle B&B is so warm and inviting, embracing the essence of Scotland in every nook and cranny – but in a classic, natural way. As we step inside, the scent of crackling logs and aged whisky fills the air. It's like getting a hug from your grandad, right when you need one. The soft glow of the fire dances across the room, casting flickering shadows on the stone walls. An inviting-looking sofa sits in front of it, so we head over there, and it isn't long before the receptionist sets hot chocolates down on the table next to us.

'Hot chocolates for the losers,' Millsy announces with fake pride.

'Ah, you say that, but we're the ones sitting here, nice and cosy, in a castle, whereas Jay and Tally are probably standing, frozen cold and shattered, at the side of the loch, suddenly having to explain to our loved ones that they abandoned us,' I point out.

'Well, when you put it like that, it's easy to see who the real winners are,' he replies. 'But hang on a minute, I thought I was supposed to be the optimist in this re... in this.'

Ick. I can't help but notice he was going to say 'relationship' and then tried to walk it back without my noticing.

'Well, your annoyingly sunny outlook had to rub off on me sooner or later, didn't it?' I reply.

'As long as I'm not going to turn into a little doom cloud,' he teases.

'Oi, I'm not a doom cloud,' I reply.

'Cara, when the pedals on the boat stopped working, you whispered "we're going to die",' he points out.

'Wow, did I?' I reply. 'Okay, I really am a doom cloud.'

'It's the balance that works,' he replies between sips of his drink. 'We keep each other realistic.'

'I suppose we do,' I reply with a smile.

I lie back on the sofa and dare to rest my head on Millsy's shoulder.

'It's nice over here, isn't it?' he says with a sigh. 'If we had a boat, we could stay here and only pop over to Gran's to eat. It would seriously minimise our Jay time.'

'Which is always great,' I reply. 'But I wouldn't want to give up my four-poster bed. My cardio is using the stool to climb in and out of that thing.'

'Ah, there is that,' he replies. 'I suppose that bed is sort of special to us, isn't it? It's the first bed we shared.'

'And as friends, no less,' I remind him. 'It's a very sexy bed to keep things so platonic in.'

'Yeah, well, I wanted to pounce on you from the first night,' he confesses. 'Not that I would've.'

'Scoundrel,' I tease him. 'And there's me thinking you were my friend but, yeah, I would've welcomed it.'

He laughs softly to himself.

'We have some good memories, don't we?' he eventually says.

'Some great ones,' I correct him. 'And some that we need to take to our grave.'

'Yeah, I'm pretty sure Flora would murder you, if she ever realised you were the one who put your hand in her wedding cake,' he reminds me.

'And you were the one who smoothed it over,' I point out.

'Aren't I always?' he replies.

The tone suddenly shifts something almost serious. If ever there was a time to have a serious conversation about this – all of this, whatever this is – then it would be now.

I open my mouth, ready to stay something, searching for the right words.

'Hopefully we get back soon,' Millsy says with a sigh. 'I'm supposed to have a lesson this afternoon.'

I close my mouth again. I guess now isn't the time after all.

**24**

I decide to make my escape from the living room, the sound of
Millsy's voice mingling with Tally's flirty laughter like nails on a
chalkboard to me. They are clearly having a great time with their
lessons, and while it's great to hear him making progress with his
accent, it feels like a punch in the chest. If I'm going to stand a
chance of winning Millsy back, then I need more time alone
with him. Being stranded at the B&B together brought us closer,
just like when we were locked in the grotto – we felt like the old
us again and that felt amazing. But for now, I need the two of
them out of my sight, ears and mind, so I make my way downstairs to the party room to find something to do.

I should have said yes, when my parents, Oliver and my gran
said they were going into Pitlochry town to do some shopping,
but I was hoping if I hung around here, I'd get a chance to spend
time with Millsy. The only other place I can think to go in the
house is the party room.

As I head down the stairs, I can't help but wonder if I'm being
selfish. After all, Millsy seems to be enjoying his time with Tally
– could there be something going on between them? And if it

isn't now, could it have happened in LA? I wonder how I'd feel, if he had been with someone else. I didn't even entertain the idea of anyone else while he was away, even after we decided to split, and my attempts at dating since then have been for his benefit, to show *him* I'm moving on, to make *him* jealous. But neither the freaks on Matcher nor Charlie – the man who is supposedly just my type on paper – could turn my head. All I want is Millsy.

My hopes of finding somewhere to hide and distract myself from the drama are dashed when I walk through the party room door and find Jay in there alone, playing pool. A mischievous glint flashes in his eyes as he catches sight of me.

I could go, leave him to it, the energy levels I would need for a sparring match totally depleted. But I'll go mad if I have to spend any more time alone in my bedroom.

'Fancy a game of pool?' he asks me.

I hesitate for a moment, but what else am I going to do? It's not like Millsy is falling over himself to spend time with me.

'If it will help me beat the boredom,' I reply, a wry smile playing on my lips. 'But no pervy lessons, like the last time. I'm not as bad as I used to be.'

It was in this very room, more than three years ago, where Jay agreed to give me pool lessons, and proceeded to do it in a really porny way, bending me over the table, in a room full of people. Long story short, he ended up with a black eye – courtesy of Millsy, but an accident. If he tries to touch me this time, I'll give him another black eye, entirely on purpose.

'I'm not as bad as I used to be either,' he says with a smile. 'I'll set us up for a new game.'

We take our positions at opposite ends of the pool table. As I grab a cue and chalk its tip, I can't help but feel a surge of excitement mixed with a tinge of nostalgia. I wonder to myself, if I could go back in time to the last time we were here, would I do it? It's funny, when you fall in love, and you think you've found the person you want to spend the rest of your life with, sometimes, for no real reason, you'll mourn the fact that you're never going to meet anyone (romantically) ever again, and it's not that you want to, not that you want someone different. It's that feeling of meeting someone, being so into them, not knowing if they like you the way you like them, but wanting them so badly, waiting with nervous excitement as you try to work out if they like you too. There's something about that feeling, when it's just you and them, and there's chemistry and flirting but you haven't really laid a hand on one another yet. Lingering in that moment, waiting to see if it's going to happen, and then it does. Wow.

I love that feeling, that romcom moment, but not to the point where I would want to be single again, to have to try to find it with someone else. So, if I could go back in time, and do all that again with Millsy, but hopefully get it right down the line, would I do it? I sigh.

'You can break,' Jay tells me. 'Show me what you've got.'

I line up the cue ball and try to focus. With a swift stroke, I send the balls scattering across the table, the impressive crack of impact echoing around the room. Okay, so none of the balls find their way into the pockets, but I can't help but smile at my improved technique.

'Not bad,' Jay says.

My little triumph is short-lived as I watch Jay step up to the table confidently. He eyes the balls with a calculated gaze, almost as though he already knows what he's going to do and how to do it. With a flick of his wrist, he takes his shot, and *of course* he pots a ball with effortless precision.

'Oh, come on, Jay,' I exclaim with a pout. 'Can't you at least pretend you're not a pro for one game or it will be over before it's even started?'

Jay chuckles, his eyes twinkling with mischief.

'I can't help being amazing, Cara,' he jokes. 'But don't worry, the game's not over just yet. There's still plenty of time for you to make a comeback.'

I pull a face, one designed to show that I know I have no chance, but I'll give it my best shot.

With renewed determination, I analyse the table – for what it's worth – searching for the best shot to turn the tide in my favour. As I strike the ball, it glides smoothly across the felt, nudging another ball closer to the edge of the pocket.

Jay watches intently, a hint of admiration in his eyes.

'Not bad,' he tells me. 'You've definitely been practising.'

'Not practising,' I point out. 'The last time we played, I'd never ever held a cue. This time, although limited, I have some experience.'

'I could train you up, to beat Millsy,' he suggests. 'Imagine the look on his face.'

'Ha,' I reply. 'I don't think I'm anywhere near beating anyone just yet.'

As Jay lines up his shot, his brow furrows with concentration for a moment. I wonder if he's finally struggling but he smashes another ball in, which is no surprise – unlike when he breaks the silence with a genuine curiosity.

'Come on then, how's life treating you?' Jay asks, actually sounding interested. 'How's work going?'

I take a deep breath, considering his question, carefully planning my answer.

'Work has been really busy,' I reply. 'I've been working on a new kind of escape room-style game – an AR app. It's been stressful, but I think we're almost there.'

Jay nods – he almost looks impressed.

'An app? That sounds interesting,' he replies. 'How does that work?'

I lean against the table for a moment.

'It's a sort of treasure hunt, around Leeds, that you can do on your phone,' I explain. 'It uses AR so it's really immersive and something new and different – I hope.'

'Wow, that actually sounds pretty impressive,' he replies. 'Beauty and brains.'

I'm a little taken aback by his, well, normal, grown-up small talk, and the fact that he actually seems interested in talking to me. He doesn't quite seem himself right now – in a good way.

My curiosity piqued, I decide to ask about him.

'And how about you?' I say. 'How's life as an ecologist?'

Jay's expression softens. Is that a hint of sadness in his eyes?

'It's been a tough time, if I'm being honest,' he replies. 'The work side of things is good but my co-worker, Kris, passed away recently, and it's hit me pretty hard. We were the same age, played on the same football team – he had a wife and kids, though. Losing him has made me reflect on the fragility of life and the importance of spending time with our loved ones while we have them.'

Huh. This really is a new Jay.

I offer a sympathetic nod and a half smile.

'I'm so sorry, Jay, that's awful,' I reply. 'You're absolutely right, about spending time with family while you can. That's exactly how I feel.'

'That's why I decided to come here, for Christmas,' he continues. 'I want to be with my family.'

I feel bad saying this, because surely not even Jay would make up something like this to be manipulative, but is he for real right now? Is that really why he's here? I decide to lighten the mood with a joke, but to dig a little deeper.

'And there's me thinking you were only here because your sugar mamma dumped you,' I tease.

Jay laughs, shaking his head.

'It's not how it sounds, you know?' he insists. 'I did date an older woman, briefly, but it didn't quite pan out as I expected.'

'Do you want to talk about it?' I ask, lining up to take another shot.

Jay's expression turns thoughtful, a glimmer of introspection in his eyes.

'I know I was joking about it but, truthfully, she wasn't the nicest person,' he admits. 'It turned out she was just working her way through all the younger men at the bar, after little more than a fling. I only saw her a couple of times and, looking back, I was little more than a piece of arm candy and a roll around in the sack – probably the best she's ever had, but still.'

The first thought that pops into my head is that this is some kind of poetic justice because that is pretty much how Jay treats women, but I'm never one to kick someone when they're down.

'I know what you're thinking, Cara Brooks,' he says with a laugh. 'A taste of my own medicine. And you're right. It was an eye-opening experience. It made me reflect on my own past behaviour, the way I've been treating women for years. I need to do better.'

I can't help but admire Jay's honesty – if it is honesty.

'Well, that's good,' I say. 'Good for you.'

A seemingly genuine smile spreads across his face.

'Thanks,' he says.

I watch as Jay lines up his shot, his focus fully on the pool table again. With a swift stroke, he strikes the cue ball, aiming for one of the striped balls near the pocket. He looks more surprised than I do, when he accidentally causes the black ball to go hurtling into one of the pockets.

'You win,' he tells me.

'I win?' I reply.

'Yep, I potted the black too soon, that means you win,' he clarifies.

I burst into laughter, clapping my hands in delight.

'I won,' I blurt giddily. 'I won and I beat a pool pro like *you*.'

'All right, don't milk it,' he insists with a smile. 'We could always go again.'

'And ruin my perfect average?' I reply, still dancing around.

'Hey, bro,' Jay says, looking over my shoulder.

I turn around to see Millsy making his way towards us, a curious expression on his face.

'I was going to ask if you wanted to get some fresh air,' he tells me, his voice trailing off as he takes in the scene. 'But I see you're busy with Jay. I'll ask Tally instead, then.'

'Oh, that's okay, I—'

'Don't worry,' he insists. 'I'll catch you later.'

As Millsy disappears from view, I try to catch my breath for a moment, embarrassingly knackered from my victory dance. I stop laughing – I stop smiling, even. My happiness from winning slowly evaporates until it's gone.

As the laughter subsides, Jay's expression softens too, his eyes filled with concern. He takes a step closer to me, his voice gentle in a way I'm not sure I've ever heard it.

'Cara, is everything okay?' he asks now it's just the two of us again. 'You know, if you ever need someone to talk to, I'm here for you.'

I think he means it. He isn't laying it on too thick, he isn't using it as an excuse to touch me. It feels like genuine concern and, even though I can't tell him, it's nice.

'Thanks so much, Jay,' I reply. 'The same goes for you, if you ever need to talk about things.'

He nods, his smile kind and reassuring.

'No problem at all,' he insists. 'I'm just a phone call away – unless you deleted my number.'

'I kept it for emergencies,' I say with a smile.

'But in the meantime, come on, play me again,' he insists. 'I'll never live it down if you don't let me win one.'

I suppose Millsy is probably already back with Tally, asking her if she wants to go for a walk with him, I might as well.

'Go on then,' I say. 'You can break this time, you might have more luck.'

'She wins one game and she starts smack-talking,' Jay says with a laugh, setting up the table again.

I suppose I'll just have to wait until tonight, when we're alone in bed together, and see what Millsy has to say about me hanging out with Jay. Hopefully it's nothing bad.

## 25

We all went for dinner in Pitlochry this evening, to a gorgeous little place tucked away just off the main street. Not only did I have the best fish and chips I think I've ever had – although being absolutely starving probably added to my enjoyment – but because there are so many of us, it's hard not to break off into small groups, so you only really chat with your immediate table mates. I got lucky, finding myself sitting between my mum and Oliver. I chatted with them both, separately and together, over the course of the night, and my dad and Gran sat opposite us, so I could really focus on my own family, and forget about the Millsy Show down the other end of the table. It was really nice, to have a bit of time off from the drama and the awkwardness – and hilariously with a bit of distance between me and Millsy, there were no dramas, no epic fails, no accidental sabotage of the evening. So I'm starting to think that the fun little scrapes we always seem to get into as a duo really are our own fault.

I was grateful to get to enjoy a good night in what has otherwise been a series of stressful events, only thinking about the lie I'm living, panicking about what happens next. Laughter, conversation, and the clinking of cutlery filled the air as we enjoyed our meal together. The atmosphere was great – but now it's back to reality, back to the house, and the afterparty is in full swing.

Mhairi, who always loves a dance, takes charge and puts on some lively music. She always gets Rod up on his feet to dance with her, even though he seems to have two left feet – not that I'm much better on the dance floor.

Rod, Millsy's dad, leans back in his chair, a mischievous glint in his eyes.

'Does everyone know the story of Millsy and Cara dancing in Cornwall?' he asks.

'Oh, no one wants to hear that,' I quickly insist.

'I do,' Oliver pipes up excitedly.

'We all went to that resort in Cornwall,' Rod starts obligingly. 'And Millsy and Cara ended up dancing for everyone.'

'I never knew that,' my mum says. 'Or that you could dance.'

'Cheers, Mum,' I say through a laugh.

'Sorry,' she says, giggling. 'But I was the one who tried to take you to various dance classes when you were a kid.'

'Erm, I like to think I'm a lot better than when I was six,' I point out with a scoff.

But not much better.

'Anyway, somehow all the old birds at the resort got it into their heads that Millsy here was a salsa teacher,' Rod continues. 'I don't know how it started, but the next thing we knew, they were all clamouring for a front seat to watch him dance, and he and Cara stepped up the challenge.'

'You definitely don't know how to salsa dance,' my mum says with a laugh. 'Do you?'

'They definitely don't,' Mhairi adds. 'I do know how and I can safely say they don't.'

'But we pretended we did,' Millsy says, smiling as the memory comes back to him.

'And whatever we did, they thought it looked like salsa dancing,' I chime in. 'We just sort of... moved... sexily? I don't know.'

'Lots of spinning, dipping and grinding,' Millsy adds. 'We'd had a lot to drink.'

'There's something I wish I'd seen,' my mum laughs.

'Sounds like a bit too much grinding for me,' my dad half-jokes.

God, that holiday feels like forever ago. It was a last-minute thing, a trip to the Cornish coast with Millsy, Rod and Mhairi, his sister Fran, and her family, but we had a great time. I don't think we stopped laughing for a second – well, apart from when we delivered our super sultry, super sexy (absolutely not) salsa performance.

'I think our Fran wet herself,' Rod says. 'It was hilarious. Oh, go on, do it again, for old times.'

'I don't remember how,' I blurt.

'It doesn't sound like you knew to begin with,' Oliver teases me.

'What song was it?' Millsy asks. 'I don't feel like I knew it.'

'It was "Sway" by Michael Bublé,' Mhairi informs us.

'How could you forget?' Rod jokes. 'Go on, Mhairi, put it on.'

She does as she's told and as the familiar-sounding melody fills the room I feel like I'm back in Cornwall.

Millsy rises from his seat with a playful reluctance, a cheeky glint in his eyes as extends his hand towards me with that charming smile of his. I can't help but feel drawn to him, to the idea of taking a trip down memory lane, to dancing with him again – pushing from my head the idea that it could be the last time.

'Do you actually remember how to do this?' I ask him.

'I'm sure it's like riding a bike,' he jokes.

As the lively beat of the music fills the room, Millsy takes hold of my hand and pulls me into the centre of the party room. With only our parents and Oliver still up, I don't feel so silly as we try to recreate our performance.

Without missing a beat, Millsy snaps into character, his movements fluid and confident, leading me through a series of spins and twirls that we invent on the spot just like we did back in Cornwall, although I imagine, like snowflakes, no two salsa performances of ours will ever be the same – it's probably as flimsy as a snowflake too. But while we may not know the authentic salsa steps, our improvised routine has – what we feel, at least – is that sexy salsa energy.

I try to keep my face as straight and as serious as possible. Millsy is much better at this (you would hope so, with him being an actor) but his sultry pout only makes it harder for me.

As we sway, dip, and grind to the rhythm, the room erupts with cheers and applause – it's as though the elderly ladies from the resort are here with us, cheering us on.

The song comes to an end and we grind to a sudden halt, our hips pressed together as Millsy holds me in a dip.

'Ladies and gents, the Cornish Salsa,' he announces.

Everyone laughs and I can't help but smile because, as silly it sounds, he seems like him. I like it when Tally isn't around, because he drops the accent, he lets the stress fade away, and he just lights up the room. This is the Millsy I fell in love with.

The next song from Mhairi's Apple Music comes on automatically – another Michael Bublé song. 'Home'.

'Encore,' my mum calls out. 'Show us what you can do with this one.'

'Now, slow dancing we've always been good at,' Millsy says as he pulls me close.

I rest my head on his chest as I hook one arm around his neck and take his hand in my other. As we sway gently to the music, it feels like we couldn't be physically closer – mentally things feel like a different story.

'Aww, you're such a cute couple,' my mum says.

'Such a cute couple,' Oliver teases in a funny voice.

'This would make good first dance material,' Rod points out. 'This or the Cornish Salsa.'

I allow myself a little laugh – not just at the idea of the Cornish Salsa being anyone's first dance, but because it's almost cruel hearing that comment right now. Not that Rod knows, of course.

I sigh heavily and I don't know if Millsy feels it, but he holds me a little closer.

It's so hard, being under the spotlight like this, the people who know us best watching us.

'Go on, give her a kiss,' Rod calls out. 'Ahh, young love.'

Millsy and I part just enough to look one another in the eye. Whether it's old habits or an unspoken pact to keep up the act, our lips meet for a second or two. I love the way his lips feel, the way they make mine tingle every time, and suddenly being under the microscopic eye of our nearest and dearest feels irrelevant. We might be pretending we're still together, but this is real. There's no faking it involved.

As the song ends, we finally part and I don't know if I feel happy that it happened or sad that it's over. I think it's one then the other, so I let out a big, fake yawn and make my excuses.

'I'm knackered,' I say. 'I'm going to bed.'

'The Cornish Salsa really takes it out of a girl,' Rod jokes. 'Actually, I'm knackered. Come on, Mhairi.'

I say goodnight and head off to my room, although I know Millsy won't be far behind me.

When it's time for bed, it's just the two of us, no family around, no one to try to make anyone jealous, no Tally, no story to keep up or accents to maintain. Living the lie is hard but, sometimes, facing the reality seems like even more of a challenge.

There is a soft glow in the room, the only light coming from the bedside lamp on Millsy's side. I'm already tucked into bed, once again giving my vaguely sexy pyjamas a go, even though it's kind of cold, and they're evidently terrible for walking around the house in. Millsy arrives from the bathroom where he must've changed for bed, closing the bedroom door behind him before he saunters over to climb in next to me. He gets in and the silence, wow, it makes my ears ring.

My brain goes into overdrive, wondering what I should say, how I should fill the silence – if I should fill the silence. Do I mention Jay, or do I just make normal conversation? God, I never thought things would be like this between us.

'Did you have fun hanging out with Jay?' Millsy asks, taking the lead, his voice lacking any discernible tone, but I can sense his underlying apprehension.

I take a deep but subtle breath.

'It wasn't a big deal,' I start, trying to find the right balance between casual indifference and honest explanation. 'Everyone else was busy, or out, and I was feeling a bit lonely. You've been so busy lately, and if we're being honest, we're totally avoiding one another. Jay was there playing pool on his own so, I don't know, it was just something to do.'

'I'm sorry,' he says with a sigh. 'I know it's a difficult situation, and an unusual one, and I don't want to avoid you. Look how much fun we had this evening. I can't imagine my life without you in it, Cara. I really, really hope we can be friends.'

I try to smile.

'We did have fun, and being friends is better than nothing,' I agree. 'But I can't promise that I won't be jealous, seeing you move on. So... there's that.'

'You don't think I'm jealous?' he replies, turning to face me. 'It drives me crazy seeing you talking to other guys, the thought of you dating someone else... I'm trying to tough through it, but it hurts.'

I hold my breath for a second or two. Is he regretting our break-up? Has he – like me – been hoping that it wouldn't stick, that we would snap back together the second we were in the same country again?

But then the dreaded 'but' enters the conversation.

'But we just need to be mature about it all,' he adds practicality.

My heart, which had been slowly rising up into my throat, drops into the depths of my stomach again.

I suppose I could leave it, let it go, keep on with the plan... or I could say something, but doesn't saying something always have the potential to make things so much worse?

'I'm just thinking, if you're feeling as jealous as you say... maybe you don't want this break-up as much as you thought? Maybe neither of us wants it as much as we thought,' I dare to say.

Millsy smiles softly.

'Then I suppose we just need to be mature about that too,' he suggests. 'We just need to take things slow, make sure we don't rush anything, and figure out what it really is that we want before it's too late.'

It takes everything I have to keep a lid on my grin, instead allowing myself a more muted – but definitely happy – smile.

'Taking it slow sounds good to me,' I reply, even though I

want nothing more than to whip the covers off him and jump on top of him. 'Why don't we do something fun tomorrow?'

I hold my breath again, in anticipation of his reply, but he answers right away.

'I was actually planning to catch the train to Aviemore tomorrow,' he says. 'The journey is beautiful, only about an hour, and then there's this charming old-fashioned cinema that's showing "*It's a Wonderful Life*", which I'm pretty sure is your favourite Christmas movie too. It would be great if you came along.'

He smiles. He knows full well that it's my favourite Christmas movie, we watch it every year without fail (I thought this year was going to be the first one where we didn't and I've been feeling really crappy about it, like the movie might be ruined for me forever because of the sad memories newly associated with it).

'I would absolutely love that,' I reply, my heart skipping a beat.

'Great,' he replies. 'Well, I told Tally to be ready for eleven – I hope that's not too early?'

Oh. Tally's coming – of course she is.

My smile must falter momentarily but Millsy doesn't notice. I slap on my brave face just in time.

'I can do eleven,' I reply. 'I can't wait.'

Deep down (although probably not that deep down, I'm no actress) I wish it could be just the two of us, no distractions, no third wheels. I just need to remind myself that this is progress, a step towards getting our relationship back on track, and that Millsy mentioned us being mature – the mature thing to do is embrace Tally's presence, so that's what I'll do.

I sink down into the bed, making myself comfortable.

'Light off?' Millsy says.

'Yeah, go for it,' I reply. 'I'd best get to sleep, if I'm up early.'

'I love that you think eleven is early too,' he replies – I can hear his smile. Then the light goes off. 'Sweet dreams.'

'Yeah, night night,' I reply.

I feel Millsy get comfortable until eventually everything is calm. There's no light, no noise, no movement.

Is this it? Is this how we get back together? I try to replay the conversation we just had in my head, but I've forgotten almost every word of it – apart from the plan for tomorrow. It's not a date, is it, if Tally is there? But if I'm there, it's not a date for her either. I just wish there was some sort of way to tell, some sign that I'm not letting my brain run away with me.

Millsy's hand finds mine under the covers and holds it lightly.

That's all the sign I need.

## 26

I practically vibrate with anticipation as we approach Pitlochry station – to be honest, I've been giddy since last night, when Millsy suggested a scenic train journey to Aviemore. I'm looking forward to the journey, to the cinema, to everything. Although, if we're being real for a moment, we could be going anywhere, to do anything, it's the fact that Millsy invited me that has me all excited. That and the conversation we had last night. It just feels like, if we can just get this right, we can be perfect again. The only problem, the only hiccup, the thing that makes all of this so much harder is the fact that Tally is coming too. Imagine how romantic it would be, just the two of us. And the problem isn't just that three's a crowd, it's that somehow it's always me who feels like the third wheel.

As we head towards the platforms, Tally stops in her tracks.

'Is there a restroom?' she asks. 'Do we have time?'

'They're over there,' I tell her. 'I can show you, I might grab a quick drink.'

'I'll see you on the platform,' Millsy calls after us. 'But be quick, we don't have long.'

I pop into the little shop and grab myself a bottle of water and a packet of sweets for the trip – because I am a child – and then head back out.

It's only as I walk across the bridge that I spot Tally, standing on the wrong platform, looking around for Millsy. And then right on cue, our train pulls in on the other one. I freeze on the spot for a split second. If I go, right now, then Millsy and I can get on the train and go alone together. My God, today would be so much better if it was just the two of us, this could be exactly what we need, our perfect moment, our chance to fix everything. I have to do it, I have to do what's right for me, so I duck as low as I can and run across the bridge, down the steps, and onto the train.

Millsy must already be onboard because he isn't on the platform, so I walk along the train until I spot him. There he is, with the conductor, obviously trying to get him to hold the door, I give him a whistle from the other end of the carriage and then a wave to let him know I'm on board. It looks like he thanks the conductor before heading towards me. Then, sure enough, the doors beep, then close, and it's just us.

His face drops when he realises I'm on my own.

'Where's Tally?' he asks.

'I... I thought she was with you?' I lie. 'She wasn't there when I came out of the shop.'

'Shit,' he says. 'Let's sit down and I'll call her. Perhaps she's in a different carriage.'

'Yeah, probably,' I say as the guilt creeps in.

'Tally,' he says into his phone. 'Where are you?... I didn't see you on the platform... oh, shit, Tally, that's the wrong platform... yeah, that one goes the other way... you could get the next train?... yeah, I suppose you would... oh, really?... okay, I'll text you his number... so sorry, Tally.'

My heart is in my mouth as I listen to half the conversation.

'Well, it seems like she went to the wrong platform,' Millsy says. 'She's missed the train.'

'Oh, no,' I reply. 'Is she going to get the next one?'

Please say no.

'No,' he says. 'She says there's no point, she'll miss the movie. She asked me to send her my dad's number so he can come back and get her, take get back to the house.'

'It's a good job I came,' I tell him. 'Or you'd be going on your own.'

'Yeah, I guess,' he says with a half-hearted laugh. 'Okay, let's try and focus on the positives.'

'Yes,' I say with a clap of my hands. 'What's the plan?'

'Well, we have "*It's a Wonderful Life*" at the old cinema,' he starts excitedly. 'Then there are loads of scenic places to take a walk, gorgeous places to eat and drink, loads of amazing shops – I know you love a giftshop. I *love* that you love a giftshop.'

I really do love a giftshop. And I love that he loves I love a giftshop too – if that makes sense.

'Wow, I can't wait,' I reply. 'Sweet?'

'And I love that you always have sweets for a journey,' he says through a laugh. 'Thank you. What kind are they?'

'Erm...' I look down at the box and laugh awkwardly. 'Nessie Poop.'

I'm amazed at my own ability to keep a straight face as I say this.

'Nessie Poop?' he repeats back to me. 'They were all out of Wine Gums?'

I laugh.

'I mean, I'm sure they're delicious,' I reply. 'They're jelly-beans. Irn Bru flavour, I think.'

'Okay, now I know you're having me on,' he cackles.

'Or maybe they're cola but, here, try them,' I insist.

'Thanks,' he replies, that delicious smile of his turned up to full, his dimples so deep. God, I want to kiss them.

We settle into our seats, the train chugging along through the picturesque Scottish countryside. I glance at Millsy, his eyes alight with excitement for the day ahead of us. I know, I know, I shouldn't have ditched Tally like that, but I'd be lying if I said it didn't seem like it was worth it. Today is going to be amazing, I can tell.

## 27

I have spent weeks – if not months – thinking that this Christmas was going to be shit. It's a funny old thing, but we all put so much pressure on ourselves to make Christmas perfect. We shop as though we're preparing for war, we go all out on presents, we make all these plans – all just for one main day, and a couple of others around it. I know, it's a special time, and it's only once a year, but there have been Christmases before, and there will be Christmases again, and there's really no need to be crying in a Tesco Express five minutes before closing on Christmas Eve because you forgot one of the ingredients for your controversial Christmas puddings, and they don't have it. I suppose what I'm saying is that we should all try not to sweat the small stuff, and to try to have a good time regardless, but then again, perhaps I have a unique clarity, seeing as though I thought my Christmas was going to be rubbish because of the complete breakdown of my relationship, and the fact that I was going to have to fake that I was okay through the whole day.

Christmas Eve is here and, dare I say it, I'm starting to feel like things aren't so bad. In fact, I'm really looking forward to it.

There's a glimmer of hope in the air, and more than a whisper of possibility that things between me and Millsy might be back on track. I'm going to stop worrying about it so much and just embrace the magic of the season, and our plans for this evening.

We're all currently on a coach, the whole gang, and I'm over the moon to be sitting with Millsy, our conversations nothing but laughter and excitement. The coach plods along slowly, taking us on the short journey from Pitlochry town to the magical Faskally Forest, which has – for one night only – been transformed into a light and sound show, with a variety of light installations, all creatively utilising the scenery of the forest, and there's even a spot partway through where you can drink mulled wine, hot chocolate, and eat all sorts of delicious warming treats from hot dogs to toasted marshmallows. It's supposed to be a really magical, beautiful experience and I can't wait.

'Why did you let me eat a third mince pie, right before we left?' Millsy asks me, rubbing his stomach for effect.

'When have I ever been able to stop you from eating anything?' I reply with a laugh. 'The man who eats biscuits while his dinner is cooking.'

'Some might say you're at your hungriest, right before you eat your dinner,' he muses.

'And others might say that's why you're cooking the dinner in the first place,' I tease.

He playfully narrows his eyes at me.

'Hmm,' he says. 'I'm going to have to think carefully about a rebuttal to that one.'

I can't help but grin at his playful banter. Millsy has always had that effect on me, the ability to make me laugh, a seamless back and forth between us always coming so naturally. I clutch my black earmuffs, ready to embrace the festive spirit like a kid on a sugar rush – and Millsy probably is on a sugar rush, so I'd imagine he feels similar.

I am on top of the world after our trip to Aviemore earlier today. Honestly it was, just, perfection. I have zero regrets about the unfortunate series of events that led to it being just the two of us because we had the best time. We walked, we shopped – we even held hands! We ate amazing food and the movie – wow. I've seen '*It's a Wonderful Life*' so many times, but this time something was different, it struck a chord with me. I know, it sounds corny, but these last couple of months have shown me what life would be like without Millsy as my boyfriend, my partner in everything, my forever plus one, and I don't like it. I hate it. I want my old life back, whatever it takes, I'll make it work. But now I'm certain and it feels amazing. I want us back tother again. Life just isn't the same without him.

The coach finally comes to a halt and we all filter off. The illuminated path that lies ahead shows us which way to go, beckoning us deeper into the heart of the forest. I know it sounds corny, but I feel like I'm in a fairy tale right now, the magic of the lights, the ambient music, the sparkly little noises that seem to come from nowhere. Yesterday was amazing, perhaps tonight can be better?

Ahead of us couples walk hand in hand, families laugh together, marvelling at the sights, and the atmosphere nothing short of heart-warming.

As we head up the path, the forest welcomes us with a symphony of twinkling lights. I'm buzzing with excitement, my smile stretching from ear to ear. This is it, the moment I've been waiting for, Christmas is here and I'm spending it with Millsy.

My joy is short-lived as I hear a familiar voice calling my name from behind me.

'Cara?' Tally says. 'Cara, can I borrow you for a sec?'

Millsy and Oliver are chatting, so I hang back for a minute. Tally approaches with a beaming smile plastered on her face but, I don't know, I can just sense something.

'While we've got a moment away from the others, I thought you might like to explain why you ditched me at the train station yesterday?' she confronts me, still with a smile. 'What was the plan, try to get Millsy alone without me? And then what? Just leave me standing there alone without a second thought?'

Tally's tone is laced with accusation, and I feel a flicker of something inside me: a combination of guilt (because it wasn't a great thing to do) and anger (because who does she think she is?).

I shake my head.

'That's not what happened,' I insist, my voice purposefully dripping with innocence. 'I just assumed you were already on the train.'

'Cut the shit, Cara,' she replies, her smile finally falling, suddenly seeming like the must un-Tally-like version of Tally I've encountered so far. 'I saw you, up on the bridge. I saw you look at me and then dash off in the other direction. The train had left, before I could catch you up. And don't think I don't see the way you look at Joey, all doe-eyed, feeling sorry for yourself because you let go of one of the best guys going.'

Oh, boy, I can feel my blood boiling.

'You need to mind your own business,' I tell her. 'This is nothing to do with you.'

Tally's eyes narrow as she smirks.

'Oh, come on, Cara,' she blurts. 'You know how much time Joey and I have been spending together – we've been inseparable for months. We have a closeness, more than you think. Maybe you should've paid closer attention, thought of him more.'

'Just spit it out,' I reply, not wanting to play games. 'What is it you want to tell me, that you and Millsy are a thing?'

Tally smirks smugly and rolls her eyes.

'Why don't you ask him yourself?' she suggests. 'It's not my place to say.'

But her tone very much is saying it, without a doubt, she is trying to tell me that she and Millsy are a thing.

'So why don't you just back off, huh?' she replies. 'I'm not a part of your silly games and your childish drama.'

She walks off, leaving me with her revelation and my thoughts. My heart sinks as her words echo in my mind. I gave Millsy the chance to be honest with me, and I suppose he did seem a bit rattled by the question, I guess now I know why. I really, really wanted us to get through this, but I can't overlook a lie like that.

With a heavy heart, I watch as Tally walks away, and then make my own way into the forest, alone, to try to get my head around stuff.

The trees, adorned with shimmering lights in every hue, stand tall all around me, casting a warm glow on the forest floor. The changing lights almost make the trees look as if they're dancing – even the trees are having more fun than I am.

It seems almost sarcastic, as a symphony of colours surrounds me, like I'm in a kaleidoscope – just, you know, a nightmare version of one. Even the most beautiful things can seem scary in a nightmare.

I pass a magical waterfall, where cascades of light tumble down the rocks, creating an illusion of liquid light. Next, I walk through a tunnel of stars, which is like a gateway to another dimension, except when I pop out of the other side I'm still just in our shitty real world. Finally, I come to a light maze. Now this seems like the perfect place to get lost, even if it's only for a few minutes, and then I'll go to find my family and stick with them for the rest of the night – for the rest of the trip, even. Ergh, I feel like a character in some tragic Christmas movie, destined to be alone with a big bottle of wine and a box of tissues.

I make my way around the twists and turns of the maze, trying to find a way through, trying my best to enjoy the lights while I'm here. I turn a corner, only to find myself at a dead end, but it's not a completely dead end. Jay is there, smoking a cigarette.

'Shh, don't tell anyone,' he says with a cheeky smile. Then he notices the look on my face. 'Are you okay? You look like you just found out there's no Santa.'

I bounce my bottom lip theatrically.

'There's no Santa?' I reply.

He laughs.

'What's up, though?' Jay asks, with genuine care in his voice.

Why is it that, the second someone asks if you're okay, you cease to be outwardly okay all at once?

'I just had a bit of a run-in with Tally, that's all,' I tell him. 'She's... yeah, I don't know. She's something. Getting in the way, mostly.'

Jay raises an eyebrow, a look of concern in his eyes.

'Is something going on between Millsy and Tally?' he asks me. 'I know, he's Mr Perfect these days, but I remember the Millsy of old – the Millsy before you. If he's... y'know.'

I hesitate for a moment, the truth hovering on the tip of my tongue, but then I shake my head, trying to convince myself as much as Jay.

'No, nothing, nothing like that,' I insist. 'It's just... it's complicated.'

'I know complicated,' he replies. Then he turns on his smile and his charm. 'But you clearly don't want to talk about it, and that's fine, but you have to smile. You have to have fun here. They might kick you out, if you look miserable.'

I laugh a little.

'If they're not going to kick you out for smoking, they're not going to kick me out for frowning,' I point out. 'But thanks for trying.'

'Well, if threats won't make you smile, then perhaps this will,' he says. He drops his cigarette to the floor and stamps it out, then he leans in to talk to me – not that there's anyone around, not for long, it's quickly obvious this is a dead end, and everyone is having too much fun to worry about what we're doing.

'I can't believe I'm telling you this,' he says as he unfastens his coat. 'And I definitely can't believe I'm showing you, but look... As I was stepping down from the coach, I don't know what happened, but I've split my trousers right down the arse.'

Jay turns his hips to show me his bum and, sure enough, they've torn open right on the bum, his boxers peeking out from inside.

I don't know what I was expecting him to say or do to cheer me up – not this, though. Perhaps that's why it's so effective.

I burst into uncontrollable laughter, the sound echoing through the maze. My smile returns, if only for a moment, and I'm grateful for Jay's attempt to cheer me up, even at the cost of his own pride which, believe me, he takes very seriously.

'But you can't tell anyone,' he adds as he fastens his coat again. He smiles, but I can tell he feels a little embarrassed to have shown me. That's actually really sweet.

But as quickly as the laughter comes, the tears are not far behind. I blend seamlessly from laughing wildly to sobbing like a baby, almost as though letting one emotion out of the door has allowed another to sneak out with it.

Without thinking, Jay grabs me and holds me close,

comforting me, patting me lightly on the back in a reassuring way.

'It's all going to be okay,' he promises me.

It's only as he's hugging me that I realise how much I need this right now. I squeeze him tightly, like he's a human stress toy, as I wait for my emotions to let up.

Eventually, I stop squeezing him and he loosens his embrace, allowing me to stand back in his arms. Then, without warning, Jay leans in for a kiss, and I recoil instinctively. His lips barely graze mine before I shove him away, a rush of anger making my face feel boiling hot suddenly, and the mother of all stress headaches kicking in.

'You're unbelievable, Jay!' I snap, wiping away the remaining tears. I turn on my heel, heading back into the depths of the maze, trying to find a way out. I wipe my lips with the back of my hand – he barely touched them, but I feel like I can taste cigarettes. My God, what was he thinking, trying to kiss me? Why would he think that was okay?

I pop out of the maze and continue on my way. My plan is to find Oliver and stick with him – in fact, I might even see if I can sleep on the sofa in the guest house tonight, because I don't want to be around Millsy or Jay or Tally. As I navigate through the forest, my heartache makes way for anger. Millsy and his entire bloody family are nothing but a pain in my arse. Maybe, once Christmas is over, I really am better off without them. The thought lingers in my mind for a minute. Is that really what I want?

By the time I catch up with Oliver, I realise Millsy is still with him. I wipe away any signs that I've been crying before I reach them.

'We thought we'd lost you,' Millsy says with a smile. He

reaches out to take my hand but I quickly whip it back. Oliver notices, and makes himself scarce.

'What's wrong?' Millsy asks.

'I don't want to hold your hand,' I tell him. 'In fact, I don't want anything from you.'

'But I thought we were going to—'

'This, all of this, it needs to stop,' I interrupt him. 'We broke up, I don't know why we're messing around like this, but it needs to stop.'

'Sure,' he says simply. 'Sorry.'

I hurry after Oliver, who doesn't know he's my bodyguard yet, but who I know will happily take the role.

Is this what I want? I'm not sure it matters what I want any more. When things are this messy, and this far gone, perhaps love isn't enough. Maybe it's time I really did try to move on.

**28**

I woke up this morning – Christmas morning – briefly confused until I remembered I was in Oliver's bed in the guest house. He slept on the sofa last night, because even though I didn't tell him exactly what went on, he used his sibling intuition to recognise that I really needed some space from Millsy. He simply went along with it, sacrificing his own comfort for mine, because he is amazing. I'm so lucky to have him and, when he finally takes his eyes off his work, whoever has him in the future will be lucky to have him too. We need more Olivers in the world.

To the rest of the family, I effortlessly styled it out as if spending Christmas Eve with my own family and waking up under the same roof as them was some spontaneous cute idea I had, so my presence in the guest house hasn't raised any alarm, I don't think.

The guest house, a delightful holiday rental in the grounds of Iona's house, is so cool and modern. It boasts three bedrooms, each adorned with tasteful furnishings, and the place is all decked out for Christmas, which is a nice touch. The beds are comfortable, the bathrooms shiny and pristine, and the living area provides a cosy sanctuary for relaxation – perhaps I should have pushed to stay in here from the start.

As the plans for today evolved, we agreed that each family would exchange gifts within their own spaces before convening in the main house. It seemed like a sensible idea at the time, ensuring that everyone had their moment of unwrapping joy before coming together as one big, bizarre, blended-ish family unit. For me, it just meant that I could enjoy Christmas morning with my own family, and try not to think about all the chaos awaiting me next door.

With the exchange of gifts complete between my immediate family members, we make our way across to the main house, dragging bags of presents with us, Santa style. Everyone seems so excited, except me, and I feel guilty for feeling so rotten, but at least I'm sticking to the script.

As we step into the lounge, I can just about make everyone out in the sea of crumpled wrapping paper. The room is in a state of joyful disarray, but full of smiling faces and good cheer. Iona is already on the sherry, which makes me smile.

From the corner of my eye, I catch a glimpse of Jay, looking shifty as ever. It would seem that he's kept what he did – or tried to do – to himself, and I certainly don't plan on telling anyone, so perhaps that's for the best. He'd do well to stay out of my way today, though.

Next, I notice Tally, the other thorn in my side, sitting with Mhairi, a smug smile firmly plastered on her face as she greets me. Her feet are planted comfortably under the table – in multiple respects – as she assists Mhairi with a jigsaw puzzle. Oh, how lovely for her. I should have known she would be just Mhairi's type – I always felt like she didn't think I was quite the right girl for this family. Perhaps I was right.

As my lot settle into the room, everyone chats, about the day, what presents they've got so far – anything and everything.

'We need to tidy up and get ready for dinner soon,' Mhairi calls out. She is always the mastermind behind family logistics. 'Time to unwrap the last of the gifts, everyone!'

'Merry Christmas, Cara,' Millsy tells me.

'Merry Christmas,' I reply.

We hug, awkwardly for us, but hopefully no one notices.

'Come on, you two, swap gifts,' Iona urges us.

'Yes, you two always get each other the best presents,' my gran adds. 'It's one of the highlights of the day.'

I chew my lip thoughtfully.

'Of course,' Millsy says. 'Here you go.'

He presents me with a box wrapped in snowman paper. I hand him a small box, wrapped in gold paper, with a fancy ribbon and bow job.

'You first,' I insist.

Millsy nods as he unwraps his gift. He looks at the small blue leather box underneath the paper before he opens it. Inside there's an aged guitar plectrum with what is hopefully an unmistakable marker pen scribble on it.

'Is it...' Millsy's voice trails off, almost as though he can't quite believe what he's holding.

'It is,' I reply. 'It's a signed Billy Gill plectrum – one of his own. I thought that it might bring you close to him, if you had something of his.'

Millsy looks stunned.

'Cara that's just... wow... I just...' He stands up and leans over to hug me again, like he means it this time. 'This is incredible, thank you.'

'You're welcome,' I say, with a subdued smile. I've never been great at taking praise, but I revel in Millsy's reaction. I bought this for him ages ago, and it's not like I have any use for it, or I can return it. Anyway, I know it will help him, so he should have it.

I begin to unwrap my gift from Millsy. I'm almost in there when he pulls his attention from his plectrum and realises what I'm doing. His face falls, which is odd.

It's hard not to feel a flutter of anticipation, like I always have when I'm unwrapping a gift from Millsy, but as I peel away the wrapping paper, my heart sinks.

'It's... ah.'

I stop myself from announcing it, while I take it in, making sure my eyes aren't deceiving me.

'What is it?' Iona asks sweetly, peering over to try to see.

'Chocolates,' I tell her.

And not just any chocolates – and I don't mean this in a good way – chocolates that we saw in a gift shop in Aviemore. I remember casually saying they looked nice, in a really casual way, and I know it's the same ones because they're in a frigging tartan box.

'Chocolates?' Iona calls back, surprised.

'Ah, but what's inside the box?' my gran asks with a smile, thinking she knows Millsy better than this.

'Erm, chocolates, I'd imagine,' I reply simply. 'The plastic is still on the box.'

'Oof,' Jay blurts. 'Awkward.'

Mhairi takes charge of the situation instantly.

'Millsy, why don't you tidy up the wrapping paper?' she suggests. 'Dinner isn't that far away.'

'Yeah, sure,' he replies.

'Well, I think we all know who won that one,' Rod says with a chuckle.

As Millsy gathers the crumpled paper, I sink into my seat,

more sad than I am embarrassed. I don't mean to sound ungrateful, a present is a present, but is this it? A box of chocolates that he bought yesterday, that's my present, after three years together, when we're still pretending to be a couple?

Of all the signs that we are over, this one has to well and truly be it. What a crap, heartbreakingly thoughtless gift.

This whole thing needs to be over now, but we've got dinner to look forward to first. Yay!

# 29

The aroma of Mhairi's meticulously prepared Christmas dinner fills the air, mingling with the laughter and conversation around the table. The food looks and tastes impressive – roast turkey, honey-glazed ham, roasted vegetables, creamy mashed potatoes, and all the delicious trimmings including Yorkshire puddings, to make us all feel at home. It's undoubtedly delicious, although I can't help but compare it to the one my mum made for us last week, which was like a personalised version of a Christmas dinner, everything made exactly the way I liked it. It was nothing short of perfect. But everyone feels that way about their mum's cooking, don't they?

We're all sitting together, across the two tables which have been pushed together to make one big table. One big table for one big family – one big family that won't exist in the new year. It's a shame, because we all get on so well. Sure, Mhairi might be a bit grumpy sometimes, and I'm not sure our grandmas can always tell what the other is saying, but I never thought I would have such lovely in-laws (for lack of a better term for them).

Mid-bite, Iona suddenly coughs, a tickle in her throat that catches everyone's attention.

'Are you okay, Mum?' Mhairi asks. 'Let me fill everyone's water glass.'

'Fill everyone's wine glass,' Rod jokes. 'No one wants water, it's Christmas.'

Mhairi fills our water glasses, like the perfect host she is, before taking her seat and continuing her dinner.

The crackers have been pulled, we're all wearing our dorky hats, the jokes have been told. All that's left to do is eat and chat.

Rod, always one to stir up conversation, brings up the topic of New Year's resolutions.

'I know it's early, but is anyone making them?' he asks.

'If you were going to make one, perhaps it should be to live more in the moment,' Mhairi tells him. 'Christmas isn't even over yet.'

'Christmas isn't that big a thing in Scotland,' Iona chimes in. 'It wasn't even a bank holiday when I was younger. Hogmanay is when we celebrate.'

'Well, I wish Ted would make a new year's resolution, to make an effort to think ahead like that,' my mum jokes. 'Further ahead than what's for dinner will do.'

'What is for dinner?' my dad asks, his comedy timing perfect.

Everyone laughs.

And then, without skipping a beat, and because I'm feeling spicy, I take this as my opportunity to talk to Millsy.

'Any resolutions for you, Millsy?' I ask, my eyes playfully narrowing. I still can't shake the disappointment of the lacklustre gift from earlier.

'Buy better presents?' Rod jumps in, reading my mind. Everyone laughs, dispelling a little of the tension from when he gave it to me. Everyone but Millsy, of course. And Jay.

'I think we all wish Millsy's resolution would be to shut up,' Jay suggests as he swigs his beer.

The sudden shift in tone catches everyone off guard. Everyone stares at him.

'Okay, Jay, you've made your point,' Mhairi tells him, trying to pour water on the ever-growing flames.

'I think it's a lovely accent,' Iona insists. She seems a little upset by the way the conversation is going.

Millsy, never one to back down when it comes to Jay, laughs to himself.

'Perhaps you would prefer my voice if I sounded like a middle-aged woman with an inheritance burning a hole in her pocket?' he suggests.

Ouch.

'Because your love life is so perfect,' Jay says with a snigger, making it obvious that he knows something.

He definitely has Millsy's attention now. Millsy looks over at me, almost accusingly, so I jump to my own defence.

'I haven't said anything to him about anything,' I insist confidently, because I know that I haven't.

'No, she didn't tell me a thing,' Jay replies casually. 'But seeing her profile on Matcher told me everything I needed to know.'

My jaw drops.

'You didn't match with me, though,' Jay says to me directly, pouting playfully, draining another beer.

Wait, what? I deleted Matcher, after my disastrous date with Liam. Unless... oh, shit. I didn't technically delete it, I uninstalled the app in a disappointed huff, I didn't think to deactivate my profile before I did so. That means that my profile has been served up to the locals wherever I've been. So Jay, who I guess uses Matcher (shock, horror) has seen me on there while we've been here.

'What are you doing?' I ask Jay angrily.

The genie is well and truly out of the bottle now. Breaking out another box of crackers isn't going to turn this conversation around.

'What are *you* doing on Matcher?' he retorts.

'What is Matcher?' Iona asks.

'It's a dating app,' Tally ever so helpfully replies – thank you, Tally!

'And why, oh why would you be on a dating app?' Jay persists.

'Are you just using it for something to do with the app that you're building?' my mum chimes in. It gives me a fuzzy feeling in my heart, that she would jump to my defence without question.

'Only if she's building a dating app,' Tally reasons.

'I can think of a more likely reason,' Jay sings.

'Wait, is this why you tried to kiss me last night?' I ask him angrily.

'You tried to kiss her?' Millsy says, the hurt in his voice impossible to hide.

You can tell from the look on Mhairi's face that she knows she needs to step in.

'Now, now, boys,' she says, attempting to defuse the tension.

'Yeah, come on, lads, knock it off,' Rod shouts. 'This shit has to stop happening every time we get together, the two of you scrapping over girls.'

'But Cara isn't a "girl",' Millsy reminds them. 'She's the woman I love.'

'The woman you love who uses dating apps,' I just about hear Tally say under her breath.

'Enough,' Mhairi snaps. 'You're upsetting Mum.'

Iona looks awful. My own gran looks worried sick and my dad has officially gone into Yorkshire man mode, which essentially involves playing dead at times of emotional crisis.

Millsy pushes out his chair angrily and storms off in the direction of our bedroom. Tally goes to stand up, to go after him.

'Leave him,' Iona tells her sternly, coughing to clear her throat again. 'Give him some space.'

The room falls silent, and we all continue to eat our dinner, lost in our own thoughts. I sit for as long as I can, pushing my food around my plate, until I can't take it any more.

I leave the table, to head for the guest house where I can try to process this on my own.

'Merry Christmas, everyone,' I hear Jay, ever the joker, say in a silly voice.

Of course the last word was going to be his.

## 30

It's Boxing Day morning and I've made a decision.

After a chat with my parents – but without telling them what exactly has been going on just yet – we've decided that we, Oliver and Gran should head back home earlier than planned, and celebrate New Year's Eve in Yorkshire.

I feel so many things right now, but the two main ones are sadness and relief – relief to be leaving this situation, and that makes me feel even sadder.

With determination in my stride, I make my way to the main house, to tell Millsy that we're going. I pound the floor with my feet, as though that's going to give me a confidence boost, but as I walk through the house, I realise how quiet it is, like someone has hit the mute button. It's eerily quiet and it rattles me slightly. But I need to keep my head in the game, I need to get through this.

I call out for Millsy, but my voice echoes through the empty silence. It's as if the house is playing a practical joke on me, hiding Millsy from me somewhere, but I eventually find him in the bedroom, sitting up in bed, looking like he hasn't slept a wink.

'Hi,' I greet him softly.

'Hi,' he replies weakly, very much in his own voice.

Come on, Cara. Get it over with.

I take a deep breath and then I cut to the chase.

'I'm going home,' I tell him. 'Me and my lot. All you and I have done is make a mess, and I'm not sure this is one we can fix by borrowing a hat or improvising a party game. We never should have pretended to still be together. It hasn't made things less awkward – in fact it's only making things more awkward. I haven't told anyone the truth yet, but I can't keep lying. I won't pretend we're still together for another second. It's over.'

Millsy opens his mouth, as if he's going to speak, but then Rod comes charging in.

'Sorry, Cara, I thought you were in the guest house,' he apologises. Then he turns to Joe. 'Something has happened, it's Iona.'

Rod catches his breath for a second.

'What's happened?' Millsy asks as he gets out of bed.

'We've been at the hospital with her for most of the night,' Rod explains. 'Mhairi found her on the bathroom floor in the middle of the night, so we rushed her straight to the hospital.'

'Where is she now?' Millsy asks.

'She's still there, in Perth,' Rod tells him. 'So we've come to gather some things for her and sort ourselves out before heading back.'

'She's there alone?' Millsy says.

'Yeah, we left them to do some tests,' Rod replies.

'Right, I'll go right now, while you guys get sorted,' Millsy tells him.

'Thanks, lad,' Rod replies. 'I'll let Mhairi know.'

Millsy hurries on his clothes with an urgency I don't think

I've ever seen from him before. He's ready to go in a few seconds. Then he looks at me.

'We'll have to do this later,' he tells me. 'But you're right, no more lies.'

'Go,' I insist. 'Be with your gran, and give her my love.'

I wait until Millsy leaves to start packing my things, not wanting the last thing he sees before he leaves for the hospital to be me emptying our bedroom here of all of my things.

I hope Iona is okay. She's such a sweet lady and, while she always seems so strong, I think it's easy to forget that she is almost ninety.

I grab my things and head back to the guest house. Leaving is definitely the right thing to do. This is a real emergency, a time for their family to come together, the last thing they need is silly drama.

I just really hope she's okay.

## 31

Resting my head against the cool car window, I gaze out at the passing scenery. God, I love the views here. I don't know how many times I've visited now but the shine has never worn off. Will I ever have a reason to visit this place again now that Millsy and I are definitely over?

As my thoughts wander, concern for Iona and Millsy surges to the forefront – again. I can't shake off the worry gnawing at me. Poor Millsy must be feeling scared and overwhelmed, alone at the hospital with his gran. I chew my lip thoughtfully, wondering if I really am doing the right thing. Should I really just be going home? Shouldn't I be by Millsy's side, making sure he's okay? Millsy needs someone right now and, break-up or not, whatever has happened, I know that someone should be me.

'Shit, I've made a mistake.'

The words escape my lips in the car, startling everyone.

'I should be at the hospital with Millsy,' I say. 'How hard would it be to go to Perth?'

My dad glances at me through the rear-view mirror, a warm smile on his lips.

'We're already on the way, love,' he reassures me.

Good old Dad, knowing what I want, even before I do.

Once we arrive at the hospital, I dash around like a headless chicken, desperately searching for the right room. After a whirl-wind of enquiries, a helpful nurse guides me to Iona's room. Through the window, I spot her lying in the bed, still and motionless. I feel sick and dizzy, but I need to hold it together.

Millsy catches sight of me through the window and I don't think he has ever seemed so pleased to see me. He hurries to the door to greet me.

'Cara,' he says, grabbing me, squeezing me tightly.

He doesn't need to ask what I'm doing here. He knows.

'How is she?' I ask.

'I don't know,' he replies. 'I've not been here long, no one has told me anything, I've just been sitting quietly next to her, holding her hand.'

'Then that's what I'll do too,' I tell him.

We take a seat at either side of Iona's bed. The first thing I notice is that she's had one hell of a knock on her head. We each take one of her hands. I stroke it gently, hoping she can feel it, and that it makes her feel reassured that everyone is doing every-thing they can to help her. I want to grab her, and wrap her up in bubble wrap, and then I want to do the same to my own gran, just in case. She looks so small, so weak, so fragile. I'm even worried about how tightly I'm holding her hand, so I loosen my grip a little.

'Hello,' she says, weakly, but with that trademark brightness in her voice, as she tries to open her eyes.

'Gran,' Millsy says. 'Gran, are you okay?'

'I've been better,' she jokes. My God, am I pleased to hear her make a joke, but she doesn't look or sound good.

'Do you know where you are?' Millsy asks her.

'Not at home with a sherry,' she replies. Then she sighs. 'Hospital. Had lots of tests.'

It's good that she's conscious, right? I was worried she was out.

'Cara is here too,' Millsy tells her.

'Hello, hen,' she says.

It takes everything I have not to cry.

'Hi, Iona,' I say, trying not to sound worried. 'Up to no good again?'

'You know me,' she replies. 'Anyway, what about you two, after last night...'

'Don't worry about that,' Millsy insists.

'But I do worry,' she replies. 'You two are okay, aren't you?'

Millsy looks at me.

I know what I said, no more lying, but this is different.

'We're okay, Iona,' I reassure her. 'Just misunderstandings and silly rows, but we're all good.'

'Good,' she says, her eyes closed, but her smile clearly content. 'I'd never seen you so happy, before you met Cara. She makes you the best version of yourself, like my Jimmy did with me, back when we met.'

'He makes me the best version of myself too,' I tell her – which is true.

'That's good,' Iona says softly. 'All you can do is love one another. I keep waiting for the news that you're getting married – I thought there might be a ring in that box of chocolates.'

I give Millsy a smile, to let him know that it's okay.

'Well, I haven't opened them yet,' I tell her. 'So maybe we'll look together when you get home.'

'That would be nice,' she says. 'I'm going to go back to sleep now.'

'Okay, Gran,' Millsy says. 'Love you.'

'Love you too, sweetie,' she replies.

Millsy reach out with his free hand, taking mine in his, and he squeezes it.

'Thank you,' he mouths at me.

'You're welcome,' I reply silently.

A few seconds later, Mhairi and Rod arrive – along with a doctor.

'I'll go,' I say quietly. 'Give you guys some space.'

'See you later,' Millsy tells me. 'And thanks again.'

'No problem,' I reply. 'Keep me posted.'

I leave the room, leaving the family crowding around Iona's bed, everyone clearly worried sick about her. I feel better for coming, but still not great. At least Millsy seems a little less stressed, not just because I dropped by, but because Iona spoke to us.

And what would be the point of telling her that we're broken up? If a happy family and the idea of a proposal makes her smile then let her think that, she needs something to look forward to, something to focus on, for when she gets out.

God, I hope she gets out soon. She looks awful. I really, really hope she's going to be okay.

## 32

'You should've had a wee at the hospital,' my dad ticks my mum off.

'You can't use the hospital for a wee,' she reminds him.

'I'm sure they would rather you used their loo than had an accident,' Oliver adds with a laugh.

'I would rather you used their toilets than had an accident in my car,' Dad replies.

Mum scoffs.

'Ted Brooks, I gave you two children,' she reminds him. 'When you've given birth twice, come back to me.'

I laugh at my parents' semi-playful back and forth. I always wondered if Millsy and I would end up like this, like an old married couple, playing teasing tennis.

God, this journey home is going to drag. It feels like Dad is driving especially slow, and I can't believe we've stopped *already*. I can't believe I'm stuck on a trip that feels like it's never going to end, on a day when I can't get my problems off my mind.

'We'll wait here,' Dad says. 'Cara, take your mum for a wee.'

'My, how the tables have turned,' I joke as we get out of the car.

'Okay, enough of that,' Mum says. 'At least I won't sit there shouting your name, insisting you wipe my bum.'

I'm going to tell myself that one is about Oliver and not me.

'Wait here for me,' she says. 'I'll only be a minute.'

I hang around outside M&S, shifting my weight back and forth between my feet. The shop is quite open, there's no way I'll miss Mum if she comes out, so I grab a packet of Percy Pigs for the road, then return to my spot.

I love a classic British service station and this one, at a glance, seems like it has it all. I like the ones where you have choices, where decisions aren't made for you. Decisions like Costa or Starbucks, or McDonald's or Burger King. The dream places have both. I love the fact they still have arcades in places like this, with claw machines and slot machines, and then there are the shops. The nice thing about still being in Scotland is that there's less general tat and more targeted souvenirs. Well, I'd rather see Irn Bru-flavoured everything and Loch Ness Monster-themed things than the random stuff you see in England, like monstrous-looking plushies, travel cushions that aren't immediately obvious what part of you they're for, and hilarious T-shirts that say things like 'I survived the M25'.

I glance around. There's still no sign of Mum and I don't know how long I've been standing here but it feels like ages.

I take my phone from my pocket and call my dad.

'Hello?' he says.

'Hi, is Mum there? I was just...' My voice trails off when I notice something. 'Dad, are you driving?'

'Yes,' he replies simply.

'Is Mum with you?' I ask.

'Yes,' he says again.

'Have you...' I pause for a moment, unable to believe that I'm about to say what I'm about to say. 'Have you left without me?'

'We have,' he replies, very matter-of-factly given that he's my dad and he's left me at a service station.

'Well, my self-esteem is through the roof,' I blurt. 'How did you all manage to forget me?'

'Who said we forgot you?' I hear Mum reply with a laugh.

'Mum, what's going on?' I ask.

'I thought it would have been obvious by now,' she replies playfully.

I hear a loud noise, then some rustling, then my mum saying to my dad, 'Quick, hang up, quick, that's the perfect thing to say, qui—' Then the call ends.

'What are they doing?' I mutter quietly to myself.

'I think it might be my fault,' Millsy tells me.

I turn to look at him standing next to me and pull a face – then I realise that *Millsy is standing next to me* and I jump out of my skin.

'Wha... what are you doing here?' I blurt. 'You were just... I left you at the hospital. How's Iona, is she okay?'

'She's going to be fine,' he reassures me. 'It was only two at a bed, so I said I'd go. It seems like she might have a chest infection, and that she probably coughed so hard in the night she passed out. She fell and, how did my dad so eloquently put it? She got her bell rung.'

I laugh, the relief I'm feeling is immeasurable.

'She's going to be just fine,' he tells me. 'I was worried sick, when you arrived, I didn't think she was going to make it.'

He sighs heavily. I reach out and rub his arm.

'Thank you, for saying what you said to her,' he tells me. 'I think it really would've upset her, to find out that we broke up.'

'Oh, of course,' I reply. 'Honestly, it's no problem. I haven't told anyone yet – I think I'm having trouble telling myself.'

I stop myself, before I say too much.

'Just, hang on a sec,' I say, my thoughts catching up with me. 'Why have my parents turfed me out at a service station? And what are you doing here?'

'Don't be mad at them,' he insists. 'I asked them to turf you out at a service station.'

'Wait, is this why Dad was driving so slow?' I ask.

'Yep,' Millsy replies. 'I think I actually overtook him at some point. Anyway, they're on their way back to Iona's house now.'

'And what are we doing here?' I ask, starting to smile.

'I thought we could have a date,' he says.

'A date?' I reply. 'Here? What, have you got us a table?'

I laugh at my own joke.

'Yes,' he replies simply. 'If you'll follow me.'

I feel my eyes widen.

Millsy leads me to a table where two plastic trays are waiting, one from McDonalds, one from Burger King.

'I know you like to choose,' he says with a grin. 'I also know that it's always beef from Burger King, chicken from McDonald's – so I got both to save time – and then chips from Burger King and a milkshake from Maccies.'

My jaw drops.

'That's good,' he teases. 'Good stance for eating.'

I laugh, bemused, as I take my seat at the table.

'Cara Brooks, I'm about to ruin your day,' he tells me. 'I am going to say words I think you would probably never want to hear me say: no more games. I'm not playing any more, so listen...'

I hold my breath, waiting to hear what he has to say.

'I didn't want to break up,' he tells me. 'It's the last thing I wanted but things were tough, I was away, you suggested it and I guess I thought you were calling my bluff, so I called yours right back,' he starts. 'That was the first round of the game. The next was how we stupidly both refused to message the other, not backing down, probably both starting to believe this was what the other person wanted, and worrying sick about it. Round three was this stupid break-up plan, to pretend to still be together, to "not ruin Christmas", but I convinced myself this was part of the game, that it was a way to tell ourselves we were over when we so clearly weren't, and the game continued. Is this sounding about right?'

'It is,' I confess.

'I didn't know I was bringing Tally with me, until the last minute, and I know that complicated things,' he continues. 'And when I just called her on the drive here, telling her that she should go home, to spend the rest of the holidays with her family, and that I wouldn't tell anyone if she did, she confessed to me that she might've said some things to make you think she and I were together.'

'You aren't together?' I ask quickly. 'You've never been together?'

'Of course not,' he replies. 'Even if we weren't going through it, you know I'd never be so unprofessional, not with this role on the line.'

That's true, and I feel stupid for thinking it.

'She said you upset her, and that's why she said it, but she didn't tell me what you said,' he continues. 'I guess that's between you and her, but I can give her your number, if you want to talk.'

'Thanks,' I say softly.

To be honest, I'm not surprised she said what she said to me. I mean, come on, the poor girl is working away from home, in a foreign country, at Christmas, and I left her stranded at a train station because I was jealous. I owe her a big apology.

'So, Matcher, huh?' he says with a smile. 'I never thought you'd go back there.'

'Neither did I,' I insist. 'But then you started pushing me to move on.'

'I was trying to act like I wasn't bothered,' he points out. 'I was trying to make out like I was cool about you moving on, because I didn't think you would actually do it.'

'I didn't actually do it,' I admit. 'I went on a few dates to prove a point, and because I thought I had to move on, but they were all hell, and there's nothing going on between me and Charlie, that was just to try to make you jealous.'

'It did make me jealous,' he admits. 'Really, really fucking jealous. I figured you really were moving on and it killed me.'

'I never wanted anyone else,' I tell him. 'Not for a second.'

'I think the thing that hurt the most was thinking that we were over, but that you were being so cool about it,' he replies. 'I thought I hated the arguing, upsetting you, disappointing you. I hated it even more when I thought that you were moving on, that you'd already stopped thinking about me that way. I actually preferred it when you were mad at me. I realised that I would rather argue with you forever than not argue with anyone else.'

I smile.

'You're saying you want to argue with me forever, but I get what you mean,' I say with a smile.

'I don't want to break up,' he tells me plainly. 'Do you?'

'I don't want to break up either,' I tell him. 'At least I didn't, until you got me that shit Christmas present.'

'Well, I have to admit, that isn't your main present,' he confesses. 'But I am guilty of only buying your real present just before our trip.'

'Interesting,' I say. 'Do I get it?'

He smiles.

'You get it if we call off this whole break-up nonsense,' he says.

'Ooh, tough call,' I tease. 'You know me, I can't handle not knowing what's inside a mystery package. It's like a tiny escape room.'

'I know, I'm worried you might say yes, just to sneak a peak,' he replies. 'So, just let me say this. I love you, I've always loved you, I always will love you. If you ever want to love me too, I'll be here.'

'I love you too,' I blurt, without a second of hesitation.

'I'm worried this is just a ploy to get your real present,' he says as he stands up. 'But okay, I've been hiding it in the car.'

I assume Millsy is going to go to the car, to get this mystery gift, but instead he walks over to me. It all happens in one swift movement, as he removes a small box from his pocket and gets down one knee.

'Fuck,' I blurt softly as I realise what is happening.

'Cara Brooks,' he says as he opens the box to reveal a jaw-droppingly beautiful ring. 'Will you marry me?'

'Yes,' I squeak. 'Yes, yes, yes.'

I jump to my feet, grabbing him, kissing him like I've never kissed him before. Kissing him like it might be the last time I ever get to kiss him, but knowing it's just the new first of many. I can hear other people in the food court clapping, cheering and whooping.

Eventually we part and Millsy places the ring on my finger.

'I can't believe you only bought this recently,' I tell him. 'How did you know we'd be okay?'

'Because my gran is right,' he replies. 'We're meant for each other, we make one another better. And we absolutely should be married.'

'I can't believe we're engaged,' I say, admiring my ring.

'I can't believe I had to pop the question in a service station,' he says with a laugh. 'Over stone-cold fast food.'

'Ah, but you didn't do it in your fake Southern accent,' I remind him. 'So it's dead classy.'

He laughs.

'You don't have to actually eat this, you know,' he says.

'Oh, I'm so going to,' I insist. 'What are you having?'

'God, I've missed you,' he says with a happy sigh. 'Come on then, make short work of the food, and then we'll go tell our family together.'

'Sounds perfect,' I reply.

And it really does.

**33**

Iona's house is buzzing with the infectious energy of New Year's Eve. The whole family is here, and I really mean the whole family.

Something this past week has given me a newfound clarity about life, and the importance of making the most of every moment, and every precious person in it.

And it isn't just getting things back on track with Millsy that has made me feel this way – although the thought of life without him really didn't seem like something I would enjoy – it's seeing Iona in hospital, feeling scared, worrying that we might lose her. We're so lucky to have both our grans still, to have so much family around us. Thinking about family got me thinking about Auntie Mary and I think I get it now. I understand why we put up with her, it's for my gran. Of course my gran loves her, she's her daughter, and I know my gran would love nothing more than have her entire family around her on New Year's Eve, so I did something I didn't think I would ever do. I called up Auntie Mary and invited her, Uncle Paddy, Flora, Tommy and the boys to join us for New Year's Eve and, do you know what, they all jumped at the chance.

As midnight fast approaches, I can feel a sense of anticipation in the air. I usually don't think too much of New Year's Eve, all that new beginning rubbish, but this year feels different. It really does feel like a new beginning, and I can't help but feel excited about what's to come.

I glance around at my family – every complicated branch of the tree – and I smile. In the interest of starting afresh and turning over a new leaf, I should go and speak to Auntie Mary and Uncle Paddy, and thank them for joining us, show them just how welcome they are. They're chatting with Rod and Mhairi, so I approach them slowly, not wanting to interrupt.

'...and that's how I saved Private Ryan.'

Catching the end of one of Uncle Paddy's tall tales stops me in my tracks. Nope, I can't face it, not right now. I quickly turn on my heel and walk away. I'm all for new beginnings, but there's no need to rush things.

I smile as I notice the grans sitting together on the sofa, chatting, all smiles. It's so good to have Iona home.

Flora and Tommy are watching and laughing as the boys run rings around Oliver – literally, they're tying him up in a piece of tinsel they must have pulled from the tree. Then I look over at my own parents, watching as my giant of a dad tries to teach my tiny mum how to play pool. I smile but then I realise who is missing: Millsy.

I head upstairs from the party room, eventually finding him by the patio door.

'Hello, you,' I say. 'Trying to escape?'

'I think we've established I'm not at all easy to shake off,' he replies with a smile. 'No, I'm just doing some things for Mhairi, all the fun little Hogmanay traditions. I'm unlocking everything, so we can open the windows and doors, to let the old year out and the new year in.'

'Makes sense,' I reply. 'Out with the old, in with the new.'

'Except the new year can't be trusted to come in on its own,' he continues. 'So all the dark-haired men have to step outside before midnight, then bring the new year in with them.'

'Oh, I think Oliver is going to have something to say about that,' I joke.

'Yeah, probably that he doesn't want to go out in the cold,' Millsy replies with a laugh. 'You think that all sounds fun? Alan, Gran's next-door neighbour who, you know, lives nowhere near here really, goes out at midnight and fires a shotgun.'

'Cute,' I say.

'But don't worry, Dad's brought his English charm too,' Millsy continues. 'A box of fireworks so big it could destroy every tree within a two-mile radius.'

'Ah, good old Rod,' I reply. 'Don't go anywhere near them.'

Millsy laughs.

'Not a chance,' he replies. 'Anyway, he still treats us like kids, still thinks he needs to hide them from us.'

'I mean, knowing us, that sounds about right,' I reason.

'Yeah, seems fair,' Millsy adds. 'How about we make a tradition of our own, or at least do it just this once? I say we take this year out together. We go outside right now and we kiss 2023 goodbye. I can't think of a better way to put this year to bed and look forward to the future.'

'Sounds great,' I reply.

We grab our coats and head outside, walking down the garden to the loch, where we eventually stop on the jetty. I smile as the cool night air brushes against my cheeks and admire the shimmering glow that the moon casts on the water. It's such a peaceful, tranquil spot – until Alan fires his shotgun, and Rod lets off his big box of fireworks, at least.

'I know I said I wanted to kiss this year goodbye, but all I really wanted to do was kiss,' he says with a cheeky smile.

'Oh, you dirty boy,' I say with a laugh. 'Go on, then.'

Millsy grabs me, pulling me close as we kiss. As our lips touch, the rest of the world seems to fade away. I wrap my arms around his neck and hop up into his arms, locking my legs around his waist. As we turn up the passion, he accidentally knocks me into the crates behind me. We freeze for a second, still joint at the lips, and I'm relieved we haven't fallen into the loch (that would be so us) but, come to think of it, I did hear a loud splash.

Millsy releases me and we both look down into the water. Is that...?

I hold my breath while Millsy uses the torch on his phone to check and, yep, sure enough, we've knocked Rod's giant box of fireworks into the loch. Absolutely classic us.

'Oh... my... God,' I blurt. 'What the hell are we going to do about this one?'

'Absolutely nothing,' he replies with a smile, taking me back in his arms, and kissing me again.

Sounds perfect.

# ACKNOWLEDGMENTS

Huge thanks to the brilliant team at Boldwood Books – especially Nia, my fantastic editor.

Thank you to everyone who takes the time to read and review my books. Given that this book is a stand-alone sequel to The Plus One Pact, an extra special thank you to everyone who bought a copy of that book – to have sold over 100k copies of it means so much to me, and to be able to bring these characters back to life has been so much fun.

Massive thanks to the incredible Kim, to Pino, and to the amazing Aud who has every last one of my books on her shelf. Thanks so much to Joey who is always there for me no matter what I need, and to James for being brilliant as ever. Thanks so much to Jess for the beautiful photos and to Darcy for always being by my side.

Finally thank you to *my* Joe – the undeniable inspiration for the Joe in this book – for absolutely everything and more.

# ABOUT THE AUTHOR

**Portia MacIntosh** is a bestselling romantic comedy author of over 15 novels, including *My Great Ex-Scape* and *Honeymoon For One*. Previously a music journalist, Portia writes hilarious stories, drawing on her real life experiences.

Sign up to Portia MacIntosh's mailing list for news, competitions and updates on future books.

Visit Portia's website: https://portiamacintosh.com/

Follow Portia MacIntosh on social media here:

facebook.com/portia.macintosh.3
twitter.com/PortiaMacIntosh
instagram.com/portiamacintoshauthor
bookbub.com/authors/portia-macintosh

# ALSO BY PORTIA MACINTOSH

# Boldwood

Boldwood Books is an award-winning fiction publishing company seeking out the best stories from around the world.

**Find out more at www.boldwoodbooks.com**

Join our reader community for brilliant books, competitions and offers!

Follow us
@BoldwoodBooks
@TheBoldBookClub

Sign up to our weekly deals newsletter

https://bit.ly/BoldwoodBNewsletter

Books are to be returned on or before
the last date below.